Praise for Andie J. Christopher

"Sharp, smart, and sexy."

—Christina Lauren, *New York Times* bestselling author, on *Not the Girl You Marry*

"*Not the Girl You Marry* is funny, heartfelt, and super sexy!"

—Jasmine Guillory, *New York Times* bestselling author

"This one's for all the prickly, witty women who need their own edge-of-your-seat rom-com."

—Talia Hibbert, *USA Today* bestselling author, on *Not the Girl You Marry*

"Andie J. Christopher is a master satirist of the absurdities of modern womanhood even as she renews our faith in the power of love."

—Jenny Holiday, *USA Today* bestselling author, on *Thank You, Next*

"Delightful, playful, and sparkling with keen, observant humor, Christopher's signature crisp storytelling sings in this forbidden-yet-sweet romance."

—Sierra Simone, *USA Today* bestselling author, on *Hot Under His Collar*

"Andie J. Christopher is a treasure to romance readers!"

—Farrah Rochon, *New York Times* bestselling author

"[A] laugh-out-loud rom-com."

—BuzzFeed on *Thank You, Next*

"Christopher's work is one of those laughing through your tears books, a laugh-out-loud romp with depth that unflinchingly peers into the soul of any woman who's ever felt the double-edged sword of their muchness making certain they'll never be enough."

—*Entertainment Weekly* on *Not the Girl You Marry*

TITLES BY
ANDIE J. CHRISTOPHER

Not the Girl You Marry

Not That Kind of Guy

Hot Under His Collar

Thank You, Next

Unrealistic Expectations

UNREALISTIC EXPECTATIONS

ANDIE J. CHRISTOPHER

BERKLEY ROMANCE
New York

BERKLEY ROMANCE
Published by Berkley
An imprint of Penguin Random House LLC
penguinrandomhouse.com

Library of Congress Cataloging-in-Publication Data

Names: Christopher, Andie J., author.
Title: Unrealistic expectations / Andie J. Christopher.
Description: First Edition. | New York: Berkley Romance, 2023.
Identifiers: LCCN 2022059134 (print) | LCCN 2022059135 (ebook) |
ISBN 9780593200087 (trade paperback) | ISBN 9780593200094 (ebook)
Subjects: LCGFT: Romance fiction. | Novels.
Classification: LCC PS3603.H7628 U67 2023 (print) |
LCC PS3603.H7628 (ebook) | DDC 813/.6—dc23/eng/20221213
LC record available at https://lccn.loc.gov/2022059134
LC ebook record available at https://lccn.loc.gov/2022059135

First Edition: September 2023

Printed in the United States of America
1st Printing

To Julie,

for helping me to learn my own mind

and change it

UNREALISTIC EXPECTATIONS

CHAPTER ONE

Communication is key. Without open lines of communication—the real, vulnerable kind that you have when you're asking for your needs to be met—any relationship is doomed.

—Jessica Gallagher, PhD, licensed clinical therapist

When Jessica Gallagher returned to her condo the day before the release of her first book, there were movers hauling out furniture and boxing up things in closets. She checked to make sure she hadn't gotten off the elevator on the wrong floor before entering the condo she shared with her boyfriend, Luke. Maybe there'd been some sort of plumbing emergency while she'd been gone, and they had to temporarily move some of their things? She checked her phone. Luke would have told her about any domestic disasters. No texts. No voice mails. Not even a missed call.

And it looked like the movers were only hauling out Luke's furniture. Her heart kicked up speed as she dodged a guy carrying the massage chair. Maybe Luke had finally listened to her about how ugly it was and was getting rid of it?

Something in her gut told her that Luke had not just decided to redecorate. "Luke?" She walked further into the apartment, stubbed her toe on a box, and almost tripped. "Son of a bitch."

She looked down into the box to find that it contained medical textbooks.

She limped into their bedroom and found Luke standing in their walk-in closet, tossing his shoes into boxes. He was in scrubs, so he must have just come off call. He should be asleep, not packing. She stood there, bewildered, for a long beat.

It took Luke a second to realize that she was standing behind him. He'd always been absentminded, but Jessica had convinced herself that it was just because he was a brilliant medical mind who didn't have the brain space to keep track of his keys or the laundry that needed to be done or take-out orders he was supposed to pick up. But, right now, it infuriated her.

"What the fuck is going on?"

That startled Luke out of his furious packing. He turned, and his normally pale skin was tomato red. Probably because Jessica rarely yelled, but she was yelling now. "I . . . uh . . . I was going to tell you—"

"Tell. Me. What?" She'd managed to quiet her voice, but she knew there was still rage in her tone. "Because it looks like you are moving out of our home. And that seems weird to me, because you haven't said anything about us moving somewhere new together. So this must mean that you are moving someplace else on your own. Which is also weird, because you haven't mentioned anything about wanting to break up. But of course this means we're breaking up. People don't just live together for a decade and then not live together but remain romantically involved. Especially when they've been talking about having a baby." Jessica took a step toward Luke, and he wouldn't meet her gaze. "Do they?"

Everything below her neck was cold and numb, and she couldn't hear anything but her own thoughts screaming at her.

"Listen—"

"That's all I do, all day. I listen to people." For some reason, him telling her to listen to *him*, when she'd been his steady confidant for the majority of his adult life, made her want to scream. She'd often felt a little superior, despite herself, during sessions with clients who talked about having screaming arguments with their partners.

She and Luke had never had a screaming argument. They had discussions and made agreements. They—well, she—expressed feelings and needs, and Luke tried to meet them. They'd never been the kind of couple to make rash decisions or even the kind of couple who went to bed angry. Because they never made each other angry. Irritated—yes. So angry that she wanted to drag him out of the closet by his receding hairline and demand answers—no.

"I was going to tell you last night, at dinner."

"You were going to tell me that you were moving out and abandoning our relationship last night, at dinner? The special dinner that we were having to celebrate the release of my book?"

Luke flinched. "You just seemed so excited about your little book, and I couldn't stand to see you upset." He made a lame hand motion at her. "Like this."

"I'm not upset right now that you're moving out. I'm glad you're moving out. If you weren't moving out right now, I would be tempted to kill you and then retile the bathroom with your rotting bones behind the new tile."

"That would really start to stink after a while . . . the decomposition."

"I would dissolve your flesh with lye." This was probably not the time to make jokes about murdering him, but that had always lightened the mood before. He'd joke about giving her an air embolism in her sleep. She'd imply that she could deadlift his body easily enough to hide it—all the while knowing that they were adults, and they'd made a commitment to one another.

"You really do watch too much true crime."

"You mean that I watch too much television, when I'm at home, waiting for you." The only reason that she'd ended up writing the book was that she had most of her evenings and weekends on her hands and shows about murder had started to give her nightmares.

Luke put his hands on his hips and looked down at his feet. They'd had this conversation before, but the stakes had never been this high. Even though she'd had her moments of feeling lonely with him, their relationship had never been about their passion for each other—she'd thought that they were both passionate about the life they'd built together. He might have chosen her because she was convenient, but she'd chosen him because he'd never once made her worried that he would abandon her. He'd never given any indication that he wasn't ready to stick around for the long haul—not until now.

But here she was, standing in her half-empty closet, looking at a man that she'd spent almost her entire adult life with become someone she didn't recognize—someone who would leave her without warning. She'd been grateful at the beginning of their relationship that he'd been kind and friendly and it seemed to come from a place of wanting to get to know her, not from any compulsion to see what he could get from her.

"Is this because we haven't been having sex?" Their sex life had never been bad, but it also hadn't rocked her world at the very beginning—or the very end, it seemed. Over the last fifteen years, they'd gotten into a good rhythm. And most long-term couples didn't have much sex. That aspect of their relationship had never been the most important thing to Jessica, and she hadn't thought it was that important to Luke, either. But the way his skin flushed, when she asked him that, told her that she'd been making assumptions about their sex life, too.

Luke finally met her gaze again. "I care about you, and I want you to be happy."

"So, you were planning to disappear without telling me?" Jessica was shrieking again, and Luke looked a little befuddled. But that didn't stop him from pulling the few articles of clothing he hadn't packed off the rack. "You think I'd be happy about you leaving without a word? Without a discussion? Without even trying to work out whatever is making you unhappy?"

"I knew that if we had a discussion, you'd get me to go to couples counseling, and we'd talk things out like logical adults. And I'd never really leave, but neither of us would ever be happy." Luke sounded so defeated, and Jessica started shaking. Her body literally could not hold on to the shock.

"It almost sounds like you feel like a prisoner . . . in our life."

Luke stepped toward her with his hands outstretched, as though he was going to pull her into a hug. As much as she could use a hug right now, she couldn't accept one from him. Not right now. Not ever again.

He caught on and respected her space, dropping his hands to his sides. "No, not a prisoner. There's a lot of good stuff here between us."

"Just not enough." Jessica didn't want to pick at his words and turn them against him. She'd never advise a client to do that when having a fight with a partner. She'd advise deep, calming breaths and questions that didn't put blame on the other party. But Luke was to blame for all the pain swirling around her body—the tears she couldn't hold back any longer and the way her knees felt like they would buckle at any moment. She didn't want to lose control of herself like this, not when she could no longer trust the person she was losing control with.

"You're my best friend, Jessica." Luke sounded despondent, but Jessica didn't really feel sorry for him. He was a thirty-seven-year-old man, and yet he didn't have the cojones to tell her that he didn't want to be with her anymore. He didn't have the integrity to own up to the fact that he was having his mid-life crisis about ten years early.

She wasn't going to address the fact that you also don't abandon your best friend without warning. "Is there someone else?"

Luke backed away from her, and he didn't meet her gaze when he said, "No."

She didn't want to believe that he was cheating, but he was doing a lot of cheater-like shit right now. Growing up with her mother had exposed her to the wide world of ways that cheaters behaved.

Jessica sighed. If he was cheating, she wasn't going to get a straight answer from Luke on the subject. Not when she'd already threatened to kill him.

"I don't want to lose you." More like he didn't want to end up being featured as the victim on an episode of *Snapped*.

Jessica wrapped her arms around herself and looked at him, dead in the eye. "Well, you did."

There was nothing left to say, so she turned and walked out of her condo. This time, the movers got out of the way.

CHAPTER TWO

> Healing from rejection takes time and self-reflection. It's really a great opportunity to become more self-aware. Be kind to yourself. Take your time. Don't let anyone push you into a new relationship before you're ready. The people you date going forward will be grateful for the work you've done.
>
> *—Jessica Gallagher, PhD, licensed clinical therapist*

"TODAY ON *DATE Hard or Die Alone*, I have Jessica Gallagher, the author of *Ten Things Not to Do If You Ever Want to See a Naked Girl Again: The Straight Man's Guide to Not Dying Alone in a Pile of Dirty Underwear.* Jessica is a licensed clinical therapist with a decade of experience, and her practice focuses on helping singles figure out their relationship patterns so that they can change them. Tell me, Jessica, what made you write this book?"

Jessica shifted in her seat, took a deep breath before speaking, and hoped that it wouldn't mess up the sound. She was much more comfortable sitting across from a client in session than she was talking to a podcast host. For one thing, the podcast studio was extremely hot, and she usually didn't have giant headphones that pinched her ears and a mountain of recording equipment between her and her client. And in session, there was the opportunity to clarify and elaborate. In the media appearances that her publicist had arranged for the release of her new book, her words were digitally memorialized. If she messed up, there was no chance to back up and clarify. If she said something that someone took out of context, she could go viral and lose all credibility.

She hadn't written the book so she could become a public figure. The book proposal had come out in a chunk after she'd had to talk one too many of her clients out of giving a tenth chance to a walking red flag, after a long week of talking other clients out of giving more chances to men who frankly didn't seem to like or respect them very much.

"Well, Diana, a lot of the young people I see in my practice are extremely accomplished in their professional lives, and they have fulfilling and rewarding relationships with their family and friends. But so many of the young women I see—especially the young women who date men—are really struggling with dating and relationships."

Diana laughed. "Then why didn't you write a dating book for those young women?"

"There are thousands of dating books for straight women, telling them how to navigate the murky waters of dating," Jessica replied. "But, in my professional experience, the young women aren't the problem. Most of them, unless they've become jaded by the dating process, are earnestly putting themselves out there on dating apps and in group activities they think likely relationship candidates might be interested in. They're working on themselves and trying to present themselves in the best light. They're giving the men they meet the benefit of the doubt far beyond the point where—in my opinion—the men deserve it.

"And the men, who profess to want to date them and who

benefit most from long-term, monogamous relationships, treat them like utter garbage. It's the men who need the advice. It's the men who need to be better."

"But men don't buy dating books. That's just the way it is."

Jessica wasn't sure how she was supposed to answer that. It was release day for her book, and this woman had just told her that no one was going to buy it. Now that she had to pay both halves of the mortgage, it would be great to earn out her advance and get some actual royalties. "Well, I'm hoping some concerned parents or ex-girlfriends will shove my book at the people who need it most."

Without missing a beat, Diana, a dating coach, not a licensed therapist, asked, "Don't you think the title of your book is a little inappropriate?"

Jessica did in fact think that the title of her book was inappropriate. However, her editor, publicist, and literary agent had insisted that "an eye-catching title like that will get you mentioned on *The Viewpoint* for sure." Instead, she was talking to a woman with no discernible training in the field of mental health or relationships—a woman who probably thought that psychology and psychiatry had been co-opted by "big pharma"—about whether she had the credibility to talk about a subject in which Jessica had a decade of experience and a whole fucking PhD.

"Well, I didn't pick the title of the book. But if it gets one feckless dude bro to open it up and explore the possibility that his methods of relating aren't going to work for him long-term and are harming the people around him, I think it's done its job."

The podcast host looked down at her phone, seeming to have lost interest in the conversation. Jessica almost wanted to say something incendiary to get her attention. Although most people thought—through Jessica's own efforts—that she had her shit completely together, she had to quell the urge to do and say outrageous things more often than anyone would have imagined. Especially when she was feeling dismissed or unheard. Especially in the past twenty-four hours when she was still feeling like tenderized meat.

She knew the urge sprang from the fact that her mother had paid more attention to the parade of boyfriends she'd traipsed through their lives than to her own daughter, and she knew that acting on it would only leave her riddled with anxiety and regret. So, instead of telling Diana that her free dating guide, "Eight Steps to Not Look like a Bridge Troll in Your Dating Profile," was a pile of patriarchal dog shit, she waited for the next question.

But she was not expecting Diana's next question.

"But, like, are *you* in a relationship?" When Jessica didn't answer right away, because her mouth was agape, the host continued. "How will readers know you're qualified to give relationship advice?"

Yesterday, after a good hour of crying in the shower, Jessica had called her publicist and insisted that she would not answer questions about her personal romantic life. As a therapist, she dodged questions about her own life like a boxer during the first round of a fight, and she wasn't about to put all of her personal business out in public. Not now. That would be something her mother would do, and her mother was the world's best counterexample.

"I don't think it's helpful to use my personal relationships as fodder for the work I do. In individual therapy, being client focused is key, and this book is reader focused."

"So you haven't experienced the behaviors that you describe in the book?" Diana really wasn't giving up on this, was she?

"All of the experiences that I talk about in the book happen to real people every day. I think my strength is breaking down what's happening psychologically when things go wrong in relationships."

There were a couple of tense moments, when Jessica was pretty sure the host was going to probe further. But then, miraculously, she moved on.

"People really do still send other people unsolicited pictures of their junk?" Diana asked.

Relieved that she could talk about something that she'd never, ever experienced, Jessica said, "Believe it or not, they do."

GALVIN BAKER HAD been single for most of his life, but he'd never felt as single as he did when he was buying groceries to cook for one. In the before times, whenever the threat of a sad desk salad as an evening meal loomed, he'd opened a dating app or texted a buddy or lady friend to eat with him. But now, his buddies would give him endless shit about his newly toxic reputation, none of the women in his phone would answer, and the dating apps would be barren.

The worst part was that he hadn't done anything truly wrong—he'd only dated one of the most famous-for-being-famous women in the world for a few months and then tried to end things respectfully.

So, he'd gone from never having to deal with a sad desk salad to rooting around the farmers' market so he could dice cucumbers for one and hide from the world. In the past few months, he'd gone from never spending an evening at home to getting very familiar with his own company.

He must have been doing what his grandmother would have called "gathering wool"—thank goodness she couldn't work Instagram and therefore didn't know that he'd been humiliated—because he didn't notice a woman staring at him from across the vegetable bins. She had shiny hair and a nice smile. She did the thing where she kept looking down and then up at him—flirting.

It had been so long that Galvin fought the urge to look around to see if she was flirting with someone else. He'd gone over the numbers enough to know that not everyone in the world was on Instagram. Not everyone in the world had seen the video and thought he was trash in bed.

So he took a risk and smiled back at the woman. He wasn't used to this being awkward, but he found himself searching for something to say. They were in Southern California, so the sun was shining. The sun was shining every day, and not having to talk about the weather was one of the best things about living in Southern California. But, right now, he really wished the weather was some sort of hot topic.

They could also talk about vegetables, he guessed. "What are you planning to make?" he asked. She looked confused, and he wanted to die a little inside. But instead, he opened his mouth again and said, "I'm making a salad, which I guess is probably as boring as talking about the weather in Southern California." He felt like an idiot. He'd never felt like an idiot with women.

Sure, he wasn't the marrying kind who would grill in the backyard and toss the football with various niblings, but he'd never had a hard time making simple conversation before.

The woman cocked her head to the side and asked, "I know you from somewhere. Are you friends with my idiot ex-husband?"

Seeing as he was short on real friends, he doubted it. And most of his friends were single. He would have remembered her. So, she probably recognized him from the video and was going to make another video talking about how he'd blathered like an idiot about salad when they met. Kennedy would probably share the video, and he would never have a dinner companion again.

"I promise we've never met before. And, if I had one of those *Men in Black* memory erasers, I'd use it right now so you could forget that I am truly a chump."

After that, she laughed. Maybe he wasn't totally hopeless. "Recently divorced?"

He felt the color rise on his cheeks. He definitely had the stink of someone who hadn't talked to strangers in a long time. "Nope. Never married."

The woman grimaced at that. "Late thirties and never married?"

She must have been talking to his mother. "Judge much?"

"Well, you're not bad looking, so it kind of must mean that something is wrong with you."

How did he get into this conversation? Now all he wanted was to find salad ingredients in peace.

"I'm sure there are plenty of things wrong with me, but I'm not really looking for a diagnosis from you."

He grabbed baby lettuce that probably cost more than a pair of high-quality cashmere gloves and an organic cucumber that had probably been cultivated with Perrier and the prayers of monks in a mountain paradise and walked away.

His real problem was that he'd probably been alone for too long. The only solution was that he probably had to get out more. He hated it.

GALVIN BAKER COULDN'T believe his luck. He hadn't been out to this bar in almost a year—the last three months of which he'd virtually been in hiding. And yet, the very night he emerged from his self-imposed isolation, the perfect woman appeared in front of him.

He rolled his rocks glass between his palms as he took in her long blond hair and million-dollar ass. She hadn't looked at him yet, and he wasn't sure how to rectify that. The old Galvin would have had her in a coatroom, sucking his dick, in the next ten minutes. The old Galvin was charming and successful, and no one knew who he was. He could sleep with whomever he wanted, in the way that he wanted—no names, no strings, no emotions. The old Galvin didn't do emotions. Emotions were the road to ruin, and he'd do anything in his power to stay off that road. And if his feeling-free existence caused harm to other people, that really wasn't his problem. He was totally up-front about what he could offer. He certainly wasn't going to take the blame when they expected more from him. He'd been clear that he was good for sex, a few months of fun, and nothing else.

But he couldn't live that way anymore. And that wasn't his fault, either, which was why it had taken him months to come to grips with the fact that his old mix of casual relationships and one-night stands—the very efficient way that didn't involve allowing anyone to ingratiate themselves too far into his life—wasn't going to work for him anymore. Not after his mega-influencer ex-girlfriend had lambasted his sexual prowess on her social media platforms after he'd ended their relationship.

The new Galvin was trying to be better, but it wasn't his choice. He was actually going to have to put in an effort, but that didn't mean he had to be happy about it. The blonde finally looked at him, so he gave her "the look," which was a holdover from the days before he was dicksona non grata, but he figured it was still worth a try.

The blonde met his gaze and returned her own sultry look before flicking her hair over her shoulder. Galvin took that as his signal to approach. When he reached her, he put down his glass and said nothing. Anything he could say at this point would be irredeemably cheesy, so he kept his mouth shut. He took his time looking the perfect woman up and down, though. She was athletic, curvy, and shorter than him by a few inches. Close up, he realized that she was a little bit older than he'd originally thought from far away. That was great for him—younger women often expected the sex to turn into a white picket fence. They still bought into the unrealistic expectations of a fairy-tale romance. Older women had their heads on straight. They never tried to paint his red flags green in their minds. Their more robust experiences taught them that there wasn't anything beneath his rakish exterior. They could have their fun and not get attached.

New Galvin still didn't want to get attached long-term. From the therapist he'd reluctantly started seeing, he knew that it was dysfunctional. Though he didn't agree that he was afraid of commitment. He just wasn't capable of it at this point because he'd avoided it for so long. He couldn't imagine himself actually wanting to talk to someone after the postorgasm haze wore off. The only feeling that settled into his gut after getting off was the slight nausea that told him it was time to leave the premises.

Finally, the blonde said, "I know you from somewhere."

Dread lodged itself in Galvin's gut. There was really only one way this woman would know who he was—if she was one of Kennedy's 450 million Instagram followers. Still, he tried to keep the facade going that he wasn't notoriously deficient at doling out pleasure. "I would definitely remember you if we'd met." He was trying to sound charming, but he truly felt like such a douche.

The blonde scrunched up her face in this cute way that made him even more attracted to her, but he knew she was trying to figure out where she knew him from. And she would never sleep with him once she knew. He actively began making an extraction plan.

But he wasn't fast enough, because Blondie decided to yell, like she was trying to get on the *Family Feud* board for the category "Men You Wouldn't Set Your Worse Enemy Up With," when she said, "You're Galvin Baker, and you dated Kennedy Mower!"

Galvin looked around to see if anyone was paying attention to him, wishing there was a kind of witness protection program for Kennedy's ex-boyfriends. Even though Kennedy was on the longest-running reality show in history and had hundreds of millions of followers on social media, he hadn't even known who she was when they'd met at a party at some actor's house. He'd only been invited because he had designed James Fahereghty's new home. He'd only attended because it would be good for business, and all the devotion that he refused to put into romantic relationships he put into his career. He may not have much of a love life, but he loved his work. Although he'd started out in residential architecture rather than commercial to spite his parents, he never regretted his choices.

Somehow, in three short months, he'd gone from a relatively unknown figure to a guest star on reality television to a widely reviled laughingstock.

"I am and I did." The old Galvin probably would have denied it and tried to gaslight this woman into believing she was mistaken, not to do her harm, but to save face. The new Galvin could own up to his mistakes.

The blonde cocked her head at him and said, "Honestly thought you would have left town and gotten a new face."

Galvin let out a tight laugh. "Yeah, the U.S. Marshals wouldn't agree to my terms regarding relocation, so here I am."

She put her hand on his arm and looked at him with immense sympathy on her face. The touch was promising, but the pity said that she believed what Kennedy had said about him and was not going to fuck him.

It was really the most brilliant thing she could have done—telling everyone in the world that he was terrible in bed. It wasn't like he could do anything to disprove it. He didn't always get phone numbers, even after a particularly stellar performance on his part, so character witnesses for his generosity as a lover were pretty thin on the ground. Even though she'd lied—at least, that's what he had to believe not to hide his head in eternal shame—he was never going to get laid again.

CHAPTER THREE

JESSICA DID NOT want to be out with her girlfriends right now. She wanted to be curled up on her couch with her long-term boyfriend, drinking the champagne she'd been saving for her cozy little release party for two since she'd signed the book contract. Instead, she was in a crowded bar, wearing a cocktail dress so tight that it cut off circulation to her extremities. She wasn't sure if this was preferable to lying on the love seat that Luke hadn't taken with him earlier when he moved out. She winced at the thought of returning to her apartment. Somehow a completely empty apartment would have been better than half the clothes and toiletries, half the kitchen appliances, and half the furniture gone. Besides, Luke had taken the good TV.

Eventually, she'd have to fill the condo with new furniture. But she didn't even know if she wanted to stay there. And she didn't know if she could afford it long-term—especially if the book wasn't a success.

But her friends weren't going to allow her to be depressed. Barbie—named for the doll—and Kelly had known her since freshman year of college, and they weren't going to let her lie in bed and watch costume dramas on the small TV Luke had left for her. Kelly was a pediatrician, but she'd told Jessica that, in her learned medical opinion, they needed to have drinks. She and Barbie, a makeup artist, had ambushed her at her condo about ten minutes after Jessica had apprised them all of her in-progress breakup. Their other friends would have been there, but they all lived thousands of miles away. However, they'd promised to cover Jessica's bar tab and restitution for any property crimes she might decide to commit against her newly minted ex with Barbie and Kelly's encouragement.

But Jessica wasn't angry. That phase of grief had passed relatively quickly. She had cycled back around to sadness and a flavor of paralysis.

"It was like being in a car crash," Jessica said. "I felt like I was watching it happen to someone else. And I couldn't feel anything. I wanted to do something to brace for impact, but I couldn't move. I could barely say anything. All I could do was screech, and it all sounded like utter nonsense."

Barbie shook her head, a sneer on her face. "I never liked Luke."

Jessica wanted to put a stop to this particular postdumping activity. From a psychological perspective, the trashing-the-ex-even-though-you-were-also-friends-with-the-ex ritual wasn't terribly useful. If she wanted to move forward, Jessica would have to just allow herself to feel all the shitty feelings that being broken up with in such a brutal manner brought up. "He's not that bad."

"And that's the issue," Kelly said. "He was never that bad, but he was also never that good."

"We were together for over a decade." Jessica knew that wasn't much of a defense for their relationship, but there had to have been something good there for both of them to stay for so long. Now that she wasn't in the eye of the shock hurricane, she could look to the recent past and acknowledge that she and Luke hadn't been really connected and tuned in to their relationship for a long time. She'd been busy with her practice and writing and editing her book, and he was constantly working and on call. It hadn't left much space for them to take vacations or even to cook dinner together.

But she'd thought that there was still enough of a connection there that Luke would at least put in one last effort before throwing in the towel. They'd been together for so long Jessica had felt completely secure in their relationship. She'd taken that security for granted, and now the very ground beneath her felt frighteningly shaky.

He was clinical about their breakup. After he'd walked out the door, she found a letter on the dining room table detailing how he'd set her up with a separate cell phone plan and transferred all the utilities to her name. She'd called him to clarify a few points, and he'd responded to her voice mail with a bullet-pointed text.

The fact that she wasn't still crying, screaming, and throwing up was a miracle. She knew she wouldn't get through this massive, stressful upheaval without a support system, so she was grateful for her friends, even though she felt as though she was walking around vulnerable—as though all of her skin had been sloughed off and people could see inside. All of the ugly feelings from her childhood that she'd worked through—the feeling that she wasn't good enough to be loved and seen—were creeping in on her. Even though she had the tools to cope, and she'd become a therapist partially to assemble those tools, she was overwhelmed.

"C'mon, now. You liked him. We all did." It was telling that Jessica didn't have more of a defense.

"Yeah, we liked him like we like brown rice," Kelly said. "Brown rice is nourishing, but no one is ever going to scream in the streets about how brown rice rocked their world. We liked Luke as long as he was good to our friend, but we always thought you deserved to be with someone who you wanted to scream in the streets about."

This was new information for Jessica. "Why didn't you tell me?" She was used to being the person commenting on other people's relationships, so having her friends do a postmortem on her own was extremely uncomfortable.

"You seemed happy enough," Barbie said. "Like, the happiest we'd ever seen you. You know . . . you're a very serious person. You've always found something wrong with the people we dated. We weren't going to say something when you started dating someone who seemed like he was really into you and who you were willing to tolerate."

"Am I really that hard on men?" Jessica knew the answer to this question. She'd always had deep-running trust issues, and she'd always been able to suss out if a man was only interested in something casual. And her instinct was a hair trigger when it came to cutting something off if it had the slightest red flag for an unhealthy pattern—like if she or one of her friends was too attracted to someone right away.

"I just have healthy boundaries. I had to develop them." What Jessica didn't say was that her friends had both come from reasonably functional homes. Their mothers hadn't shown up at Parents' Weekend and started hitting on the other kids' married dads because they'd just broken up with their latest loser boyfriend.

"You told me you had to break up with one guy because he was 'too good' at kissing," Barbie said.

Jessica wanted to stop this conversation. "He wasn't looking for a serious relationship, and I didn't want to get attached because he knew what to do with his tongue."

"What I don't get is why you were looking for a serious relationship while we were still in our twenties. Your twenties are for banging randoms for the story, not meeting your person."

"I saw my mom bang enough randoms when I was growing up to last me a lifetime. And I have the stories to prove it."

Kelly pressed her lips together as if she was trying not to say something but really wanted to comment on Jessica's aversion to casual hookups vis-à-vis Laurie Gallagher.

Barbie had no such compunctions, though. "That's bullshit. You were never going to be as irresponsible as your mom. But you didn't have to save your cherry for . . . Luke." That last word dripped with disdain.

"You know very well that I didn't save my cherry for Luke. I've just always been selective." She stuck her tongue out at Barbie. "Besides, the orgasm gap is particularly egregious when it comes to casual hookups."

Both of her friends nodded their heads. They'd heard Jessica bring up the orgasm gap before, and their experiences bore it out.

"But Luke isn't the guy that you give up your twenties for," Kelly said.

"You gave up your twenties to become a doctor." Jessica knew she sounded defensive, but she was feeling defensive.

Kelly wasn't deterred, though. "That's my point. Luke gave up his twenties to become a doctor, too. And you gave up your twenties to support him in that. And now that you're actual adults and can lift your head up to enjoy how hard you've worked, he wants to leave and find something more exciting. Probably something younger, with perkier tits and less emotional baggage."

Jessica didn't want to be upset that Luke was probably going to trade her in for a shinier, newer model. If he hadn't already.

"Being young doesn't necessarily make life any easier. Every twentysomething who comes to see me is carrying a lot more than a sunny social media profile could ever convey."

"But they don't have to spend any money on Botox." Barbie had been getting Botox since they were twenty-eight. It was practically required in her line of work.

"They might have more collagen in their skin, but I would never want to be twenty-one again. Plus, most of my younger clients are a lot more self-aware than I was at that age—some of them are more well-adjusted than I am now."

"Any twenty-five-year-old that Luke ends up with is probably doing keto. They will not put up with the Millet Man for long."

"I didn't realize that I was eating brown rice every day and pretending to like it until he walked out the door. As soon as he was gone, I realized that our condo didn't feel like a home without the both of us in it." Every choice she'd made was in service to a relationship with a man who hadn't loved her all that much. She'd thought that the most self-loving thing she could do was avoid her mother's mistakes and attain a level of security. "I put security ahead of passion, and all the security disappeared in an instant."

Barbie put her hand over Jessica's and squeezed. "But now you have a chance to find the passion."

Kelly waved down the server for another round. "Maybe he did you a favor."

"Ugh. I really don't want to date again." Jessica wasn't in a place where she'd consider dating for at least a few months, but stories from clients and friends had filled the entire two hundred pages of her book.

"Listen, sometimes the teacher has to become her own student," Barbie said as she finished her second martini. "Besides, it's not that bad. I only had to up my meds once the last time I was on Hinge."

"This is why I only fuck guys I work with," Kelly said. "If they get it in their heads to act like an ass, the hospital grapevine will prevent them from getting laid at work anymore."

"But what about the interns? None of them will have the Dossier of Unfuckables," Barbie added.

"Ew. I don't do interns. But you could fuck an intern, Jessica. That would drive Luke absolutely insane," Kelly said, greeting the returning server and their drinks with a smile.

"When I do start dating again—which will be a long time into the future—I'll probably have to do the apps. It's not like I work with any men, and all my hobbies are pretty girly."

"You could try hiking," Barbie suggested.

"I think that would warn more men off because of my weak

constitution." The last time Jessica went on a hike, she had to stop in the middle and throw up because of the exertion.

"Get a trainer and fuck him," Barbie suggested. "Two birds. One stone."

"As a therapist, I really think you should consider seeing a therapist," Jessica said. She was joking. Kind of.

Jessica didn't want to do any of this. She might have been deluded, but she'd really thought that she was going to be able to bypass all of this dating bullshit. And she could admit to herself that she'd felt a little bit superior—like she had it all figured out. But she didn't. She wasn't qualified to give the kind of advice that she'd so recently filled a book with.

CHAPTER FOUR

JESSICA NEEDED TO pee. And then she needed to go home and sleep for about a thousand years. Last night, she'd had a dream about waking up with white hair and a frail body, surrounded by the loving family that it was now questionable she would ever have.

Now that she was single and firmly in her late thirties, she was more likely to end up in a *Golden Girls*–type living situation. Instead of waking up to loving grandchildren reminiscing about baking cookies or crocheted blankets, she'd be waking up to her best friend Kelly roasting Barbie about what a slut she was being in and around the retirement community.

As she made her way through the almost-empty bar, her gaze snagged on a man sitting alone, staring into a glass of amber liquid. He was slumped over the bar, holding the side of his head with one hand. There were two empty glasses in front of him, and the bartender cleaned glasses while giving him a pitying look. She stopped short, which was weird because her bladder was seconds from bursting.

She walked past him, toward the bathroom, but she noticed his big hands as she went by. He didn't raise his head or look at her, just continued staring into his drink as though it held some sort of answer. She caught his scent, and it made her think that she knew him from somewhere.

The man was still there when she left the washroom to make her way toward the restaurant's entrance. She went on her tiptoes and saw that her friends were no longer standing outside the restaurant. Their Ubers must have shown up. They'd offered to share a car, but Barbie lived in West Hollywood, and Kelly lived downtown. It had been a long, strange forty-eight hours—the first in a series of what were sure to be long, strange days—and she needed to get on with her plan of sleeping for a thousand years.

As she passed the man at the bar again, she realized where she recognized him from and that it would probably be rude not to at least say hello. She stopped next to him and said, "Galvin?"

It took him a second to react. When he looked at her, she remembered why almost every girl she knew in college tried to sleep with him and only spoke his name in a breathy whisper. Not her—she'd taken one look at Galvin Baker and known he was more trouble than her heart could take—but he sure was pretty to look at.

His eyes were the color of a vintage Coke bottle, and his hair still had a tousled, fluffy thing going on that made it look as though he'd just rolled out of a bed at the Four Seasons with a couple of supermodels. His sharp jaw contrasted with his extravagant mouth, and his lips turned sinful when the corners turned up.

His gaze flicked over her body, appraising. She stepped closer to him without meaning to. Still, he didn't say anything.

She shifted on her heels, feeling awkward as he took her in. She was extremely conscious of the fact that she was wearing a short, tight dress in that moment. It felt even shorter as he looked at her, and had it suddenly gotten hotter in the bar?

The silence between them became awkward, and she said, "I figured that I should say hello." That probably sounded stupid, but Jessica had little experience talking to new men outside of new therapy clients. There was sort of a script for that. Out in the wild, she was usually at a loss.

For his part, Galvin said nothing, which made Jessica even more flustered. "I recognized you, and I saw you sitting alone when I went into the bathroom." Jessica really needed to stop talking, but she couldn't seem to turn her mouth off. "You looked kind of sad . . . uh . . . lonely maybe. And you're probably on a date. Of course you're on a date." Her skin was so hot, she could probably grill meat on it at this point. "I'm just going to go."

As she turned to leave, he grabbed her arm and she stopped short. He really did have big hands, and she liked the feel of his hands on her. Finally, when she turned around, he spoke. "You recognized me?"

"Yeah, I mean . . . there was a time you were pretty much everywhere." Jessica wouldn't have said they were friends in college, but they were in the same general crowd. And she would have remembered him even if they'd never hung out, because Luke had always *hated* Galvin. It had been striking because

Luke was a pretty easygoing guy who didn't hate anyone. That was one of the things she'd loved most about him. There was never any drama with Luke, not in their relationship, not in his life. Until yesterday. But he'd hated Galvin and taken potshots at him every time they were in the same room.

He dropped her arm, and she missed the contact immediately. "Oh, God," Galvin said, looking sheepish. "You saw it."

"Saw what?" They were definitely talking about two different things, and Jessica realized that Galvin did not recognize her. "I saw you sitting here, but I didn't see anything else. Is there something to see?"

She was rambling and elected to stop speaking.

"The video."

Her mind immediately went to "sex tape," and she definitely hadn't seen a sex tape with Galvin Baker. That would be memorable. Her entire body heated thinking about what he would look like now without his clothes on. She'd only seen him shirtless once, on spring break their senior year, and the image was tucked in a corner of her mind. He'd been long and lean and tan back then. Now, it certainly looked like he'd filled out. His physical presence was overwhelming—especially given the fact that Jessica had tried to train herself not to notice that kind of thing. She wasn't shallow, like her mother.

She'd always looked beyond appearances, and that had yielded a long, stable relationship that she'd been so proud of. Maybe she was noticing and appreciating Galvin Baker's fine physical attributes as some sort of reaction to her breakup. That was the only explanation she could think of for feeling an overwhelming attraction to a lonely-looking fuckboy and probable amateur pornographer.

Regardless, she needed to end this conversation that she never should have started in the first place. "Saw what video?"

He sighed heavily, and Jessica felt guilty for asking. Whatever this video contained, it was a sore subject for him. She had enough of her own emotional turmoil to deal with. She didn't need to delve into Galvin's world. It probably contained debauchery that would make Mick Jagger circa 1975 blush. But, before she could tell him that she didn't need to know about the video, he said, "My ex-girlfriend defamed me and my dick on her Instagram Stories."

Jessica changed her mind about what she wanted to know or not know about Galvin's situation immediately. Galvin and his dick—well, really more his mouth if college campus legend was accurate—had been legendary. He'd probably built a lot of his self-image on being a proficient, if not steadfast, lover. Having someone publicly malign his prowess would probably be a blow to his ego. It seemed like he needed a friendly ear—and Kelly and Barbie would never forgive her if she didn't get the scoop. They'd both probably seen the video, and they would expect her to grab the opportunity to get context.

Instead of making her apologies and calling an Uber, she sat down next to him. He seemed relieved, and Jessica was glad that she didn't just run off into the night.

"I didn't see the video, but we knew each other in college." When his gaze didn't light with recognition right away, she added, "I lived with Kelly, Barbie, Mia, and Tara."

That string of names seemed to ring a bell, probably because he'd hooked up with three out of four. "Jessica?"

She pressed the tip of her finger to the side of her nose and winked at him. It was kind of flirty, but she was allowed to flirt now and then. There was absolutely nothing wrong with flirting now that she was single. And if it lifted his mood around the defamation of his dick, all the better.

"You're not going to tell anyone about this, are you?" he asked. Jessica felt a pang of guilt about her earlier intention of gossiping about Galvin with her friends. He wasn't a client, but people came to her with problems all the time outside of a therapeutic relationship. Although she'd used some heavily anonymized anecdotes in her book, she would never reveal someone's private business if they didn't want her to.

"I can keep a secret—unless your dick murdered someone or intends to cause someone imminent harm." Jessica chuckled when he looked puzzled. "I'm a therapist. Mandatory reporter." When he still looked befuddled by the words coming out of her mouth, she said, "Never mind."

"A therapist, really?" He looked impressed rather than disgusted, which was good. She didn't know why she was so relieved that he wasn't in the "therapy is for the weak" camp. That camp had been shrinking for decades, but she was always surprised how often she came across someone who wanted to debate the merits of her life's work. "You were always a great listener."

Jessica's skin heated as she took in his words. She never thought that he'd noticed her. Even though her looks had never been an issue, she'd always been pretty reserved in social situations, preferring to linger around the edges and observe than be the center of attention. And Galvin had always been right there, in the center of attention, with center-of-attention girls. So the fact that he had paid attention to anything about her was disarming.

He kept looking at her and he rubbed his thumb across his bottom lip before speaking. "If you haven't seen the video, I kind of don't want to tell you what happened. I don't want to change the way you're looking at me."

Her internal temperature increased by about a thousand degrees. Jessica shook her head, trying to dissolve the frankly impure thoughts she was having about someone entirely inappropriate—whether she was in a relationship or single. Galvin Baker would eat her alive.

She was reserved with her heart because she knew how fragile hearts could be. And some people might be into casual hookups and could prevent themselves from having feelings, but that wasn't for her. She knew her strengths, and her ability to create emotional distance only extended as far as her office door. The most disheartening thing about being newly single after a long relationship was that she was going to have to play the games and join the apps for the first time. She knew that it was just how things were done, but it made her want to crawl into a hole and never emerge.

She especially didn't want to face the highs of meeting people she could see a future with, quickly followed by the lows of getting ghosted over and over again. She talked to people riding that roller coaster every day, and it hurt her emotionally even though it wasn't happening to her. It might have been the reason she'd clung to the contentment and relative safety of her relationship with Luke for so long. Because she was susceptible to the romantic dreamy outlook that had completely derailed her mother's life—and hers. She just knew the consequences of having unrealistic expectations of what a real relationship would look and feel like. And she refused to fall for the Hollywood paradigm for love and relationships.

She actually really needed to know about the contents of the video that seemed to bother Galvin so much. She needed for the video to reveal something awful about him so she wouldn't be attracted to him anymore. If she could get the "ick," she could stop thinking about his dimples, his bottom lip, and the way he smelled. If she didn't nip it in the bud right now, she'd end up having a crush, and that would be truly stupid of her.

"Tell me about this video." Jessica put on her most empathic expression. "Obviously, I'm not your therapist, but I can try to be a friend."

JESSICA GALLAGHER WAS really pretty. Like, *really* pretty. He couldn't believe that he hadn't remembered who she was when she'd walked up to him. She hadn't seen the video, which meant that he might have had a shot with her if he hadn't fucked it all up.

Though, she was pretty, but she wasn't really his type. Never had been. She was way too smart to get involved with someone like him. Even when they were eighteen years old, she'd seemed to have her shit together. And no interest in him. But even though he knew that he didn't have a shot now, he couldn't help but notice that she'd gotten better with age. Her long, brown curls and eyes that toggled between brown and an earthy green hadn't changed since college, but he specifically remembered that she'd always dressed really conservatively, in dark colors, as though she wanted to disappear into the background.

Now, however, she dressed to emphasize her curves, and her whole energy was different. Like she was at home in herself. She'd even been flirting with him. The one time he tried to talk to her in college, she'd glared at him over a copy of a textbook that she'd been reading while her roommates were getting ready to go out for the night. Tonight, she'd winked at him.

He was the one who hadn't changed much since college. Sure, he'd gotten older and had the patina to prove it. But he hadn't changed his behavior. Until the video, he'd been dating and hooking up as though feelings weren't really part of the equation. He never got in deep—had made it a point to keep things shallow—and now he was flirting with a therapist?

She'd asked about the video, but he didn't want to tell her. He wanted her to keep looking at him with compassion. But she could Google search it easily enough if he declined, and it was better that she heard the story from him.

"So I was dating this influencer, Kennedy Mower?" Jessica didn't look like that was ringing any bells, either. Jessica was probably so self-contained that she didn't even have social media. "Her dad is Benjamin Mower, the movie producer?"

The recognition dawned on Jessica's face. Of course she knew of the Oscar-winning producer. She was probably the type of woman who only watched Academy Award–nominated films. Though she'd been as sweet and awkward as the female main character in a romantic comedy a few moments ago—which he found charming for some reason when it was her—she probably thought that rom-coms were not worthy of her time and attention.

"Oh yeah, his daughter sells detox teas on Instagram now, right?" Jessica asked, clearly not impressed with his choices.

Galvin nodded. "Yeah, we met at a party for James Fahereghty." Her eyes got wide when he mentioned the movie star. "Not my usual crowd, but I designed his new house."

For some reason, he didn't want her to think that he hung out with Hollywood people in his everyday life. The more he thought about his relationship with Kennedy, the more embarrassed he was by the whole thing—not just the ending. He'd never felt comfortable hanging out with her and her friends, and he hadn't liked the feeling that every moment with her could be caught on camera and dissected by people on social media.

Sure, he'd been in magazines before because of specific commissions—the *Architectural Digest* spread about James's house included—but he wasn't famous. People didn't know him by name outside of a relatively small community of architects who worked in high-end residential real estate. In the larger world of architecture, his parents' firm—which only designed commercial projects—was much more well-known.

He was just beginning to break out. Or, he had been before the debacle with Kennedy. No one had fired him, so he was still busy for the next two years. His parents already didn't approve of his choice to go into residential work, and they'd already made it clear that this level of notoriety was "an unacceptable embarrassment." It pained him to think of getting the "I told you so" that his parents were dying to give him if his career petered out because of his association with Kennedy.

But Jessica wasn't looking like she was judging him. Of course, this was probably just her professional face. She might be judging up a storm behind those almost-hypnotic eyes. He felt drawn to her in a way he hadn't felt in a long time. He wanted to stick his face in the space between her neck and shoulder and commit her scent to memory. It wasn't just that she was pretty. She was compelling and layered, like a bottle of Burgundy from a very good year.

He resisted and forced himself to tell her the rest of the story. "We weren't ever that serious. I don't usually do serious." That last part left him with a little bit of shame. He'd been thinking about the fact that he didn't do serious and the reasons why since his breakup. For the first time in his life, he'd been forced to do actual self-examination. Other than disagreeing with his formerly very supportive parents about his career, he'd had it easy his whole life. And now, he was falling apart at the very first sign of struggle. "But she thought we were going to get engaged, and I broke up with her. I thought she took it well, but she went home and made a video saying that I never made her come."

Jessica's eyes got big at that part, and it made it even more painful to tell her the story. The one thing he'd always tried to do was to be honest, even when it hurt. Which was sort of what had gotten him here, with his reputation in tatters. Maybe if he had let Kennedy down more easily, they both could have moved on.

Or maybe he really was trash in bed, and that part made him feel shame and took a sledgehammer to his confidence. He'd never worried about that before. He knew where the clitoris was, and he'd always thought that he knew what he was doing with one. But Kennedy's video had brought it into question. He'd never been interested in a long-term commitment, but he'd always thought that his casual relationships were mutually beneficial. If they weren't, if he'd been lying to himself, he felt like a real asshole.

"Well, is that true?" Jessica asked, surprising him. Most people believed Kennedy, and Galvin frankly didn't blame them. But he'd slept with plenty of women who were effusive in their praise of his willingness to do anything for their pleasure, though he didn't quite feel confident that they were telling the truth anymore.

"I don't think so."

Jessica gave him the side-eye and ordered a drink from the bartender. It was almost closing time, but Jessica was pretty, and Galvin had noticed the bartender noticing her. Galvin said, "Put it on my tab."

"It's diabolical if she wasn't telling the truth." Jessica smirked, and it made Galvin want to kiss her. He knew it wasn't the right moment, and he was pretty sure there wouldn't be a right moment.

Yet, he was still incorrigible enough to say, "I'd love the opportunity to prove my innocence to you."

CHAPTER FIVE

JESSICA ROLLED HER eyes at Galvin. "You might be flirting with me, but you don't mean anything by it. You probably flirt just as easily as you breathe. You probably get out of parking tickets using the same line." She wouldn't let him turn her head. It wouldn't be sensible to flirt back. God knew she could use the practice now that she'd have to date again, but Galvin Baker wasn't an amateur flirt. He was professional level.

Instead of doing what her traitorous hormones were telling her to do—flirt with him, kiss him, bring him home and fuck him just to prove that she was still desirable—she waved a hand at him and said, "I'm not sure why it matters. It's not like everyone in the world follows Kennedy . . . or would believe her."

"Kennedy has half a billion followers on Instagram," he said. He drank the last of his bourbon and waved the bartender over. "Two more."

"I really shouldn't have *another* drink. I might do something dumb and let you try to clear your name with my vagina." The fact that those words had just come out of Jessica's mouth was a sure sign that she'd exceeded her limit. And the fact that she'd been dumped and had a book published in the span of forty-eight hours certainly did not help. She was losing her grip on her words, and actions would follow if she had another drink and spent any more time with Galvin.

"Oh no. These are for me. Keep me company, though, will you?" Galvin looked at her, and she was certain that his gaze should be classified as a weapon. He'd never looked at her like that in college, and for that she was incredibly grateful. Because—deep inside—there was a part of her that would have done anything for someone who looked at her as though he wanted nothing more in life than to kiss her. As though she was the only woman he could see.

She knew that it wasn't real. He couldn't see her. They barely knew each other. It was just hormones cascading through her mind and body that made her want to touch him. That was a warning sign, the biggest red flag.

Her nervous system was already completely fucked up from the highs and lows of the past two days. She was tired and a little bit tipsy. Seeing Galvin had brought on a wave of nostalgia for a time when the biggest life issue was picking a graduate program and not whether she would die alone. Going from life being full of opportunity and possibility to having the life she wanted disappear without warning.

Spending time with Galvin Baker was maybe the dumbest thing she could do with her night. She was too vulnerable to not fall for whatever he wanted to tell her. She wasn't sure she would believe Kennedy Mower's claims about Galvin's prowess in the bedroom. It was possible that he was great at getting women into bed but terrible at getting them off, but Jessica had a feeling that he knew what the fuck he was about. Jessica was more likely to believe that Galvin had broken Kennedy's heart, and she'd struck out in a way that would really hurt him.

Galvin was probably only flirting with Jessica because he was feeling unmoored. The last thing he needed was her flirting back. She'd be a better friend to him if she put up a boundary right here and right now.

"I'm not going to leave you alone right now, but I'm also not going to fuck you," Jessica said. It was firm. It was emphatic. Galvin busted out laughing.

"I've never been turned down so hard before, and women have been turning me down for months. You're killing me." He put his hand on his chest, and Jessica noticed how nice his hands were. They were big, and the way his veins marked his skin made her want to reach out and touch him. She'd never been hit this hard by raw lust before, and it simultaneously made her want to run away and lean into him. "Are you usually this harsh with your patients?"

Jessica shook off her thoughts, hoping to turn them around to something helpful for him and not destructive for her. "I'm harsh, but fair." When he didn't say anything and continued looking at her like he could see every bit of every thought and feeling she'd ever had, she said, "I just think that you seem like the kind of person who needs people to make firm boundaries. You're so charismatic that people end up doing what you want and then resenting you for it. I think that's probably what happened with Kennedy.

"You were probably perfectly clear that you didn't want

anything serious with her, but she probably didn't hear that because of the way you make people feel."

"How do I make people feel?" The little smirk on his face told her that he knew exactly what kind of influence he had over people.

"Your attention is on me right now, and I can't keep track of my thoughts." Jessica didn't mean to say that, but it was out now. She shook her head. "You know you're attractive."

He took a few moments to answer. The bartender brought over his bourbons, and Jessica grabbed one. She'd already said too much. Her buzz was wearing off, and a little light sedation was in order.

"I have a question for you, Jessica."

"What?" Jessica didn't know what he was going to ask but knew that it wasn't likely to be very appropriate.

"Do you know how attractive you are?"

Jessica didn't often think about her own appearance. She liked what she saw in the mirror well enough, but she didn't want to spend her life preoccupied with her looks the way her mother had been. But now that she thought about it, she'd modified the way she dressed and did her hair because of things that Luke had said over the years.

"That's a shallow question," she said. Galvin scowled at her response, which made Jessica feel defensive. "It's not what really matters in the long run. Beauty fades and getting caught up in it is one sure way to make it fade faster."

"What about enjoying the moment?" Galvin asked. He leaned back and looked her up and down. She felt like there was a heater inside her abdomen that flushed her whole body.

"I'm more interested in a life I look back on and feel proud of." She'd never lived for the present moment. And she'd seen what living for the present moment had done for her mother and some of her clients. "And I'm not the one crying into my whiskey."

"No, you're watching me cry into my whiskey, which seems worse."

Jessica laughed ruefully. "Well, my ex-boyfriend moved out of our place without any warning yesterday, so you might have a point."

"What the fuck?" Galvin sounded chagrined. "Why am I sitting here telling you my sad story, when you have, like, real problems?"

Jessica shrugged. "I guess that I'm just used to focusing on other people's issues."

"This seems like a real big issue not to focus on." Galvin turned his body more toward hers. And even though this was objectively not the right time to be attracted to someone new, and Galvin was objectively the wrong person to be attracted to, she felt his attention in the pit of her stomach. He had long lashes and a very kissable mouth. She swayed toward him. "How long were you together?"

"Since college."

"Holy shit." Galvin whistled. "You've been with the guy since forever, and he just walked out? Do I know the guy? I kind of want to kick his ass."

"He was in your fraternity, so yes, you do know him. Luke Grayson."

Galvin sneered. "That fucking guy?"

Jessica was surprised by Galvin's reaction. Almost everyone

liked Luke. That was Luke's thing—he was laid-back and likable. "He didn't like you, either."

Galvin paused, and Jessica waited to see if he would elaborate. Instead, he said, "I can't believe you spent over a decade with *him*."

"What do you mean?" Jessica was genuinely curious. Galvin and Luke couldn't have been more different, but Jessica didn't see why that would have prevented them from being friends. In her experience, friendships between straight men weren't as intimate as friendships between straight women. But that sometimes made them less fraught.

"I mean, you put up with him for *years*. You probably have more of an idea of why he's an asshole than I do."

I didn't think he was an asshole until he broke up with me. "Like I said, him leaving came out of nowhere. We weren't married, but we were settled, you know?"

"Shit." Galvin shook his head. "I'm sorry."

"Yeah, me too." Jessica swallowed the rest of her drink. It went down the wrong tube, and she choked a little. He patted her on the back until she could breathe again, and his touch lingered.

"I'm going to buy you a few more drinks and then some food. And maybe more drinks."

"This place is about to close." Jessica wasn't sure of the wisdom of that choice. But she'd gotten dumped by the so-called love of her life making wise decisions.

"I've got some places we can go. Places with tacos." He waggled his eyebrows as though he was promising sex instead of food, and her skin heated. He was kind of adorable.

Galvin looked at her with a disarming earnestness. Being

around him felt good. The way he looked at her and flirted with her made her feel attractive, and she realized she hadn't felt that way in a long time. She knew that relationships were hard work, but she'd been working really hard for a really long time to make her relationship with Luke feel sustainable, and maybe that was the problem. She'd been the only one working, the only one invested. Because she hadn't wanted to let go of her relationship. She hadn't wanted to risk ending up in the kind of dating hell that her clients bemoaned. She didn't want to end up the victim of the behaviors she talked about in her book.

Even though spending any more time with Galvin was probably going to lead to her having a story to tell for her next book, she didn't want to leave it here. She didn't want to walk away. When Galvin looked at her, his eyes filled with mischief and adventure, she didn't want to say no to him. In fact, it was impossible to force her mouth to make the words.

"Okay."

CHAPTER SIX

GALVIN WAS SHIVERING when he woke up, which might have had something to do with the fact that he was almost naked and sprawled out on a very cold tile floor. His face was stuck to said floor, and the skin on his cheek stretched unnaturally when he tried to lift his head. But that was the least of his problems. It felt as though his head was a construction site and all the heavy equipment was parked where his thoughts should be.

He sat up and looked around the bathroom he had slept in. He remembered everything from the night before, but it was the kind of hazy, alcohol-obscured memories that he had to reach out for, and that reaching was kind of painful at the moment. He pressed the heels of his hands into his eye sockets as he saw himself drinking tequila shots with Jessica Gallagher at a bar and then dancing to a club mix of Adele. And then taking more shots. And dancing some more.

There were tacos in there somewhere, too.

But the memory of kissing Jessica on a dance floor under colored lights slammed into him. Jessica wasn't the sort of girl he usually had those kinds of nights with. He waited for the remorse to show up, but it didn't arrive. All he wanted was a clearer memory of that kiss. Since he'd seen her at the restaurant, he'd wondered what she would taste like. And now he knew, but he didn't know enough. He didn't even know if she'd liked kissing him and wanted to do it again.

She'd said, pretty emphatically, that she wouldn't fuck him. And they hadn't done that. If they'd fucked, he wouldn't have woken up on the floor of her bathroom in his boxer briefs. He looked around for his clothes and didn't see them, so they must have come off someplace else. And then he remembered that she'd taken off most of his clothes and said they weren't fucking, so he could keep his underwear on. She'd been so funny and cute that he hadn't really cared whether or not they had sex. A first for him.

And now he just hoped that she wouldn't be upset with herself—or him—for letting all that happen after she'd told him that they were definitively not going to pound town. He was glad they hadn't, but Jessica didn't seem like the kind of woman who made impulsive decisions. She probably had a spreadsheet for every choice she made in life. She seemed like a checklist person. He didn't know that for sure, but it wasn't a huge leap. Last night hadn't been about thinking about all the reasons that they were deeply incompatible. It had been about drinking, dancing, and kissing.

He got up off the floor and opened the door to the bathroom slightly. Jessica wasn't in the bed. In fact, it was already made. Pillows fluffed and everything. He did find his clothes, neatly folded on the lone chair in the bedroom.

Once he was dressed, he ventured out of the bedroom and found Jessica in the kitchen, wearing yoga pants and a cropped T-shirt. She had her curly hair in a high bun that practically demanded he stare at the skin at the back of her neck. He now knew from experience that it was soft and very kissable.

Seeing her this morning, not rumpled, but not dressed up for a night out, he wanted more than anything to have a night like the last with her again. This time with less alcohol and more nudity. She hadn't seemed to notice him entering the room, so he cleared his throat.

She started a little, as though she'd truly been lost in her own thoughts. When she turned to face him, he felt entirely naked again. Like she could see right through him. But she was inscrutable. He couldn't tell what she was thinking, and it was going to drive him mad. He just knew it.

"I'm so sorry," she said. "I'm not sure what came over me last night, and I'm so embarrassed."

He crossed the room quickly to her, needing to be near her, to reassure her. That urge was pretty foreign to him. He wasn't what any of his exes would call emotionally supportive. In fact, one of Kennedy's main complaints was that he always seemed off in his own world and never knew when she was upset. He'd tried to explain that he couldn't be that to her. But she hadn't believed him and kept complaining. Finally, he'd broken things off.

Now that he'd had a lot of time to think about what he'd done wrong in that relationship—in all of his relationships—he kind of saw her point. He hadn't been emotionally engaged with Kennedy on any level. Dating her had been fun at first—kind of a novelty. He'd thought that the sex was a wash, but her video made him wonder.

It didn't make sense that he was feeling tenderness toward Jessica. She wasn't his girlfriend—not even close. Even though she'd kissed him later—after tequila shots—she'd been so clear that she didn't want him. Maybe that had only happened because of drunkenness and proximity and her very recent breakup.

And she wasn't giving him anything to go by at the moment. But then he realized that he hadn't said anything after her effusive apologies. "There's no need to apologize."

She scoffed. "After getting drunker than I've been since freshman year in college and mauling you?" She looked down, and her skin flushed. Galvin felt a hit of gratification that he had some effect on her. "I stripped you out of your clothes and just—like—rubbed you."

Galvin smiled at her. "I liked it."

"Is this what dating is like now?" Jessica turned away from him, and he did not like that, so he went into the kitchen. She smelled freshly showered, so that must mean that she had another bathroom, or he'd been passed out on her floor while she showered, and he'd missed the chance to see her naked.

"You smell good." He hadn't meant to say that, but he didn't want to get into the topic of how dating was now. To be honest, he really didn't like it that much, either. But it wasn't as though there were a lot of options. He rarely had to go on apps, but he did habitually slide into DMs. And people were so weird.

"You don't." Jessica looked at him pointedly, and he backed off. She was almost certainly right. Booze and dance club sweat wasn't a good smell on anyone. "I'm sorry. That was mean."

He smiled at her. "No, it was honest."

"Are you hungry?" It was clear to him that she was going to back away from anything serious this morning.

His stomach growled, answering for him. "I could eat a horse."

"You know, I've never understood that phrase. Like, why is eating a horse your only option?"

"You never played Oregon Trail in elementary school? When you're out of meat and half your family has died of dysentery or drowned trying to ford a river, you'll probably have to eat the horse." He didn't know why he couldn't stop talking to her, even about something kind of stupid, but he knew that he didn't want to stop talking to her. He felt like he couldn't stop talking to her. It was probably just that she was a therapist, so her job required her to be good at getting people to open up. But he didn't think it was just that. He felt like he'd known her forever, when they'd technically only ever been acquaintances.

He didn't even know much about her. But he liked everything he knew—the way she smelled, the way she kissed, the way she looked at him skeptically when he said he was so hungry that he could eat a horse.

"I totally forgot about Oregon Trail," she said with a laugh. He liked her laugh, too. "Like, such a fucked-up game to let children play. Morbid."

"It's no wonder every woman our age is obsessed with serial killer stories. We got started young with gaming out all of the bad things that could happen."

"I love true crime," she said. And he wasn't surprised. "The criminal justice system is incredibly flawed, but there's something about knowing the depths of people's capacity for evil that fascinates me. I think it's the same reason that I love my job. People's capacity to do fucked-up things to people they profess to love will never not surprise me."

"Were you surprised when Luke moved out on you?" Galvin wasn't sure why he'd asked that question. It wasn't appropriate, and he fully expected her to ask him to leave. But he wanted to know.

Instead, she turned to him. He didn't allow himself to be caught up in her pretty green eyes. "Totally. I had no clue that he wasn't happy."

"Were you happy?" Yet another question that he had no right to ask but was dying to know the answer to.

"I don't know. And I don't know if happiness is even the goal."

"If we're not here to be happy, what the fuck are we here for?" Galvin had always chased happiness, and he'd been pretty content with his life before the video.

"We're here to grow and learn." He could sense she was about to go into some sort of therapy lecture.

"But what about pleasure?"

"We can't go around seeking pleasure all the time. We also need meaning."

"Also?" He didn't know why he was antagonizing her, but it was making him feel very alive. "So you admit that we need pleasure?"

JESSICA SHOULD TELL him to leave. Right now. She'd already embarrassed herself last night by kissing him—and then whatever else they'd done. She'd always known that there was more of her mother in her than she wanted there to be. But she'd always been careful not to indulge that side of herself. She'd carefully considered every guy she'd ever hooked up with, and she'd settled on Luke as a suitable long-term partner.

And she didn't look at settling as a bad thing. People often made compromises—in partners, jobs, places to live—and mostly were able to convince themselves that they wanted what they had settled for because what they had settled for was good for them. Luke leaving and her running into Galvin had forced Jessica to *see* all the places that she'd settled in her life.

She looked around the apartment she'd shared with Luke. She hated the stark, modern lines of the place. There was no color, no personality. She wanted warmth and color and soft, cozy furniture that she could sink into. Before they bought this place, she'd wanted to move into a cozy little Spanish-style Hancock Park bungalow. All the doorways had been arched, and the floors had been a dark, rich color. The kitchen had been light and airy but tiled in an almost shocking blue.

But Luke had hated it and said that it would be impossible to keep clean. Jessica had agreed because the color and warmth were probably only attractive to her because it had mimicked her mother's personal style. And she'd trained herself to turn away from anything that her mother might find attractive.

Like Galvin. Her mother would think he was the most gorgeous man to ever walk the earth. She would be right, because he was even gorgeous moments away from keeling over from a hangover, in rumpled clothes. She'd lied a few moments ago when she'd told him that he didn't smell good. He smelled great—like, she would have wanted to wake up to that smell in her pillows—and that terrified her. She shouldn't have offered to make him breakfast.

But, then again, he hadn't been terribly put out when she had told him to keep his boxer briefs on the night before. The kissing and touching had probably been more about humoring an old friend going through a breakup than any lust for her on his part. He was probably only staying now because she would feed him before sending him on his way.

"I'll make some eggs." She moved to get the eggs, but he stopped her by standing between her and the refrigerator.

"Do you want eggs?"

She ignored the heat coming off his body. "I eat eggs for breakfast every day."

"Why?"

He was starting to irritate her now. "They're good for you. High in protein, and they keep me full."

"But do you like them?"

She didn't not like them, but that wasn't the only thing that mattered. She couldn't count the number of mornings she woke up wanting a chocolate croissant but went ahead and ate eggs instead. Because the chocolate croissant would taste good in the moment, but it wouldn't satisfy her long-term. Galvin was a chocolate croissant. He had tasted good last night, but now she only wanted more. And he wasn't the type of man who could ever sit still and satisfy her real needs. He probably did all of the things that she told men not to do in her book, but he'd gotten away with it until recently because the package was just so pretty.

She should really give him just a little bit more credit. It wasn't just that he looked pretty. He had a great deal of charm. Like just now, the way he was looking at her made her want to say, "Fuck the eggs. Fuck me. And then let's get a dozen doughnuts and eat them in bed before you fuck me again."

"Eggs are all I have in the house." She had to shut this down before she said any of the things in her head. She didn't really mean any of them. She didn't really want him. Her nervous system was just completely shot from everything that had happened in the last few days.

"I can get you something else," he said, and she knew he was trying to be helpful and accommodating. She shouldn't find it sexy that he was arguing with her over breakfast, but she found she liked the friction.

It made her skin tingle that today wasn't like every other day.

The amazing thing about being in a relationship for fifteen years was that she'd felt a kind of security with Luke that she'd never had in childhood and adolescence. And that security had reconfigured her into the type of person who liked knowing what was going to happen next. She wasn't the kind of person who craved novelty and excitement in anything but the safest and most predictable ways.

She wasn't her mother's daughter. She knew better than to fall under the spell of a fuckboy. But she was dangerously close to letting herself investigate her attraction to Galvin Baker in a very hands-on way.

"That won't be necessary," she said, trying to sound just a little bit imperious. "If you want something other than eggs, you're welcome to go find it elsewhere."

Instead of having the desired effect of pushing Galvin out the door, her comment made him smile and roll his eyes. "Like you said last night, I'm not one of your patients. And I'm not a child. I know I could walk out the door and have last night be just a weird thing that happened between two old friends who ran into each other when we were both in a weird place."

"I think that's exactly how we should both look back at it," Jessica said. "Fondly. From a distance." The last thing she needed was a crush on someone like him, but he would probably be flattered if she told him all the things about him that were wrong for her. Those things were precisely what made him so attractive, and he knew it—despite his current minor crisis in confidence.

But, instead of leaving, he came closer to her—not encroaching into her space too much, but just enough. He'd probably been so successful with women in the past because he could read body language. And Jessica didn't need multiple graduate degrees in psychology to know she was throwing off "skittish" as a whole vibe. He knew not to make any sudden movements.

"I don't actually think you want that."

"So, you're mansplaining my feelings now?"

"No." He sighed, heavily. He was going to give up and leave, and she would never have to deal with the way he made her tummy flip over ever again. "I had fun last night."

"Waking up on a strange woman's bathroom floor is your idea of fun?"

"Not really. But kissing a beautiful woman who happens to be an old friend is." She must have made a face when he said "beautiful," because she didn't like when people noticed how she looked. "Waking up on the floor was probably not the best thing for my aging back, but the way you looked at me last night is going to put a spring in my step."

"Does that kind of bullshit line usually work for you?" There was no amount of charming eye twinkling that could overcome the corniness of that line.

"I'm not trying to work you. I'm trying to open your mind to the wide world of breakfast pastry."

At this point, it was easier to acquiesce to changing her breakfast routine than it was to keep arguing with him. "Fine."

GALVIN LOOKED OVER at Jessica as she drove them to his favorite breakfast place. He had never met a woman so immune to him—at least, she was immune to him without the disinhibiting effect of tequila shots. Usually when a girl made it clear that she didn't like him, he moved on. But there was something about Jessica's prickliness that intrigued him. Especially after last night, when she was all over him. It was probably just repeated exposure, but he couldn't stop himself from needling her. And, honestly, eggs sounded kind of great. But he wanted them with bacon and pastry to soak up the residual booze in his system.

There was also something so resolute and put-upon about how she was going to make him breakfast that it made him want to get her out of that cold, empty apartment. He didn't want to feel protective of her. They weren't close, and she didn't even seem to like him very much. But he couldn't choose his feelings.

Jessica drove around the block where the restaurant was located, looking for parking three times before breaking down and using the valet, which he'd suggested the first time they'd driven around the block. So stubborn.

Once they were seated, Jessica looked at the menu, not at him. And he felt guilty for a brief moment. She'd been through a lot in the past seventy-two hours. He knew what it was like to have his life rocked because of something that an ex had done. Maybe he should have left her in her half-empty condo to eat eggs in peace.

"I'm sorry," he said, and she seemed a little startled to hear him say it. "I shouldn't have given you a hard time about breakfast."

"Why not? I know that I'm rigid and stuck to my routine." She shrugged, and he wanted her to continue. Because, from what he could remember about her, she'd always been the "mom" friend—the one who made sure no one got too drunk or did drugs of uncertain provenance, the one who peeled her friends away from guys who might have had nefarious intentions.

"It's not a bad thing." Even though Galvin had a reputation for being sort of a cad, he'd always been a stickler for routine himself. People were always surprised that he was so ruthlessly neat and meticulous, but he'd always been that way.

She looked at him and bit her lip as though she wanted to say something else. Given that she'd only revealed that Luke had broken up with her after a long conversation, he guessed that vulnerability about her personal life was something hard-won. But he wanted that from her. He was comfortable with her, and he wanted her to feel the same way with him. "You've always had your shit together, and I'm guessing there's a reason for that."

She hesitated for another moment, but he waited for her. Something in his gut told him that whatever she had to say would be worth the wait. "My mom was a total mess when I was growing up."

"How so?" Now that she'd said one thing, he wanted more.

As greedy as she'd been for his touch the night before, he was greedy for her disclosure now.

"She was always hopping from boyfriend to boyfriend, job to job, shitty apartment to shitty apartment. And I felt like I was more of an inconvenience than anything else. I learned not to get too attached to friends, neighbors, teachers—"

"That had to have been so hard." He, on the other hand, had lived in the same house from the time he came home from the hospital until the time he'd left for the dorm. His life had been so utterly boring as a teenager that he pathologically sought out novelty as an adult. And that was what had gotten him into trouble. "I can see why you'd value stability and common sense over pleasure."

She looked at him thoughtfully for a beat. "You're pretty emotionally tuned in for an asshole."

Galvin laughed. "I'm trying to be less of an asshole these days, but I'm not sure I'm succeeding. I did cajole you into having a meal with me, after all."

"But I needed it. You saw that I was just going to eat sad eggs and be sad in my house, and you tried to make it better." The server approached the table and took their drink order. Galvin resented the interruption to whatever Jessica had been about to say. He hadn't realized that he needed as much of an ego massage as he did.

Luckily, she continued when the server left. "There might be hope for you to become a better boyfriend. I mean, if that's what you want."

Before the video, he'd always thought he was a decent boyfriend—as long as the relationship was short-term. But he'd realized in the wake of his public humiliation that he'd been selfish and shallow, and he didn't like that about himself. He wanted to change, and he wasn't sure when he'd started to want to change. But looking at Jessica's face after the server brought over her latte and his black coffee, that desire solidified. She wasn't the impetus for him wanting to be a better man—she was the confirmation.

"I think I do want that," he said. "How are you feeling about the whole Luke thing?"

She paused in thought again. He liked that about her. Another thing on the growing list of things that he liked about her. "I'm actually okay. I know that there will be waves of grief and anger, but I've realized that Luke and I hadn't been connected in quite some time."

Galvin wondered, despite wanting to keep his intentions toward Jessica mostly honorable, if "connection" was code for sex. Because Jessica was incredibly sexy underneath the staid exterior. The way she licked a touch of foam off her lip. The way she moved.

He didn't even have to think about the way she kissed for his skin to heat. "I hear that's a problem in most long-term relationships."

"That's why it's important to look for more than just sex in a long-term relationship. I mean, sex is important—especially if you're monogamous—but you actually have to like the person, too. Or, ideally you would. I know of plenty of couples that sustain their connection through a mix of antipathy and fear of being single. It isn't healthy, but humans aren't really designed to do the healthiest thing. We're mostly just terrified skin bags."

That made Galvin think of his parents. He'd never understood why they stayed together even though they could barely stand each other. They certainly could have run a business together without staying married. They'd made the right noises about the importance of family while he was growing up, but they weren't really close.

He didn't know if it was some kind of misguided loyalty or the fact that they had so much in common when it came to their work. Sometimes, he thought that splitting up would have been too much bother for them. Their lives were too enmeshed for them to untangle, even though they made each other miserable.

"Where did you go?" Jessica's question jolted him out of his maudlin bullshit thoughts.

"Just thinking about my parents. They don't really like each other." He didn't know why he was telling her the truth now, when he didn't even have bourbon as an excuse.

Instead of launching into some explanation for how his parents hating each other had fucked him up when it came to relationships and he had to lean into the discomfort, she nodded and looked at her menu. "How many chocolate croissants do you think we should get?"

CHAPTER SEVEN

JESSICA WASN'T GOING to delve into Galvin's psyche any more deeply than she already had. He was trouble. She knew he was trouble, and she wasn't in the market for any trouble. Not in her personal life, not ever. He wasn't a client, and she wasn't responsible for getting him to see that his fear of commitment came from a fear of turning out like his parents. But she wanted to ask what it was like for him when he bailed on relationships. Did he feel trapped? Did he start to pick apart everything about his partners? What was his deal?

His deal wasn't any of her business. Right now, all she had to think about was pastry.

Galvin chuckled. "I think you're a secret hedonist."

"What do you mean?" Jessica wasn't a hedonist, secret or otherwise.

"Most people would order one pastry and see if that was enough." Galvin's green eyes seemed to pierce the wall that Jessica carefully maintained between her baser desires and her behavior. Even though she was hung over and should be thinking about her extremely recent breakup, the slow heat that his gaze elicited in her body couldn't be ignored. "But you know that you need at least a croissant and a half to slake your hunger."

"Hmm." She couldn't form words, so she made a sound and looked away from him. She looked around the crowded café, filled with couples and some groups of women who appeared to be debriefing on their weekends. She should really be doing that instead of having brunch with a man she'd felt up the night before. It didn't matter that he'd seemed to be into it. She'd felt him up like a horny teenager—it was so embarrassing. She didn't know why he was continuing to humor her—continuing to flirt with her. This went far beyond the kind of compassion one might feel for an old acquaintance who'd had a bad day.

As she was lost in thought, she saw the last person she wanted to see—Abby, her publicist. The one who'd set up all of the awkward podcast interviews, and the one who'd encouraged her to share more about her personal life so she could be more relatable, despite Jessica's resistance.

She looked away immediately, hoping that Abby wouldn't notice that she was here with someone who wasn't her boyfriend. She'd told Abby about the breakup, but she didn't want anyone to think that she was getting over Luke by getting under a notorious fuckboy.

Luke had been cute in college—in a sort of boring, frat boy way. But he was a surgeon, and that training had taken a toll on his looks. She cringed, internally, at thinking something so shallow about someone she'd loved very much. But it was true. Luke had aged like a banana, and there was no use trying to see beyond his receding hairline and sallow complexion now.

During their relationship, she'd done her best to ignore the fact that he'd made shitty remarks about ten pounds of weight gain and expected her to still be hot for him no matter what. Now, that was useless.

She really shouldn't compare, but Galvin, on the other hand, was in the fine wine category of aging. Maybe there was something to be said for avoiding serious commitments. It probably left more time for the gym and skin care. She'd never have to tell Galvin that scrubs weren't appropriate dinner wear, especially ones with bloodstains on them. He even looked good in a suit that she'd crumpled up and thrown on her floor. Sort of like one of the roguish-looking heroes on one of her mother's romance novels.

Jessica was still contemplating Galvin's good looks and trying to remember why they didn't matter at all when Abby approached the table. She felt as though she'd been caught cheating on a test, and her face heated.

"You're a public figure now. You really should put on makeup before you leave the house. And what the fuck are you doing with this guy?" Jessica swore that Abby's favorite punctuation mark was the f-word. Even though they didn't know each other that well, it didn't alarm Jessica the way it used to. She found it kind of charming now, but it had taken some getting used to.

Jessica didn't quite know how to explain this. For all that Abby knew, she was still in deep mourning about the demise of a happyish relationship with her college boyfriend. It was weird that she was eating breakfast with a man who clearly wasn't said boyfriend with second-day stubble and wrinkled clothes. Jessica didn't socialize with clients, so her being here with a man she was not in a relationship with did not make sense.

She decided the best course of action was keeping her answers short and honest—they could have a discussion about her breakup later, in private. "Eating breakfast?"

She hadn't meant for her answer to sound like a question, and her hesitance made Abby examine the tableau a little more closely. "Who is he?"

Galvin looked up at her with his most winning smile. What he didn't know was that Abby could freeze the balls off an NFL player with one glare and had done so in Jessica's presence when he didn't wear the suit Abby had told him to for an interview about his memoir. "Galvin Baker."

Abby squinted at him like she knew him from somewhere. Considering why he'd recently been in the public eye, that was a bad thing. Jessica wanted to protect him from Abby's wrath, and that made her stop to think. Galvin was nothing to her but an old acquaintance. Sure, they'd had a weird evening together when they were both in a weird time in their lives and it had turned weirdly sexual—at least on her part. But that was the end of it. After this breakfast, they'd go their separate ways and probably never speak again. She was probably only protective because he didn't need Abby's scrutiny. Her publicist was there to protect Jessica's image, and it didn't need protecting from Galvin.

But while Jessica was pondering the way she wanted to come to Galvin's defense, even though he didn't need it, Abby figured out who he was. "Oh, you're Kennedy Mower's ex. The one with the sad penis."

Galvin's face paled, and before she could stop herself, Jessica said, "Galvin's penis isn't sad." Oddly, that didn't bring the color back into Galvin's face. If anything, his neck turned red, and he looked as though he wanted to crawl under the table.

"That was really loud, Jess," Galvin whispered, and then it was her turn to flush. She looked around, and a few people were staring.

"Abby, sit down," Jessica said. It didn't help that the most powerful book publicist in town, responsible for forty-eight of the fifty-two number-one books on the *New York Times* Best Sellers list in the past year, was standing around in a restaurant filled with reality television hopefuls who probably thought their lives were worthy of at least three memoirs, with a raised voice.

Unlike most of the time, when Abby never listened to anyone, she took the empty seat at their table. "This is bad."

"What's bad?" Galvin asked, his composure and the easy confidence that he usually wore like a finely tailored suit back in place. "We're just two friends having breakfast."

Abby scoffed. "You, sir, look rode hard and put up wet." Jessica chuckled at Abby's colloquialism, until her shrewd gaze turned onto Jessica. "And you don't look much better. Is this a rebound? You could do a lot better. What are you doing canoodling with Sad Dick Energy over here?"

"No one says canoodling," Jessica said, trying to distract Abby. And the stellar professional who was doing her a huge favor by taking her money to work on her book when she usually had a wait list about seven years long. "And, even if people still said canoodling, we're not doing that."

"We were canoodling last night," Galvin said, and that earned him a death glare from Jessica. He seemed impervious, though.

Now Abby seemed truly incensed. "Well, now I'm glad we didn't go with the 'Jessica Gallagher has such a stable relationship that you should listen to her advice' angle."

"I told you that it was best to keep my private life private." Jessica felt a little smug about that at the moment.

"He was a fucking douche anyway," Galvin said. Jessica was beginning to think that he was a really supportive friend. She appreciated him a whole lot in that moment. "You're going to be way better off without him."

It was Jessica's turn to flush. There was a subtext of admiration for her in his words that she wouldn't have expected after everything that had happened the night before. Even though he'd needled her this morning about her rigid breakfast habits and abhorrence for hedonism, she could feel that he genuinely liked her.

Abby looked as though she'd blown a few circuits in her brain and needed to process some more, but she was looking at both Jessica and Galvin shrewdly. Jessica didn't trust that look at all.

"We ran into each other last night at the bar. I was out with Barbie and Kelly, drowning my sorrows. Galvin was drowning his sorrows alone, and so we decided to pool our sorrows to drown them more effectively."

"And did it work? Did y'all fuck?" If there was one thing about Abby, it was that she got straight to the point.

Galvin answered for them both. "Unfortunately no."

"Maybe for you." Abby also gave as good as she got, and she

wasn't buying any of Galvin's charm. Jessica didn't buy it, either, but over the past eighteen hours or so she had gotten the sense that there was more to him. Abby looked at her. "The last thing you need after breaking up with a man who couldn't find a clitoris on a clitoris farm is Droopy Dick Dave over here."

Galvin looked too pleased at the dig on Luke's sexual prowess to care much about Abby's new nickname for him.

"He could find a clitoris."

"Yeah, he just didn't want to, which is worse."

Jessica was a little offended at Abby's assumption about her unsatisfying sex life. It was true, but it kind of stung. And, before the breakup, Jessica had thought of a boring relationship as a good thing. They hadn't had to work at things because they were good. She couldn't stop beating herself up over the fact that she hadn't noticed anything wrong with them until he was literally walking out the door.

"I thought you wanted me to trot Luke out for publicity?"

Abby rolled her eyes. "Listen, when he was the perfect surgeon boyfriend, I wanted him out there, singing your praises. Or just on your arm, looking hopelessly in love with you. He looked good on paper, and I could have hooked him up with some hair plugs and better clothes. He would have been a sign to men everywhere that—if they used your ten handy tips—they might end up with a stone-cold fox like you."

Jessica did not buy into Abby's argument that she was a stone-cold fox. She pulled herself together well, but her hotness was the least interesting thing about her. Her unwillingness to rely on her appearance alone to sell her "brand" was sort of anathema in L.A., but she stood by it. She cared about substance, and that made her different from her mother. She didn't go around chasing stuff that just frittered away.

But what she had gone chasing had moved out of their home a few days ago. That had to be why she was questioning herself. It had to be why she was having warm feelings toward a man who didn't have any of the qualities she needed in a long-term partner.

She looked at Galvin then, really looked at him. Even though his suit wasn't perfectly pressed, he was at ease in his skin. Everyone in the café had probably seen the video blasting his performance in the bedroom. Most of them probably thought that he was the one who could wander the fields of Clitoris Farms in Vulva, Virginia, and come away without harvesting even a single orgasm.

But he'd kissed her like he knew what he was about. Her skin heated and the core of her became heavy just thinking about the way he'd kissed her, about the way his hands had cupped her chin and ghosted over the skin at her collarbones and upper back. The way his need to touch her more had been palpable and how he'd held back—because she'd told him to—pressed into her mind and made her forget that Abby was sitting at the table.

"You guys, like, *like* each other, don't you?" Abby sounded completely disgusted.

"What? No!" Jessica responded to her publicist's accusation without thinking. But she did like Galvin. Despite the fact that they were incredibly ill-suited as romantic partners, he'd given her something she'd needed last night and this morning. They hadn't fucked, but he'd made her feel as though she was desirable on one of the worst days she'd had in a very long time. It would never happen again, but he'd been a true friend to her. "I mean, I like him. But we're not involved or anything. And we won't be. We can't be."

She was rambling, so she stopped talking. It would be better for everyone that way.

"She's all right," Galvin said with a crooked grin in place. She didn't like what that crooked grin meant. The way he looked at her right now made her feel as though she was a bug under glass.

IN THE LAST few moments, Galvin had figured out that Abby was more bark than bite, and that Jessica was flustered by him. He liked that she was flustered by him, and he wanted to explore that later. But he had the sneaking suspicion that her friend and publicist Abby would be a significant gatekeeper to him spending more time figuring out all of the things that made Jessica blush and ramble.

"Stop grinning like that," Abby said. "It's distracting my client, and I need her focused."

"On what?" Galvin asked. "We were just having breakfast, and she didn't mention anything about the two of you having a scheduled meeting."

"She doesn't keep you abreast of her schedule, because you are not her boyfriend." Abby sighed and pinched the bridge of her nose. "And I need to figure out how to spin this if you two are seen out together so I can minimize the damage to her public image and book sales if it gets out that she wrote a dating advice book and got dumped the day before it was released. It's a fucking nightmare. She'll be a meme. Do you want her to be a meme?"

Galvin was the tiniest bit chastened. "No. I don't want her to become a meme." And he didn't. Jessica was pretty, smart, and cool—she always had been. But spending time with her had made him realize that she was more sensitive and vulnerable than he'd thought.

"This is why I didn't want to talk about my personal life in the first place, Abby." Jessica sounded frustrated. He hated that.

"And I agreed to you not talking about your personal life in the press because Luke was a bore. And there's only so much magic I'm capable of." He couldn't help himself, but he grinned at Abby again because she also disliked Luke. Her voice dripped with disdain when she spoke about Jessica's ex, which meant that she had good taste.

"Well, he's gone now. Neither of us have to be bored by my ex-boyfriend anymore." Jessica sounded defeated, and he really didn't like that. It made him want to find Luke and punch him in the face. He was unfamiliar with the urge to defend someone else's honor. He was more of a lover than a fighter. He hadn't even sent Kennedy an angry text when she'd tried to destroy his chances of ever getting laid again. Instead, he'd moped around for the last few months—which was pathetic, but at least it wasn't toxic.

"Listen, is there any chance that Luke would talk to the press about your breakup?"

Jessica pulled a face that he was sure she didn't intend to be cute, but it was very, very cute. She bit her lip, and he almost groaned. "Not unless the press tracks him down in the operating room."

"And not a single one of my press contacts had any idea who you were dating or how long you were dating them, because I made sure that none of them knew that." Abby paused, and Galvin wondered what she was trying to get at here. "And your social media is locked down to private—"

"Yeah, but we made an Instagram for the book. You told me I wouldn't have to let randoms see into my personal life." Jessica sounded worried.

Abby didn't respond because she appeared to be lost in thought. She leaned back and looked back and forth between them. Galvin could almost see the calculations she was making fly past her head.

"Abby. No." Jessica seemed to have figured out what Abby was going to say before he did. Which was why he looked like a deer in headlights when Abby said, "Okay, so you're going to date Galvin. Publicly."

CHAPTER EIGHT

THAT'S THE WORST idea I've ever heard," Jessica said. "He is not my type." Galvin put his hand on his chest as though she had hit him, and Jessica said, "I am not your type, either. You date Instagram models." The idea that one little video about his sad dick would make him date a dowdy, uptight, frankly plain-looking psychotherapist who wore cotton panties that came in a three-pack instead of a contraption that started with straps over her tits and ended with a thong was preposterous.

"I'm not sure whether to be relieved or hurt. On the one hand, I'm sort of insulted that you don't want to date me for PR purposes. On the other hand, I'm kind of relieved that I don't have to deal with her after leaving here today." He pointed at Abby, who bared her teeth at him. Then, he leaned closer to Jessica and said, "And, for your information, I'm an equal-opportunity cad."

Jessica was a little surprised that he was insulted. She would have assumed that it was all relief that their weird night wasn't going to spin off into a series of weird nights.

"I don't really like this idea all that much, either," Abby said. "But it's not like the old days when we only had to worry about paparazzi. Now, there are gossip podcasts and social media accounts and blind items everywhere."

"Abby, we don't need this," Jessica said. They'd only met once they'd started working together on the book, but they'd grown friendly over the past few months. Abby had said that she'd wanted to work with her ever since she'd seen a YouTube video of Jessica giving a presentation on how adolescent trauma shaped behavior on dating apps.

Abby had reached out to her when she'd seen the announcement that Jessica was writing a dating book. Jessica hadn't been on board at all, at first. But one night, she'd been alone while Luke was on call and was watching a terribly unqualified dating coach with no credentials giving advice to men on TikTok. It had incensed her so much that she had started jotting her ideas down in a way that wouldn't have fit into an academic paper that she could present at stodgy conferences.

Abby had then run with the book proposal—setting Jessica up with the editor who'd purchased the book.

And though her friend was a total barracuda when it came to her business, she had the sense to let the idea of fake-dating Galvin percolate with Jessica for a few moments. Jessica used that time to chew on both her croissant and the idea of dating Galvin for PR.

Even if people believed it, how would it make her look? She'd never wanted to be a rehab for broken men—again, too much like her mother—but had dating one who hadn't seemed to be broken at the time worked out for her? Luke was the most predictable man on earth, until he wasn't.

“This would be good for your image, Galvin,” Abby continued. “Enough people saw you on that show that I would imagine dating is not going so well for you right now? The idea that you could go from dating a no-talent trust-fund baby who spends hours a day Photoshopping selfies so that her BBL pops to dating an actual, human woman with a job would probably make your dating life easier—after a carefully orchestrated, amicable breakup.”

“That’s exactly why no one would believe that he’s dating me, Abby. He’s a hot architect guy who dated Kennedy Mower, and I’m boring, bland, and I wear granny panties.” Jessica hadn’t meant to put a voice to her insecurities. That helped no one. But she didn’t want this to go any further, and Abby was delusional if she thought that Galvin would agree to being seen as her boyfriend.

It was one thing for him to humor her last night, but he wouldn’t actually want to spend real time with her.

Galvin held up his hand and said something that shocked Jessica to her core. “Hey, you’re talking about my friend there,” he said, looking at her. “And you are anything but boring. Reserved? Yes. Boring, no. And I happen to like your granny panties very much.”

Jessica gasped. She was embarrassed enough about their little pantsless romp the night before, and she had hoped to get away from this exchange without Abby finding out about the details of their hookup.

“Well, he smells like bourbon and coochie, so I assumed he’s seen your panties.”

“He didn’t get anywhere near my coochie,” Jessica said, a weak line of defense if there ever was one. “And I haven’t even seen his dick, so don't you dare ask if it was sad in a crowded restaurant."

Abby shook her head and stared at both of them as though they had disappointed her greatly by not having a one-night stand. "Listen, if you want to cease being undatable to anyone with a social media account," she said, looking at Galvin, "and you want to earn out your book advance"—she looked at Jessica—"you'll pretend to date for the next three to four months."

"That's a long time," Jessica said, which was ironic considering the length of the relationship that had just ended. But it felt like a long time to keep up a ruse of being in love with Galvin, without falling in love with him for real. Because she knew that she was always so close to becoming her mother, to becoming someone who cried on a therapist's couch about some man who had done her wrong instead of the one handing out the tissues.

Galvin chuckled, and that got her attention. "You were in a relationship for over a decade with the least interesting man in the world, and you make a couple months with me sound like a life sentence without the possibility of parole."

"You can't possibly be okay with this suggestion." Jessica refused to believe that Galvin would participate in anything so farcical. "I can't think of any two people who don't fit more than we don't fit."

"C'mon, there are members of biker gangs and gun-toting, toothless insurrectionists that are less desirable than me."

"I wasn't talking about how desirable you are, Galvin. You know what you look like. But that doesn't mean that people would believe that someone who looks like you . . . who has everything going for them the way that you have going for you . . . would be interested in dating someone like me."

His face softened then, and Jessica immediately regretted spelling things out for him. She hated the look of pity he gave her. “Wow, I can’t believe that people come to you to solve their self-esteem problems.”

Abby, who had been uncharacteristically silent, said, “Those who can’t do, teach.”

“Yes, that’s exactly why I can’t date, fake or otherwise. I never claimed to be an expert on doing dating—just what men shouldn’t do in dating.”

“You think it’s easy dating as a guy?” Galvin asked. “It’s not easy for anyone, and that’s why I always keep—kept—things light and superficial.”

“Well, that was the before times,” Abby said.

“Would you be nice to him? That video was slander, and people only believed Kennedy because she sells them their favorite detox tummy-tightening tea.”

“Thank you,” Galvin said.

Jessica glared at him. “And you really shouldn’t have been trifling with the feelings of someone young enough to be your daughter from a teen pregnancy.” Curiosity had gotten the best of her, and she’d broken down and Googled Kennedy and the video while Galvin was still passed out on her bathroom floor that morning.

“When you put it that way, I’m disgusted with myself,” he said. From the night before, she knew that he really did want to grow and change with respect to relationships.

“You shouldn’t be, but you should be willing to acknowledge your mistakes and grow from them.”

Abby cut her hands across the air to shut everyone up. When Galvin shut his mouth before responding to Jessica,

Abby continued. "Here's the thing. You both need something that you can get by dating for a little bit and taking some cute Instagram selfies together. You clearly know each other well enough to bicker, and I can make the beginning of your relationship suitably vague, so that no one will ever know that he couldn't putt a hole in one last night, and you're only dating to rehab his image and make sure yours doesn't get ruined."

"Do you really think it would help?" Jessica was still unsure that dating Galvin would have any impact on her book sales.

"Yeah, if I can spin a story out of it." Abby seemed a little pissed that Jessica doubted her professional opinion.

"What kind of story?" Why was Galvin so seemingly open to dating her for the 'gram?

Abby tilted her head toward Galvin. "Well, we could say that you did some serious self-examination after Kennedy's video came out, and really looked at your own behaviors. Then, you ran into your old buddy Jessica one night, and the two of you hit it off. She wasn't aware of the video, but you told her that you were willing to change how you relate to people. Jessica laid out terms that matched the dating philosophy that she laid out in her book, and you agreed."

"That doesn't sound very romantic," was Galvin's only response.

For her part, Jessica thought the story made her seem like both a pushover and a prig. "I hate this."

"It's a better story than 'Dating Advice Writer's Boyfriend Moves Out Because Her Book Doesn't Work.'" Abby had a point, but Jessica truly wished there was another way.

"You know, our college reunion is coming up, and it would

truly irritate Luke if we showed up together. He may even try to win you back," Galvin said.

Jessica was fairly certain that there was nothing Luke could do to win her back. Part of her was relieved that he'd moved out, because she would have married him if he'd asked. And she was starting to think that she wouldn't have been happy. They'd had a lot going for them for a long time, but just because a relationship met her basic needs didn't mean that she was optimizing her own happiness.

She'd spent decades not even thinking about happiness, per se, just repairing the damage from her unstable childhood. And maybe that wasn't any way to live.

Still, she disliked the part of herself that wanted to fake-date Galvin and rub it in Luke's face—the part of her that would take pleasure in his distress. After all, she'd once loved the guy. Or at least cared about his happiness just as much as her own. She was just upset right now. That kind of time in a relationship didn't allow for feelings to just flip on a dime, overnight.

Was she only considering this because of Galvin? Because she was truly attracted to him?

That was definitely part of it, but there was more. Part of her had always craved more adventure than she'd ever allowed herself. The same part of her was jealous of her clients, who really put themselves out there and made themselves vulnerable. Not that a fake relationship with Galvin would really make her feel vulnerable. It wouldn't even truly be an adventure. It would be more like a caper, an escapade. She would be lying to people in hopes that they would buy her book, so that they could have a love life more like hers.

It was not like she would ever fall in love with someone like Galvin. She would never let it get that far. She'd gotten through college without one single crying, screaming, throwing-up breakup. Outside of her hour crying in the shower, she couldn't remember the last time she'd shed tears other than some empathy crying with a client—which was really more like catching a yawn from someone yawning in your face.

"I don't know, Abby." Jessica shook her head. "Wouldn't it be worse if people realized that we were just dating for the 'gram?"

"Oh, definitely." Abby never sugarcoated anything, but Jessica could use a little vanilla glaze right now. "That's why we're talking short-term, vague beginnings, amicable breakup."

"If Jessica's not into this idea—"

Jessica was relieved that Galvin was respecting her boundaries here. Unlike a lot of the guys who dated her clients, he'd been pretty good at that from the beginning. He'd prodded her to talk to him and to broaden her breakfast options, but he hadn't touched her without permission or presumed that he knew better than she did. If they were truly in a relationship, it would be almost healthy. The fact that he didn't want to force her into anything made her think that this could possibly work.

"What would Galvin get out of this?" Jessica asked. It seemed like she would get most of the benefit.

"He would get to not be the asshole anymore." At this, Galvin gave Abby a dirty look, and to him she said, "I mean, Jessica could give you some hands-on lessons out of her book."

"I think we should do it." Jessica surprised herself by saying it, but it was true. Carefully planning every aspect of her life hadn't exactly worked out for her, and this wasn't truly an adventure—like jumping out of a plane or something—but it might save her a little humiliation. It might even be fun to spend more time with Galvin—sort of like having the fling she could have had in college, but never tried to.

GALVIN COULDN'T BELIEVE that Jessica would actually agree to something like this. It didn't make any sense. Granted, he didn't know her all that well, but he would never put "Will Date Someone to Save Her Image" on his bingo card.

"Are you sure?" After last night, he wanted to spend more time with her. He was attracted to her, and it felt different for him. Like, he was interested in what truly made her tick. Maybe the therapy was working, and he was becoming a better man. Or maybe she was just special—or at least had the potential to be special to him.

"I think it makes sense." Something unsure crossed her face, and she added, "Unless you don't think people will believe that you're dating me."

He didn't know where she'd gotten the idea that she wasn't immensely appealing, but he suspected that it had come from Luke, and it made him want to punch the guy even more than his baseline desire to punch the guy. "I'm more worried that no one will believe that you're dating me. I'm pretty toxic right now."

"That's correct. You are the Three Mile Island of men right now." He wasn't sure that Abby was helping her case any, but okay.

"That's true," Galvin agreed. The publicist did have a point. "Why would anyone buy your book if you live by that philosophy and end up with a guy who publicly sucks?"

Jessica chewed on the last bit of her pastry, took a sip of the latte that was probably about three seconds from cold by now, and said, "I actually think that it works better. The book is all about advice for men. What if you contacted me a few months ago, I shared an early copy with you, and you instantly tried to reform your player ways, winning my heart? That could work."

Abby sat back in her chair. "I think it's brilliant."

Jessica smiled, and that was the thing that convinced him to agree. "I guess I should probably read your book," he said.

Abby looked at him with a grin that said she thought she'd done a great job cooking up this probably stupid scheme. "You can buy a copy at your local bookstore." She stood, swinging her large Hermès bag over her shoulder. "Shop indie."

CHAPTER NINE

GALVIN DIDN'T READ a lot of nonfiction. He liked mysteries and thrillers, and he'd always thought that he would make a great spy. Until he learned that spying was not all about wooing other covert agents into spilling international secrets by making them delirious with pleasure and champagne. It was probably for the best, since all of James Bond's lovers ended up dead, but Galvin still enjoyed indulging in the fantasy once in a while.

He also supposed that his penchant for designer suits and dry martinis came from his childhood obsession with Bond films. He used to watch them with his father, and it was one of the only things they'd ever done together. Galvin had been athletic like his father, but he'd run cross-country instead of playing football. He'd been kind of scrawny as an adolescent, not filling out until he'd gone to college, and he'd always felt that his dad looked down on him because he wasn't Mr. All-American.

Despite what people came to assume about him later, he

hadn't really dated in high school. He was always the nerdy friend girls asked for help with trigonometry homework. For prom, his friend had taped a sign to his back that said, "I need a prom date," and Angela, one of his track teammates, had taken pity on him after three periods.

He never thought he'd been bitter about those experiences until recently. His therapist suggested that he'd taken on the role of Lothario in his romantic life because he didn't want to risk being open and vulnerable with someone and then be rejected. He'd suggested that Galvin still felt like kind of a nerd, even though he didn't look that way on the outside. His habit of not allowing relationships to get too deep was a defense mechanism so that no one would see him for who he truly was. The flashy suits and expensive car were a smokescreen.

Galvin resisted that. It was incredibly immature to be haunted by the specter of his high school self as he was tipping into middle age, but Jeremy, the therapist, said that it was common. People shaped their adult personalities around their childhood trauma all the time.

Once Galvin saw that, he couldn't stop noticing it in other people. Today, he was wondering how Jessica's life experiences had made her so unsure and careful when it came to love and romance. He wondered what had made Luke seem like a good choice, even though he was truly an arrogant, two-faced shithead.

He lay down on his plush couch in the Spanish-style bungalow that he'd purchased a few years ago, with a very dry martini next to him and an open mind.

Although he was reading Jessica's book for research, he hoped it would serve up some insight as to why Jessica was the way she was. He also wanted to figure out if there were any clues about why he was so wildly attracted to a woman who could see right through his bullshit.

Maybe the therapy was just working, and he wasn't as interested in easy as he was before. It had only been a couple of months, but Galvin was nothing if not a good student. But as he flipped through the pages of Jessica's book, he was disappointed. Not in her—the prose was lively, and he could almost hear her voice recounting the anonymized experiences of clients and friends (with their express consent, of course). He was disappointed that a lot of the tips were so elementary. And there was an air of condescension about some of the advice that he didn't feel from Jessica face-to-face.

And then he got to an anecdote he recognized—the one about him. She'd anonymized his name, but he recognized "Greg" as himself immediately. It was in the chapter entitled "Don't Expect to Be Taken Seriously If You've Dated Her Friend." And the entire chapter talked about how Greg had systematically dated his way through every sorority house on campus.

He'd actually forgotten about the time he'd studied next to Jessica in the library and tried to hit on her. As he read her recounting, the memory came back to him. He'd sat next to her because he'd seen her around and she seemed to ignore him. That was like catnip to him then, and he'd thought that he'd be up for the challenge.

How wrong he'd been. Jessica had told him that she knew at least ten girls that he'd hooked up with, and she hadn't seemed impressed by that—in fact, she'd been disgusted. And then she'd gone back to her studies. He could feel the shame now, as though this interaction had been yesterday.

But logically, he didn't really have anything to be ashamed about, did he? Being attractive to women was a novel experience in college. And hooking up was de rigueur. It wasn't like any of the women he'd been with had wanted or pushed for more. At the time, he'd thought that they were all after a good time, not a long time. Except for Jessica, who'd dated her college sweetheart—he hated characterizing that fucking guy as a sweetheart—until a few days ago. But maybe none of those women were looking for a serious thing in college with him specifically once he'd hooked up with enough people.

Still, it was really sex shaming to correlate vast sexual experience with being unsuitable for a relationship. Jeremy had told him that it was important to have compassion for his own mistakes—something he hadn't learned from his perfectionist parents—and he knew why he'd gone a little wild in college. Girls being interested in him had been novel and he'd gorged himself. Sort of like how he'd never gotten any sugary soda at home, and when he went to a party at his cousin's house he'd had so much real Coke that he'd thrown up.

No girls had any interest in him in high school. When he arrived at college, he started working out with weights, got a good haircut, and upgraded his wardrobe. Even though he was still the same person, the outside had a new polish. In a way, he'd gone undercover as a guy that women wanted. And he'd reveled in it for over a decade.

He was starting to think that a lot of those relationships were just sugary soda, and the whole Kennedy thing was ipecac syrup—the past few months were him just throwing up and throwing out his old conceptions of himself.

Although he still didn't agree with the subtext of Jessica's thesis about him—that he should have embraced monogamy in college—he could see that his behavior afterward had caused people to not take him seriously as a partner. For a long time, that had worked for him, until it didn't.

But the idea of a long-term relationship, where his partner knew everything about him and saw him for who he was, was still a scary prospect. He was afraid of rejection, even though he knew it wouldn't kill him. But the skinny nerd who couldn't get a prom date without a gimmick still lived inside him.

And Jessica? Would she take him seriously if he agreed to a PR relationship and tried to turn their fake relationship into a real one? Or would she judge him unworthy based on his past behavior? Was she really as judgmental as Book Jessica? Or was she the woman who threw up her hands to dance and kissed him with total abandon?

Maybe she was both?

He didn't know, but he certainly wanted to find out.

EVEN THOUGH SHE'D looked up some basic information about Galvin's ex, Jessica went back and forth about watching the video. It didn't really matter what Kennedy had said about Galvin, but she felt as though she should at least look at the video for her own awareness. It would be pretty hard for people to believe that her love had rehabilitated Galvin—a concept that Jessica did not believe in regardless—if she did not know what she was rehabbing him from.

If she didn't see it, she could at least say that she didn't need to know what was in it because she knew the man that it was about. Every relationship was its own individual thing. Someone who behaved poorly with one partner could have a completely different experience with another. Or maybe the video had been a wake-up call that Galvin had needed to become a better boyfriend. It wasn't as though Kennedy had accused him of anything that could even remotely be categorized as abuse, had she?

It was that question in her mind that nagged her as she tried and failed to move the furniture in the condo around so that it wouldn't look quite so empty. By the end of that futile endeavor, she was sweaty and tired, but the question of whether Galvin was some sort of monster in disguise was like a cricket under the floorboard of her psyche. She couldn't make it shut up.

She suddenly had a great deal of sympathy for people who came in with obsessions that they couldn't rid themselves of. Of course she never judged people for their obsessive thoughts about the partner who'd made it clear that they didn't want to be in a relationship or "the one that got away," but she'd never been quite able to identify with the feeling. She'd never been obsessed before, and she probably wasn't right now. It was just a weird time, during which she was considering something colossally stupid. The kind of thing that you only read about in romance novels—fake dating.

She finally got her computer out when she realized that part of the reason she couldn't stop thinking about the video was rooted in Luke walking out without a true explanation. She didn't want to be confused or caught unaware again. In fact, her mind wouldn't let the Kennedy video go because it was actually something she could find and process. Luke had left her with nothing but the furniture she'd purchased for their life together, and her brain wasn't ready to sort out her feelings about that yet.

It was probably why she had such a visceral attraction to Galvin right now. It was an intense thing that felt safe—well, safer—to feel compared to anything regarding the end of her relationship. Why obsess over the fact that you had to re-envision your entire future when you could obsess over what an infamous fuckboy that you were fake-dating for PR had done to deserve said infamy?

She clicked play and immediately felt insecure. She'd known a little bit about Kennedy from her previous internet search, but she'd never engaged with her content before. Jessica just wasn't the target audience for tummy tea and sunless tanner. Instantly, she realized why Kennedy Mower made millions selling products to women who looked at her and felt like they were not enough.

Jessica had worked long and hard on her self-esteem. She'd had to, with a mother who had picked apart her appearance practically from the womb, but her inner work was no match for the fact that Kennedy Mower looked like a movie star, supermodel, and actual angel all wrapped into one.

The idea that this woman didn't have whatever sauce it took to keep Galvin's attention made her wonder if he needed vision correction. But then she started talking, and Jessica understood why he might grow tired of her.

It was not that the way she talked was bad or wrong. It was just very obvious that Kennedy was very young. Not jailbait young, but young enough that she and Galvin were not looking for the same things in life.

As Kennedy broke down the reasons why she'd only continued to date Galvin out of pity, and why she thought he needed a prescription for Viagra and that he lacked "creativity"—secondhand humiliation threatened to make Jessica pass out.

She could see why Galvin was messed up about this whole thing, and her heart went out to him. She was relieved that he hadn't seemed to do anything truly manipulative or abusive, but she didn't know that she could do anything for the poor man's image.

She was also slightly less attracted to him, which filled her with relief. She would just have to remember how she'd felt watching this video every time Galvin tried to turn his charm on her. If she could do that, she wouldn't be tempted to do anything stupid, like kiss him again.

CHAPTER TEN

GALVIN WAS FILLED with confidence when he knocked on Jessica's door a few evenings later. He was going to take her to the hottest restaurant in town, where they might be seen by people who knew him but did not know her. They were going to "soft-launch" their relationship on her Instagram page—no faces or tags, but some linked hands and maybe a photo in silhouette.

In a week or so, he would start Liking and Commenting on all of her posts about the book. His breakup with Kennedy had been featured on *Who? Weekly*, so hopefully the podcasters would pick up that he was in a new relationship when he and Jessica finally posted a selfie at their college reunion in a few weeks.

After that, they'd post a few more times, and then they would have an amicable breakup sometime after Jessica's book went from frontlist to backlist.

At least that was Jessica's plan. The more Galvin thought about her and how he felt when he was around her, the more he wanted to see if there was something beyond a tenuous friendship between the two of them. He was certain that she saw him as a bad candidate for a relationship, but he was up for the challenge.

He thought.

He certainly felt stupid standing outside her door with flowers. He got a weird look from a neighbor, and it made him doubt himself. He'd never doubted himself so much before, and he was having trouble following his therapist's advice and viewing it as a good thing. Apparently, self-doubt was healthy, because questioning our own automatic assumptions led to greater self-awareness.

But it felt pretty fucking terrible.

He knocked again, wanting to steer clear of any more nosy neighbors. The last thing he wanted to do was make Jessica the victim of gossip among the people in her building. This scheme was supposed to make her life easier, not harder. If he made her life harder, she'd get rid of him the first chance she got. He could see her being ruthlessly efficient with her relationships, which kind of turned him on. But he also feared her.

She opened the door and looked between him and the bouquet of flowers for a long beat. He instantly regretted bringing them with him. It was weird, and it had felt weird when he was buying them. He should have listened to his gut.

"I'm sorry." It was the only thing he could think to say. And he wanted to kick himself for it.

"Why are you apologizing?" she asked, and he got a sinking feeling that this was going to be one of the worst dates in history.

It was probably best to just be as transparent as he could be without revealing that he was treating this like a real date. "The flowers are too much."

She scrunched her forehead in this adorable way that made him want to kiss her. "No, no, no." She opened the door wider and motioned for him to come inside. "I just didn't expect that."

Seeing her off-balance made him forget about his own uncharacteristic nervousness. "I just felt like flowers were customary on a first date."

"According to our backstory, this isn't our first date." She seemed very concerned with the particulars here, which left him regretting this failed romantic gesture even more. "This has to be at least our tenth date." She made an undecipherable gesture. "The flowers make sense if we were waiting an appropriate amount of time to have sex."

He didn't know where to start with what she'd just said. There was an appropriate amount of time to wait to have sex? And she thought it was ten dates? He'd never gone on ten dates with someone before having sex—if they weren't ripping each other's clothes off by the end of date three or four, there was really no reason to continue dating.

No wonder she and Luke had formed a relationship. If they'd waited for ten dates to have sex, then they were probably best buddies by then. She would have felt bad breaking up with that cold asshole by then. But he didn't want to say any of that. That was not the note he wanted to hit with this date.

He put on his most charming smile. "I'd bring much nicer flowers if this was a sex date."

She laughed and rolled her eyes, which delighted him. "I'll put them in water."

"Cool. I figured we could photograph them and put them in

your stories." He tried not to beam at her, but he really liked to hear her laugh—even more when he was the one who caused it.

"You really are better at this social media thing than I am. Maybe Kennedy did teach you something?"

She might as well have punched him in the gut. He now knew that it was strange that he'd dated only younger women for the past decade, and he was embarrassed about it. But he'd hoped that Jessica wouldn't notice or think ill of him because of it. As a therapist, wasn't she supposed to be nonjudgmental?

He hated disappointing people, and he'd been fighting that fight for most of his life. And part of the reason he'd dated younger women in the past was that they were more easily impressed with the low bar he'd known he could meet. None of them truly expected him to be the One, so he could focus on being Mr. Right Now, instead. He hated his past self for being so shortsighted that he never thought he'd want to be the right guy for anyone, that he'd never thought he could be.

And he didn't even truly know if he wanted to be the right guy for Jessica. He knew he was intrigued, and he was mad at himself for squandering his chance for her to see him as a real possibility for a real boyfriend.

But he couldn't do anything about it now.

"Do you really recommend waiting ten dates for sex?" Even though this question wouldn't make him seem like any less of a cad, his curiosity got the better of him. And moving on to sex as the topic was squarely in his comfort zone.

Jessica bit her lip, and hesitated. That gave him a chance to notice how great she looked. She'd looked great in yoga pants at brunch, but she was a knockout tonight. The black dress she wore emphasized her curves. It had spaghetti straps, and when she turned around to find a vase, he noticed it was backless. The thought that she could not possibly be wearing a bra filled his mind with images that would certainly only be appropriate for a tenth date.

Her hair was up again, and the back of her neck tortured him along with the graceful line of her spine.

She shrugged, and he was mesmerized by the way the muscles in her back moved. "I guess it depends. I actually try not to give advice to my clients when they're really there to gain understanding of themselves and their patterns so that they can change from a place of empowerment."

"That's not what I asked." He'd stepped closer to her without realizing how close he'd gotten—close enough to smell her. He lusted after her, and there was nothing he could do about it. Not at the moment.

"Yeah, I don't tell my clients what to do. I want them to make good choices for themselves. And it's usually not a good choice to sleep with someone you intend to have a meaningful relationship with right off the bat. It makes you ignore things that you shouldn't and get more attached than circumstances warrant."

"Bullshit."

She jumped at the sharp expletive. "I mean—it's not like you should wait to have sex with someone you don't see yourself in a long-term relationship with, so I'm not shaming you."

Even though her words hurt him, he dug that she had spirit and didn't just agree with him all the time. Maybe that was why he was so attracted to her. She didn't roll over and just accept whatever he said as the truth.

And she was right. He had avoided long-term relationships

for most of his adult life, but he had his reasons. Reasons that she would probably recognize. But he wasn't going to dump them on her. He wanted her to see him as more than a recalcitrant rake. He wanted a chance to blow Luke's memory out of her mind, forever.

But he didn't agree with her that it wasn't important to make sure the sex worked right away. If he was thinking about a long-term, monogamous commitment, the sex had to work. It was a waste of time to date someone for weeks or months without knowing if that worked.

"Only one of us is qualified to give dating advice, sir."

He liked when she called him "sir." He was putting that in his notes for later. After he convinced her that her "no sex before you know their social security number" rule was bad, they could talk about mutual kinks. "Yeah, and only one of us has been in more than one romantic relationship."

"YOU'RE AN ASSHOLE," Jessica said. "And that's my professional diagnosis."

At least he looked like he regretted saying that. She should kick him out of her apartment. Slap him right across the face. Who the fuck did he think he was to be insulting her relationship history? And they'd spent enough time together over the past few days that he knew that she felt self-conscious about her breakup with Luke. He knew she was questioning every choice she'd ever made. But he couldn't stop himself from poking at her.

Then, he did the one thing she didn't expect—he smiled at her. "You really are a pistol, aren't you?"

"Don't act like it's cute." Him thinking she was cute and acting condescending, it just made her angrier with him. "I'm not cute. I'm pissed off."

"But you're always cute, not just when you're pissed off. Just cuter when you're shooting daggers at me out of your eyeballs."

"That should make you more afraid than horny."

"See, that's where you're wrong, and it makes me doubt that you know what you're talking about when you say that people should wait to have sex until after marriage."

She pointed at him. "I did not say that, and I didn't mean it that way."

"But you judge people who can't wait until the first date is over before they rip each other's clothes off?"

"I'm not judging them." At least she wasn't saying anything directly judgmental. But her training experience taught her that couples who jumped into bed too quickly often burned out just as quickly. "It just helps to know someone before fucking them."

"Helps what?"

"It's good to know whether or not someone is a good person before becoming blinded by lust."

Galvin snorted a little. "I think I'd be more clouded by the lust before I've had sex with someone. The only thing having sex with someone too quickly under your metrics has done for me is clarified that I'm with the wrong person."

Jessica bit her lip, because she had rather harsh feedback for him based on that last statement. But she wasn't going to say anything out loud, because she wasn't a clinical-grade asshole like him.

"What are you not saying?" Of course he wasn't going to let her get away with it.

"You don't want to hear what I'm not saying."

He was standing too close to her. "I wouldn't have asked if I didn't want to hear it."

Jessica took a deep breath. "You probably lose interest once you sleep with someone because there's shame working somewhere, and you are more interested in the dopamine of the chase than you are in the actual relationship."

She thought he was going to walk out the door. She really tried not to psychoanalyze the people in her civilian life, but Galvin had insulted her and tried her patience. But instead of walking away, Galvin looked at her curiously. "Tell me more about shame over predinner drinks?"

Even though she was still mad at him, his willingness to ask questions made it impossible for her to cancel her date. "Lead the way."

CHAPTER ELEVEN

"HOW DO YOU feel right after you 'finish' with someone?"

She was a little bit gratified when Galvin choked on his water after she asked her question. "We're going in the deep end right now?"

"No time like the present." At some point during the ride to dinner, she felt like the power shifted between them, and she'd regained the upper hand. He hadn't made any more digs about her breakup and had kept the conversation light. This adversarial dynamic between them wouldn't be super healthy if this were a real relationship, but right now, they were more like colleagues or teammates. She needed to suss out his strengths and weaknesses so she would know how to best have his back.

He looked as though he was giving her question some serious thought, and she appreciated that. He actually seemed like a very thoughtful person, which made it so curious that he was so thoughtless when it came to his past treatment of romantic partners.

"I feel like I want to break the sound barrier putting on my clothes and leaving."

"So, no cuddling?" Jessica leaned closer to him so they wouldn't be heard by any other diners nearby. She'd been dying to try this restaurant with Luke, but he hadn't been able to get a reservation for six months. She smirked thinking about the fact that she'd been in charge of calendaring social events, so he'd probably space on the reservation and be charged a $250 no-show fee. He was cheap, so he'd really hate that.

"I don't like how you're looking at me right now," Galvin said, snapping her back into the moment. "Why do you stay and cuddle after sex?"

Jessica wasn't used to people being able to ask her questions, and she wasn't sure she liked it. She did, however, like the hot rolls they brought out at the restaurant, so she ripped one open and popped a piece into her mouth.

Galvin had a satisfied-looking grin on his face. "You're all flushed."

"I'm not used to this being a two-way street." It hadn't even been a two-way street with Luke. She thought for a moment about why she liked after-sex cuddling. "I guess that it reassures me of the connection."

She thought a little bit more. She'd needed the cuddling more than the sex in the months leading up to the breakup, and the affection had been scarce. Instead of thinking about it, she looked at his big hands as they ripped apart a fresh roll. She wanted his hands on her, and lust hit her.

She didn't know how long she stared at his hands, but it must have been an awkward silence. "Are you okay?" she heard him ask.

"Sorry, I drifted." She was really off her game if she couldn't be present while someone was talking to her. "I was thinking that Luke couldn't get us into this restaurant for like six months, and he'll probably get stuck with a no-show fee because he doesn't know where he's supposed to be from day to day without me telling him."

Galvin smiled. "Yeah, that checks out. He always was a fucking man baby."

"You're going to have to tell me why you hate him so much someday."

He grimaced. "I'd rather tell you about my post-nut depression."

"You know the shift in hormones really does cause that. It's totally real."

"So, I'm not some sort of emotionless monster because I just want to be alone after I come?"

"No." Jessica shook her head. Most people were gratified to hear that the things that they were ashamed of were totally normal. "Have you ever just told a partner you need a few minutes before cuddling?"

"I feel like that's a dick move."

The waiter came to take their drink order, so Jessica couldn't respond right away. Galvin picked a wine but looked at her for affirmation that she was okay with his selection, which she was fine with as long as he was paying for it.

When the server left the table, she said, "It's no less of a dick move to say you need to collect yourself for a few moments than it is to rush out the door, probably being weird the whole time, without communicating why you're being weird."

"That makes a whole lot of sense." Galvin nodded. "I'm going to try that for next time."

The rush of jealousy that Jessica felt thinking about Galvin having a next time with someone else rocked her a little bit. Of course there was going to be a next time, and it wasn't going to be with her. She got the impression that Galvin had a certain respect for her, and he liked her enough to be her fake boyfriend, but that had more to do with his hatred for Luke, didn't it?

The server returned with their wine and took their order. Galvin raised his glass in a way that was sort of quaint and would have been romantic in any other context.

"To asking for our needs to be met."

JESSICA REALLY NEEDED his help. She might know more about the human psyche than anyone else he knew, but she knew virtually nothing about social media. Throughout dinner, he'd had to hold himself back from kissing that little crease in her forehead that formed every time he told her something new about it, like that Instagram Stories were different from posts. He didn't get into the different forms of video, because that would have taken them until after the restaurant closed.

Their meal was perfect, and she'd posted a few shots of the table and their hands on glasses of wine, which was the whole stated objective for the night. He didn't know how his other objective—the part about getting Jessica to see him as boyfriend material—was going. The fact that she knew about the anxiety he felt after sex was probably not a point in his favor. She hadn't seemed to judge him, but he hadn't put his best foot forward by admitting to that.

And while she seemed to be at ease during their meal, she wasn't flirting with him the same way she'd flirted the night they'd run into each other at the bar. They hadn't done shots, though, so that might explain why she wasn't trying to rip off his clothes as he walked her to her door. In fact, she really hadn't touched him all night.

"You really didn't have to walk me to my door," she said as she got out her key fob. "Now you have to get another car to take you home." She got the door open, turned around, and looked up at him. "Thank you for a lovely fake date."

Not quite ready to say good night, he braced one hand in the doorframe—not enough to prevent her from closing the door but communicating his intent to say something else—and leaned close to her face. She didn't move away, but she started just a little. "I don't think our night's quite over, do you?"

"We had dinner, took photos, and you walked me all the way home, even though you didn't have to," Jessica said. "I'd say we're done."

"Do you think it's a little weird that we didn't touch each other all night? Except for holding hands for your Instagram?"

"I think everything about this situation is weird, don't you?"

"Touché. But if people are going to believe that we're into each other, we're probably going to have to touch a little bit."

Jessica didn't look upset by this. Her skin had a pretty flush to it, and her heat drew him in. Her lips opened slightly, and her breath sped up. He leaned in closer, and she didn't back away. "I want to kiss you right now."

"You do?" She sounded so cute and bewildered by him. He probably liked that more than he should. "Like, for practice?"

Galvin shook his head slowly. "No, Jessica. I want to kiss you because I want to."

"Oh." He'd rendered her nearly speechless, which made him

smile. He liked that he affected her on some level. It made him feel like their dynamic was more equitable, and he wasn't just a victim of an unrequited crush. He'd had plenty of those during his adolescence, and he'd hoped to leave the feeling behind him. But the way she made him feel had that same intensity. In the days since he'd last seen her, she'd hijacked more of his thoughts than she should have. He didn't even know her, and he thought about her all the time.

"Does that 'oh' mean that you want me to kiss you, too?" She hadn't opened the door wide or gone up on her tiptoes to close the gap between their faces, but he knew she was cautious. She was making calculations in her brain about how this would affect their scheme, how she would feel after it happened, and probably how it would affect him emotionally.

But this kind of chemistry didn't lend itself to rational thought. It just was. Sure, they could ignore it and try to pretend that they didn't feel the things they felt, but what a waste that would be.

The relief that poured through him when she nodded her head and opened the door a bit wider rivaled the lust he felt at that moment. He didn't hesitate, but he didn't dive in and devour her the way everything in him was urging him to. He brushed his lips against hers and breathed her in. She tasted like wine and burnt sugar—rich and decadent in a way that belied her austere aesthetic. She wrapped her hand around the back of his neck and pulled him into the entryway of her condo, and he closed the door behind them.

She gasped into his mouth when he spun them around and pushed her body against the door. She'd softened against him until she felt molten and boneless, and that fed his craving for more of her.

He didn't want her to think he was trying to fuck and run, so he whispered, "We're not going to have sex tonight."

"We're not?" she asked on a moan. He brushed the sides of her torso with his hands, trying to memorize the shape of her. Goose bumps appeared on her bare arms, and he kissed the biceps closest to him.

"Tonight, I just wanted to kiss you. And I'm going to want to kiss you more. In public so that people will know that you're mine, and in private just for you and for me."

She didn't respond, and maybe that meant that she needed more convincing. So he crushed her mouth with his. She matched him and they were soon writhing against the door, pressing their bodies into one another like the horny millennial teens from their previous lives, trying desperately not to break an abstinence-only purity pledge they'd signed in health class after someone came in and told them that any sex before marriage caused certain death.

His dick was so hard that he had to grit his teeth every time it came in contact with her belly. "Jessica, you're killing me."

"I kind of want to kill you right now." Her voice was a growl, and he felt the charge of it in the base of his spine. Everything about her affected him. And he liked almost everything about her, even the stuff he teased her about. She was so buttoned up but also held back this feral thing inside of her. "I've never been so turned on in my life by a kiss."

He chuckled. "And the dry humping. Please don't forget the dry humping."

"Yeah, but we're not having sex, and so now you need to leave so I can go in my room and make myself come."

His knees went weak when she said that. "You expressing your needs is so incredibly hot."

"What do you need right now?" It was even hot when she asked him what his needs were.

He sighed and pulled back from her slightly, putting his hands on her shoulders. He took a moment to take in her swollen lips and pink cheeks, so he could call it up for his own self-care when he got home. "I really need to leave right now before I break my promise, drop to my knees, and eat your cunt."

She started at his coarse words, but then smiled at him. "You know, you're a dirty boy. And I like it."

In a distinctly not dirty-boy move, he leaned in and kissed her forehead, tasting the sweat on her skin. He wanted to taste her everywhere so badly that it hurt. But he didn't say that to her. He was going to savor her and take her on every surface of her condo and his home.

They were going to make their fake relationship look real, because it was real. And tonight, he'd proven that his real feelings weren't entirely one-sided.

CHAPTER TWELVE

GALVIN WOULDN'T TELL her what they were doing for a second date, but he'd sent her an address and text asking whether she had any food allergies. He hadn't texted her about their kiss and heavy petting session against her door a few days before, which she supposed made sense. They were two consenting adults who were attracted to each other, and they'd made out a little bit. Twice.

That didn't mean it would happen again, and it wasn't worth obsessing over. But she couldn't stop thinking about it. In between client sessions all week, she would drift off and remember the feel of his lips against hers, the urgent touch of his hands on her body through her clothes. Every time those few moments drifted into her mind, a flush of heat suffused her entire body. The lady at the coffee shop she bought her ten a.m. latte at even asked her if she had a fever.

She wasn't sick, physically, but her mental health was questionable right now. She was too old to be having giddy feelings about a dude—especially one as fickle as Galvin. She hadn't even had crushes like this in high school. That was because she'd never been able to stay at one high school long enough to form an all-encompassing crush that wouldn't go away no matter how hard she tried to focus on other things. Her mother's lifestyle hadn't allowed for her to get too attached to any place or person.

The day after the kiss, she'd tried to teach herself to knit using a YouTube tutorial. That was a failure because there was a hot guy teaching the tutorial, and his muscular hands made her think of Galvin palming her ass while she dry-humped him.

She also tried going to the gym but got distracted when a guy who looked a little bit like Galvin was doing squats and grunting. She couldn't help herself, it sounded like sex.

And she wasn't even going to get started on how often she'd had to relieve herself since the kiss. She hadn't been lying to Galvin when she told him that she was going to masturbate as soon as he left. By the time she was done, she'd had to charge her vibrator. Some of her recently divorced clients described a similar level of horniness as soon as they separated from their partners, and she'd read some literature. But it was nothing in comparison to feeling wave after wave of lust for someone new after over a decade of trying to keep an ember alive with someone she knew well.

It got her thinking that maybe this experience would make her a better and more empathic professional. She didn't talk about her own personal experiences in session, but maybe she would be able to hold space for more messiness with more authenticity once she'd navigated this for herself.

That was all she could say to herself by way of comfort as she got pants feelings when her Uber driver hit a pothole on the way to her date.

The address turned out to be another one of the hottest restaurants in town.

Galvin certainly knew how to navigate a hard-to-get reservation.

But when she walked into the restaurant, the dining room was empty. She checked her phone to make sure she was in the right place, but a host appeared and said, "Right this way, Ms. Gallagher."

Jessica's curiosity was piqued. If Galvin had rented out an entire Michelin-starred restaurant for their second date in a fake relationship, this was far too much. And it wouldn't do anything for their plan of dating for the 'gram. All of a sudden, she was more nervous than turned on. As she followed the host through the dining room and toward what she assumed was the kitchen, she put one hand on her chest and tried to breathe deeply.

By the time the host opened the swing doors and motioned her through, she was pretty sure she wasn't going to pass out. All of this was so unlike her—the lust, the giddiness, the thinking about a stupid hot kiss—and she wasn't sure she liked it.

But she forgot about all of her misgivings when Galvin was suddenly in front of her, grasping her arms and pulling her in for a kiss. She braced herself for an onslaught, but it was a light kiss. And then he pulled back and looked at her quizzically. "Are you okay?"

That shook her out of her stupor. "Okay? Yeah, sure."

His forehead crinkled up. "You sure? Did something happen with one of your clients? We can reschedule if you don't want to hang out."

Luke had never given her that kind of consideration. He'd rarely asked about her work. In his view, he had the more important job because he fixed internal organs. She was only trying to help people fix their thoughts and lives, so his profession overshadowed hers. And when he was available, he'd expected her to make herself available. So while she'd had a lot of alone time when he was at work, she'd felt like she couldn't take a time-out for herself when they were together. At least until she'd gotten a book deal, and Luke had really started pulling away from the relationship.

"Thank you for asking me that," Jessica said. Galvin really did have the potential to be a great real partner for someone. If he was this good at attending to someone else's needs who he wasn't in love with, he would be a superstar boyfriend to someone he was really into. "But I'm fine, and you probably spent too much money renting this place out—"

Galvin made a motion with his hands that made her stop in her tracks. "I spent no money and only one favor."

"Really?" Jessica asked. "How did you manage this?"

"I designed the executive chef and his fiancée's new house, and we became friends." Galvin looked behind him, and that was when Jessica realized that they were not alone. There was a tall, handsome chef that she recognized from seeing him judging a cooking competition show on the Food Network—Will something or other—and a bombshell standing very close to him who she assumed was his fiancée. "Jessica Gallagher, I want you to meet Will Harkness and Alex Turner."

Both of them smiled at her, which eased the last of her nerves. She waved. "It's nice to meet you both."

Alex looked at Galvin. "I almost didn't believe you when you told me that you'd found anyone in this town willing to date you."

"Just like I was surprised that Will didn't dump you after you threw that fit over the entryway tile," Galvin said.

Will just shrugged. "I'm used to it by now. Keeps things spicy."

Alex gave her fiancé a dirty look, and he laughed.

Jessica turned to Galvin and asked, "Am I here to do some impromptu relationship therapy?"

Galvin laughed. "Nah, we're here for a cooking lesson."

"I've never even cooked for you. How do you know that I need cooking lessons?"

He cocked his head. "I don't. I'm not trying to insult you or insinuate that there's anything wrong with your cooking." He sighed and seemed to deflate a little, which made Jessica feel instantly guilty. "I just thought that this would be a fun way to connect. And that we could put the food in your stories and get more views."

"Shit, I'm sorry."

"It's okay." Galvin paused and gave her one of those looks that made it feel as though he could see right through her. "I'm beginning to wonder if Luke was more of an asshole than even I thought."

"Luke wasn't always an asshole. At least not to me." There was no real passion behind her defense of her ex. She didn't know why she was defending him anyway. She had assumed that Galvin had planned this lovely date because he thought she was a bad cook, even though he had no reason to think that, because Luke had been critical of her cooking. "But he did always have 'suggestions' for how I could improve at things."

Galvin made a weird face, and so did Alex and Will. Jessica felt embarrassed to be having this conversation in front of strangers. But neither of them looked like they pitied her.

"Don't worry," Alex said. "That's just run-of-the-mill emotional abuse—pretty much a random Wednesday—in my line of work."

Grateful for the opportunity to be the one asking questions, Jessica said, "Oh, what do you do?"

"I'm a divorce attorney," Alex said. "Sounds like you are well rid of your ex and might need my services."

"We were never married." Jessica shook her head, thinking about how stupid she now felt to have been with the same guy for fifteen years and have nothing to show for it.

"Too bad. It sounds like I would have had a good time making sure he walked away without even his dignity."

"I'm afraid that I'm the one without the dignity. He walked out the day before my book came out."

"You're an author?" Alex asked. "I'm always looking for a good book to read."

"It's a dating book." Jessica looked meaningfully at Will. "Unless I'm reading the situation wrong, I don't think you'll be needing it."

Galvin put his arm around her, and she was proud that she didn't even startle this time. "Besides," he told Alex, "it's for straight men, so it would be more helpful to Will if he ever decided that you were too much of a harpy to marry."

"Are you always this mean to your clients?" Jessica asked Galvin.

Galvin shrugged. "They've already paid me."

"But I could still kick your ass out of my restaurant and ban you." Will had a very deep, pleasing voice. It made sense that he was on TV a lot. Alex gave him a look that said she was thinking the same thing with a more prurient twist.

"Jessica is also a brilliant therapist," Galvin said. She felt her skin flush with the praise, even though he didn't know whether she was brilliant or a disaster.

"So she's here to fix your scrambled brains, rather than as your date?" Alex said with a smirk.

"No, I'm here as his girlfriend." Jessica thought about taking it back as soon as the words were out of her mouth. She was his fake girlfriend, and it felt weird to say that she was his girlfriend given that she was someone else's girlfriend the last time she'd said that word. And they'd been together so long that she hadn't had to clarify their relationship with anyone for a long time.

Being in a new situation, with new people, felt vulnerable and foreign. It felt like she was an adolescent in a new school, fielding questions about who she was and what she was and just waiting to see what the kids in this new place would find to bully her about.

She thought that she'd gotten past the issues of her youth and processed everything. But Luke's leaving had made her realize that she'd played it safe her entire adult life. She'd never broken up with him because she'd accepted that she'd simply never find better. She'd convinced herself that passion was for the emotionally immature, because she hadn't wanted to risk opening herself up to the kind of heartbreak that passion often reaped. And she'd always stayed away from Galvin and men like Galvin—the ones that made her heart skip several beats—because she never wanted to feel like that girl who wanted to make friends but learned to watch every word again.

Galvin squeezed her arm. "Are you okay?"

Jessica shook off her inappropriately timed introspection. "I'm fine. Why don't we get cooking before Alex lights you on fire with a blowtorch?"

"That sounds like a great idea," Will said, his tone just a little bit sarcastic. "I lock away the blowtorches whenever Alex is around, though."

"I burn one crème brûlée—"

IT WAS HIT-OR-MISS when they'd first arrived at the restaurant, but Galvin was relieved that he hadn't totally fucked things up. He'd only thought that it would be fun, romantic, and different to have a private cooking lesson from one of the country's best chefs, and Jessica had seen it as a critique of her cooking skills—of which he had zero knowledge.

Jessica had seemed shocked by her own reaction, and he didn't think it was wise to get into it in front of people she didn't know, so he'd dropped it after their little exchange. But the whole time they were cooking, he rolled it over and over in his head. The only thing that made sense was that Luke had done something to exacerbate any preexisting insecurities that Jessica had. In so many ways, she was so self-assured, but he was beginning to get the impression that at least some of that was a front.

He watched her line up carrots to dice them so carefully that she could have been judged on *Top Chef*. It was so strange that it sent heat down his spine. He didn't know why the fast, accurate way she cut vegetables turned him on.

The way she watched Will when he demonstrated how to

deglaze the pan made him jealous. The way his feelings ping-ponged back and forth in a matter of minutes made his head spin. He worried that he wasn't being present, and he couldn't stop himself from touching her as she moved past him in the kitchen. The small smile she gave him made his heart beat fast. He knew they were there to learn to make something special together, but he had a weird feeling that they didn't need to cook to be exceptional together.

Despite the rocky start, they had fun. Will had walked them through preparing his famous osso buco, and Jessica had seemed to enjoy it. He was glad—Will and Alex were good people, and they were some of the only friendly acquaintances who hadn't stopped taking his calls after his breakup with Kennedy.

Since the restaurant was closed, there was no valet, and Jessica and Galvin walked to his car so he could give her a ride home. The night was quiet—no one realized that L.A. was an early-to-bed town until they moved here—and the silence seemed to stretch out into tension as the conversations that both of them were having in their heads crowded the space between them.

"I don't get you and Luke," he said.

He expected Jessica to get immediately defensive—she had every right to be—but she kind of deflated next to him. "Looking back, I'm not sure I do, either."

"You spent so much of your life with the guy, and he—" Galvin wasn't about to explain that some guys just had really punchable faces. Jessica didn't need to hear that right now when she was obviously still getting over the breakup. And that made him even more mad. The more time he spent with Jessica, the more he wanted from her. He wanted their fake relationship to morph into a real one. Given how she was still so prickly about Luke, there was no way that jumping almost immediately into a relationship with Galvin would be her next step. She'd probably need a year to process, a year to explore, and about a millennium before she would give him a shot. And then she'd find an emotionally mature adult, probably a divorced dad or something, to settle down with.

Galvin didn't even know how long he should wait until having sex with someone new. And he was probably only so fixated on her because they hadn't had sex yet. He would probably freak out afterward and prove Jessica and everyone else right about him. He didn't have what it took to be in an adult relationship, and he was getting way too old to be having meaningless flings. He lacked depth, and the last thing Jessica needed was to be a proving ground for his inability to commit.

"I guess I hadn't realized it until tonight." Jessica had been quiet so long, and he'd been so lost in his own thoughts, that her words seemed to come from nowhere. "I didn't realize how much that relationship conditioned me to doubt myself. When I was in it, I couldn't see that the dynamic had always been more weighted to what would make Luke happy."

That made Galvin angry. More than almost anyone he knew, Jessica deserved to be happy. The fact that Luke hadn't even wanted to try doing that made him want to punch something. But he didn't say anything, because he wanted Jessica to continue.

"And it's weird to not know that you're not happy until your late thirties, isn't it?"

Galvin shrugged. "You're the therapist, so I think you're in a better position to know what's weird and what isn't."

"It feels weird." They stopped at his car and he opened the passenger door before jogging around the front and getting in. Instead of starting the ignition, he looked at her, thinking that maybe the person that everyone talked to about their problems could use someone to talk to. "It doesn't feel weird to be here with you, though. It feels right."

She looked at him expectantly, and he realized that she probably thought that he hadn't turned on the car because he was going to put the moves on her.

And it wasn't that he didn't want to. He just didn't think it was the greatest idea. For the first time in his adult life, he wanted to be seen as a real possibility for a real relationship, and he was sure Jessica wouldn't see him that way if they had sex right now.

"You know what would make me feel better?" she asked, and he almost growled in frustration. Because he did know, and he wanted to give that to her. "Why are you shaking your head?"

He hadn't even noticed that. "I want nothing more than to kiss you right now, and I know it would feel really good for both of us. But I don't think it's a good idea."

"I think it's a great idea."

Galvin sighed. He didn't want to turn her down, but he knew that kissing would not just stay kissing. He'd almost dry-humped her through her front door the last time he'd kissed her, and they weren't even anywhere private at the moment. "Listen, there's nothing more I'd like to do than make out with you like a teenager in the back seat." He motioned his head toward the back of his car. He'd never had sex in it, but he'd done the calculations before purchasing the vehicle, and the measurements worked. "But I think you'll regret it, and you'll hold that regret against me."

Jessica pouted, and he was even closer to giving in. "Don't do that."

"Do what?" Wasn't this what he was supposed to be doing? Being considerate?

"Act like you know what's best for me." She sounded real frustrated, and it didn't make it easier not to kiss her right now. "I know what's best for me."

"And you think that's me?" Galvin definitely didn't think he was the best thing for her, now or ten years from now, but he would do whatever he could to give her what she needed.

She paused, biting her lip, and he wasn't sure if he was relieved that she was rethinking hooking up or disappointed. "I don't know if you're what's best for me, but doing what's best for me hasn't really gotten me anywhere."

"And you think doing me will?" He wanted to kick himself for sounding so insecure.

"We're such a mess that we kind of make sense." She laughed. "But the only time that I haven't been going over what went wrong with me and Luke since the day he left was when you were kissing me."

So he was definitely a rebound, and he had to decide if he was willing to live with that. He made the huge mistake of looking at her, and that decided it—he would take her now and deal with the pain of whatever came after.

CHAPTER THIRTEEN

JESSICA HAD NEVER liked waiting for anything. For as long as she could remember, forward momentum had been the only way to keep herself calm. Whenever she stopped, she felt powerless and out of control. And she knew that becoming comfortable with discomfort was the only way to grow. But knowing something on an intellectual level didn't make it easier to embrace when her sense of safety had been eroded so much in the past few weeks.

Waiting for Galvin to decide whether or not he wanted to kiss her was a whole other brand of torture than waiting for board certification exam results or waiting in line at the DMV. It felt life-or-death, and it was terrifying that a man she didn't know that well had this kind of power over her. This was why this kind of chemistry was unsustainable. She didn't care that he was bad for her or that he would leave the moment that he had an orgasm with her in the room. She didn't care that she needed him to keep up the facade that she had it all together.

She had nothing together. She was held together by glue and tape—and it wasn't even duct tape.

He looked at her, though, and even that made her feel alive. When was the last time she'd felt so alive just being around another person? Maybe not ever. Definitely not around Luke. God, Luke! The way she'd folded her own wants and desires into tidy little packages and put them away for her entire adult life based on the whims of a man who could walk away like that? It made her even more afraid of what she was beginning to feel around Galvin.

Before she could rethink herself out of it, he leaned toward her until their lips touched. Then he stopped and waited to see if she would pull back. She should have but couldn't bring herself to do it. She was choosing life, even if it resulted in pain.

His lips were cool and dry, and his breath smelled faintly of the cocoa and coffee liqueur in their dessert. Like that dessert, he was indulgent. And she luxuriated in the anticipation.

"You're sure?" She hated that he was treating her as though she was fragile. She definitely was fragile, but he didn't have to treat her that way.

"Galvin, I want you to kiss me. I need you to make me forget." She knew she sounded as though she was begging, but that was just where she was at right now.

He didn't make her beg any more. Even though she'd been waiting for him to kiss her, she was not prepared for how feral he would be when he finally did. The other time they'd kissed, it had started out slow. But not tonight. Her mouth would be bruised and swollen when he was done with her. And the other night, he'd been hesitant to really touch her, but he leaned over the center console tonight and grabbed her bare thigh with one of his big hands. He squeezed the flesh and pinned her to the seat.

She wrapped one hand around the back of his neck to pull him closer to her. Her skin was on fire and the center of her pulsed with the beat of a song that sounded like pure need.

He explored her mouth until they were both gasping, and then he moved to her cheek. While she never wanted the kiss to end, she wanted to see what he would do next. All of a sudden, she didn't care that they were parked on a residential street, where someone could pass by while walking their dog. She wanted everything that he was willing to give her right now. Her mind was deliciously blank, except for thoughts of how good his mouth felt against the skin of her neck and how much she wanted him to touch her everywhere.

She felt wanton, like a siren. It was a completely foreign feeling and one she'd been trying to avoid her entire life. But something about Galvin and when he'd walked back into her life made her brave enough to throw herself into the abyss without a parachute. She might fall, and hitting the bottom of whatever they were doing would hurt, but she'd been in pain before. Only she'd become so used to the pain that it hadn't felt like pain anymore. It had just been normal. That kind of pain was deadly.

Right now, she ached for more of Galvin's touch, but she also felt the pain of knowing that she wouldn't have it forever. That someday soon they would walk out of each other's lives and she might never feel this kind of lust again.

"Are you still with me?" He whispered his question in her ear. His hot breath raised goose bumps all over her skin.

"Yes." Her voice sounded thready, the need apparent.

He kissed a spot on her neck, right below her earlobe, that

made her shiver. "If we were somewhere private, I would spread your legs, and pull your panties down. I can smell how turned on you are, and I want to taste it."

She'd never been with a dirty talker before. Luke fucked silently, and he hadn't even liked it when she made noise. But she now completely understood the appeal. With just a few words her entire basement was completely flooded, the simple picture that he'd planted turning her upside down with want.

"You can't talk to me like that." If he continued, she would be riding him in the driver's seat, with no care at all for the consequences.

"Why not?" There was a smile in his voice, one she felt against her skin as he kissed her collarbones, as though he was marking her as his with his mouth. There was something possessive about it.

"I won't be responsible for my actions if you don't stop talking to me like that. And that's sort of my thing."

"I don't know. I like the thought of you not responsible for your actions." He slid his hand further up her thigh. It was millimeters away from the hem of her panties. She moaned, and he chuckled. "You're so very hot, and you don't let anyone but me see you this way."

"What way?" As much as it was dangerous for her to egg him on, it made her feel powerful. She wanted him to be as undone by this juggernaut of feeling between them as she was. She wanted to unravel him and then wind him back up. Only to do it all again.

Instead of answering, he slipped a finger inside her underwear. She gasped, and for a quick moment, her mind cleared. Until she looked around and saw no one on the sidewalk or street. Galvin had stopped stroking her inside her panties when she stiffened up. But he didn't pull his hand out from under her skirt. He didn't stop raining kisses over her cheeks and the corners of her mouth.

"It looks like I'm giving you a kiss good night." His voice was low and soothing. He sounded as though he had so much control. How was he not hanging by a thread? "As long as you stay quiet, I'll make you come."

This was—by far—the wildest thing she'd ever done sexually. And she realized that it probably wasn't wild at all to Galvin. But still, he wasn't rushing her or goading her into anything that she would regret later. She'd probably regret allowing their relationship to become sexual at all later, but she really couldn't live in the future right now. Except the very near future, where she was coming all over his fingers when anyone could walk up.

"Please."

Just one simple word was all it took for him to press his middle and index fingers hard into her clit. "You're so wet for me, Jessica." He said her name as though it was a prayer. "It's not going to take any work at all to make you come apart." If he'd said it in a different tone, it would feel as though he was mocking her, but he wasn't. He seemed to be in awe of how turned on she was. It made her spread her thighs to give him more room to maneuver. "Pull your panties down for me."

She had to release her death grip on the door handle and the back of his neck to do it, but she managed. All she wanted was more of him. When her panties were down to her ankles, he pulled them over her shoes. She didn't know where they went, and she didn't care when he pressed two fingers to her center and penetrated her with them.

She gasped, and he stilled. "Okay?"

More than anything, she needed him to move. She wanted friction both inside and on her clit, and she wasn't sure she could verbalize as much right now. Instead, she nodded.

"I need the words, Jessica." This time, he sounded like he was giving her an order.

Willing to do anything to make him keep going, she said, "Yes. I'm here."

He started moving his hand, and she rocked her pelvis against his knuckles to get more stimulation. She felt helpless and infinitely powerful at the same time. "Do you want me to rub your clit? Is that why you're rubbing your bare pussy all over the upholstery in my car? It's going to smell like you unless I get it detailed."

She stopped moving then, not embarrassed, but shocked at his words. "I'll pay to get it cleaned."

He laughed and pressed his thumb against her clit. She felt as though she'd been struck by lightning. "Move against my hand," he said. He sounded like he was in complete control, and it turned her on. If he'd sounded like she felt, she wouldn't be able to let go. But he had himself under control, so she could revel in the sensations buffeting her body.

He was right, it didn't take long for her to come apart. She was on the edge of it, and then it was there. The orgasm turned her into a blank slate. She couldn't remember what it was like to feel pain, and she no longer knew what the ache of loneliness felt like inside her chest. For a few seconds, while she pulled her legs together to keep his hand still and inside her, there was nothing outside of the car. She was a mass of energy and part of everything all at once.

She knew how dangerous it was to connect with another person like this so quickly. She'd had patients throw their whole lives away to feel like this over and over again. But, in that moment, she didn't give a shit.

She wanted to say something encouraging, given how his last relationship had ended. But she couldn't seem to find the words—or any words.

He spoke first. "That was—"

"It was—"

"Perfect," they both said together.

"You're perfect." That burst her bubble enough that she laughed. "I'm not, but the moment was."

He didn't say anything but dried his hand on her panties and then offered them back to her. "The old me would have kept these like a trophy, but they look expensive."

She furrowed her brow and considered telling him to keep them. The fact that he wanted to was so hot it was almost worth buying a new pair. But he'd already made her come in the front seat of his car while talking about how she was making a mess on his seats, so she took them back and slipped them on. When they were on, she figured that he would turn on the car and take her home, and she wondered if he would expect them to continue the carnal festivities. Instead, he surprised her by pulling her close, wrapping his arms around her, and kissing her on the forehead.

CHAPTER FOURTEEN

GALVIN HAD NEVER thought that making out like teenagers was fun—even when he was a teenager. He'd always been caught up in the end point of the seduction—the main event. Even when he'd been wet behind the ears, he'd been focused on the destination rather than the journey. Now he knew that it was all ego. He'd been so caught up in getting women to say yes to him that he'd forgotten how much fun it could be to fool around.

He'd driven Jessica home after he'd made her come in the front seat of his car, and he hadn't gone upstairs. He told her that the night was perfect, and they both had early days, but the truth was that he was scared of how much he liked her. The fact that he was content to get her off and didn't want or need anything in return actually frightened him. His whole life, his sexual relationships had been quasi-transactional. Mutual pleasure and maybe some good times, and a swift end once things became staid or boring.

But that night, he'd just wanted to make her happy. And part of him didn't want to turn tail and run once the postorgasm glow faded, so he hadn't let things get that far with her. After that night, they'd continued to see each other—and had hard-launched their relationship on Instagram on the beach the night before.

And he'd made her come with his mouth, his hands, and a few of her highly advanced toys. But he hadn't let her return the favor. No matter how much he wanted to. Every time he let himself stop to think about it, he would get hard thinking about the sounds she made and the way he could make her body arch in what almost looked like pain right before she came. He finally understood why people got into Tantra and why his grandma always said, "It's better to give than to receive."

Though Grams probably didn't mean it in this context.

He felt like he was losing his mind, and he knew that it wasn't sustainable. Jessica was growing more and more confused by his refusal to let her even give him a hand job, and he knew that she wouldn't buy his explanation.

She would tell him that he needed to lean into the discomfort and confront his fears about what would happen if they had the sort of sex that led to them both crossing the finish line and he freaked out. But he couldn't do that to her. Even though he would have viewed her as a conquest—a worthy one, but a conquest all the same—just a few months ago, she was more to him than that now.

"I CAN'T BELIEVE Abby talked me into doing this." Jessica had hoped she wouldn't have to do any publicity for her book. However, it was part of her contract.

She paced in the tiny storage room that the bookseller had put her in to sign stacks of book copies. Her gaze caught on the copy of the blown-up author photo that the store had used to publicize the event and sneered. The door opened behind her, and her heart leapt into her throat. She'd thought she had a few more minutes.

"It's not a bad photo." Her heartbeat stayed as fast as it was before when she heard the deep timbre of Galvin's voice.

She turned and faced him. His smile made her glad that he was there. "It's not. I just don't want to do this."

His grin faltered. "Stage fright?" He shook his head. "You have nothing to worry about."

Oh, God. What if she had nothing to worry about because no one had shown up? "It's empty out there, isn't it?"

He stepped toward her and stopped her progress with his big hands gripping her upper arms. "It's full. Every seat. But you don't have anything to worry about, because you're going to be great."

"How do you know?" Jessica had always avoided public speaking. This was worse than the podcast, when she only had questions from one underqualified dating coach. Now there was a room full of people asking for advice. "If I wasn't required to do this by my book contract, I would run out the back door."

He didn't smile at that. In fact, the lines between his eyebrows deepened. "You're going to kill this. If the people out there don't drink up your advice and put it into practice, they're bonkers."

"Is that your clinical diagnosis?" She felt her face taking the shape of a smile. Somehow his confidence in her took a weight off her shoulders.

"No, I just want you to relax and have fun."

She shook her head. "This will not be fun. I promise you that."

The bookstore's event coordinator came in to retrieve her just as Galvin opened his mouth.

As he walked out to find his seat, he mouthed, *You'll do great*.

Jessica took a deep breath and walked onto the dais. She immediately regretted not asking someone to join her as a conversation partner. She would rather be interviewed by a thousand TikTok dating coaches than talk about her book and try to give people the hard sell. But she could still feel the imprint of Galvin's hands on her arms and the confidence that he had in her. She knew she shouldn't be making comparisons, but she'd never felt as though Luke had her back to the same degree.

She launched into her elevator pitch of the book but stopped when someone in the crowd laughed. She found Galvin in the crowd, and he gave her a thumbs-up, which told her they were laughing with her, not at her.

After that, she relaxed, and her prepared speech went quickly. She was almost willing to do it again, when a man who had his arms crossed over his chest for the whole talk and had not laughed even once raised his hand to ask a question.

"Lady, what I don't understand is why I have to put so much effort into impressing a female. It's not like any of them cook or clean anymore. Plus, I'm only five foot eight, and women get bent out of shape about it when they meet me."

He took a deep breath and Jessica started to answer. "Well, I—"

"And dating costs so much money. Why do I have to buy a female dinner when she probably won't even slob my knob?"

Jessica wanted to tell him that not calling women "females" was probably a good start, but she didn't want to make this more combative than it needed to be.

She'd started to gather her thoughts when the man continued. "And why would I listen to you instead of a man who's successful with females?"

The last thing that Jessica expected was for Galvin to stand up and point his finger at the man. "Would you shut up?"

"Who the hell are you?"

"I'm her boyfriend." Jessica wasn't going to think about the warm sensation that washed over her when he said that.

The guy sneered and said, "Figures."

"It figures that you don't have anyone who loves you." That was a pretty low blow, and Jessica was about to stop Galvin when he continued. "I bet you don't even believe in miracles, do you?"

"What the hell are you talking about, dude?"

"It's a miracle when two people find each other and see each other clearly at the same time and decide to take a chance on loving each other. Because falling in love is always a chance." Jessica's heart leapt when he said that. She could fight her own battles, and she could have talked this guy down. But she liked that he was standing up for her.

"For my wallet—"

"Just shut the hell up. I don't know why you came here, but if the only thing you have going on in your life is coming to a stranger's book signing and being a dick, you have bigger problems than whether to pay for dinner."

Jessica expected the man to say more, but he stood up and walked out of the bookstore. To her surprise, the other audience members clapped. Face flushed and embarrassed, once the crowd died down, Jessica said, "Any other questions?"

CHAPTER FIFTEEN

THE MORE TIME he spent with her, the more addicted to her he was. Over the past few weeks, he'd started to text her during the day with jokes and news stories that he knew she would be interested in. And they weren't even dating for the camera anymore. She listened to him talk about work when he came to cook her dinner and offered solutions when he was dealing with an unreasonable interior designer who wanted him to do something that would compromise the structural integrity of the house they were working on.

And most of the time, neither of them even mentioned the purpose of their relationship—public relations. It felt like a real relationship, and he'd never wanted one of those quite as much.

He was getting out of the shower after hitting the gym on Saturday morning, thinking about how nice it would be if he and Jessica had gone together and could be having shower sex while fighting over where to go for breakfast, when she texted him.

Jessica: 911. Emergency. Need you to come over now.

His heart started beating faster and he walked out of the bathroom with just his phone, but there weren't any little bubbles indicating that she was going to text him with more detail. What if she was hurt? What if her condo was on fire?

He shook those two thoughts off. She would call the actual 911 if either of those were the scenario. The more likely one was that someone had somehow found out about their arrangement and was going to expose them.

Galvin: What's going on? Is there something bad in the news about us?

Jessica: Nope. Worse.

He couldn't really think of many things worse than that that would warrant a distress call to him instead of medical personnel or the fire department, but she didn't make him wait this time.

Jessica: My mother is here. She is asking about my new boyfriend, and I need to produce you immediately or face the consequences. (She will not leave until she meets you and hits on you.)

Jessica hadn't talked about her mother or her upbringing that much, but he knew enough to know that it wasn't so great. She hadn't mentioned her father at all, and any conversation that touched on her relationship with her mother usually included lots of eye rolls and sighs. And the part about her hitting on him made his stomach hurt.

His parents were exacting and critical, and they persisted in one of the unhappiest marriages of all time because it was good for their co-owned business. But he'd never worried about either of his parents trying to poach a woman he was dating. That was some truly messed-up shit. No wonder Jessica had majored in psychology and then become a therapist. It might have taken that much academic training to figure her own shit out.

And he knew that she didn't have it all figured out, either. But she was more clearheaded and self-aware than 99.9 percent of the people he knew. If she was panicking because her mother had shown up, her mother must truly be a monster.

The thought of Jessica in distress had him dressing nicely—but not in the jeans that made his butt look the best, in order to avoid any butt pinches from Mrs. Gallagher—and hurrying over to Jessica's place. He got stuck in traffic, so he was irritated and sweaty by the time he got to her apartment.

He'd very rarely met any girl's parents, and he'd never been this nervous when he had. Not that many of his girlfriends had even extended the invitation. He'd never been disappointed in that fact before, but with some perspective he realized that it didn't say great things about him that no one had ever wanted him to meet their family.

But he couldn't change the past; he could only be there for Jessica in the present moment and hope she wouldn't judge him by his history. He shook off his nerves and knocked on the door.

He didn't know what he'd expected from Jessica's mother, but the woman who opened the door with a pink cocktail in her hand—at eleven a.m. no less—was not it. She was like a white version of Jessica almost, but she looked as though she'd lived a much rougher life. It was classist of him, but she looked like she'd crawled out from under the table at a dive bar, wearing a Def Leppard crop top and daisy dukes that looked like they would need to be surgically removed.

He was terrified.

He must have stood there staring for too long and not in a way that Mrs. Gallagher liked. Her smile faded, and she looked over her shoulder and yelled, "Does this man speak? Please tell me you're not dating a—"

Jessica slid toward the door, just in time to stop her mother from saying something that he was sure would be truly offensive. "Galvin can speak, but it would be fine if he couldn't."

She looked truly frazzled—wild-eyed and fragile at the same time. It made him want to kick this woman out of her apartment and out of her life. He didn't want anyone who made her feel that way to ever come close to her.

This urge to protect her was new, but it was much more comfortable than the fear that he would get too scared and break up with her. This need to keep her from harm actually made sense.

"Hello, Mrs. Gallagher—"

Jessica opened the door wider so he could step through, but her mother didn't budge. "Please, call me Laurie."

Once he got closer to her, he realized that the cocktail teetering in her grip was definitely not her first. She must have noticed that he was noticing her outfit, because she said, "Do you like my outfit?"

"It's—uh—it looks—well ventilated."

Laurie's face dropped, but Jessica choked back a laugh, and he was glad he'd said it. Maybe his lack of carnal interest would mean that Laurie wouldn't hit on him.

"Jessica didn't say anything about expecting a visit from you. What brings you to L.A.?"

Galvin had never met Laurie before, but he'd definitely met people like Laurie. He didn't know her, but he knew that she would love it if he asked her about herself, and he would never have to answer any questions about himself as long as he flattered her a little and kept her talking.

"Well, Jessica never invites me to visit."

He bit back a biting response about how he didn't think Jessica needed a day-drinking buddy who would hit on her boyfriend. He didn't know for sure that Jessica even wanted her mother to think that Galvin was her boyfriend, and Laurie hadn't actually done anything awful yet. She was just made up entirely of vodka, cheap perfume, and bad vibes.

"I just hadn't seen my little baby in so long." Laurie turned to Jessica then and squeezed her face between her hands, cramming the stem of the cocktail glass against Jessica's ear.

The look of distress on Jessica's face became worse, and Galvin scrambled for any idea of what to do. "You know what? I could use one of those cocktails."

Laurie looked at him and let go of Jessica. Her face lit up so quickly, he would have thought he'd asked her if she wanted an extra million dollars. "You'll join me for a cosmopolitan?"

"Yeah, why not? It's a Saturday. Let's turn up."

When Laurie danced her way to the kitchen, he locked eyes with Jessica, mouthing, *I'm sorry.*

She just shrugged and rolled her eyes. It was going to be an interesting afternoon.

JESSICA HAD NEVER worked with anyone who had killed their mother, but she understood the impulse toward matricide. She'd definitely walked clients through the process of cutting a toxic parent out of their lives before. But, for some reason, she'd never been able to do it herself. Whenever Laurie turned up on her doorstep—always unannounced—Jessica let her mother into her life to wreak her particular form of havoc.

Every time she was around her mother, she felt like a helpless child who didn't have any say about where they lived and when they moved. Her mother's whims felt like the weather. She couldn't do anything to change it, so she might as well batten down the hatches and hold on.

When her mother had shown up this morning, Jessica had panicked and texted Galvin. Over the past few weeks—despite trying to keep her emotional if not physical distance—she'd come to rely on him being around and available. In a lot of ways, she'd spent more time with him recently than she'd spent with Luke during the last year of their relationship.

As soon as she'd sent the text, she worried that she'd overstepped a boundary. They were only fake-dating and hooking up. This wasn't a deep, emotional connection. Despite repeating that to herself over and over, she'd sent the text.

And he'd come.

When her mother opened the door and Jessica saw the look on Galvin's face, she was immediately embarrassed. Her mother looked like a horrifying, biker chick nightmare, and it made Jessica feel exposed. Her mother had always dressed as though more skin meant paying the rent, and it often had. But Jessica had noticed early on how none of the other mothers wanted to be friends with Laurie, and that made it much harder for Jessica to make new friends.

Laurie, for her part, had never seemed to notice. Or, if she did notice, disdain about the way she dressed and flirted with pretty much everyone just made her amp up the town bike image she tried to cultivate even more.

But then Jessica saw a sort of understanding dawn on Galvin's face, and his charming public persona came back over him almost immediately. He even accepted her mother's offer of a morning cocktail and took a small sip every time Laurie turned her scrutiny on him—which wasn't very often because Laurie was on about how much Jessica sucked as a person today.

"I thought when you got rid of that boring guy, you'd find someone fun." Laurie had never liked Luke, and the feeling had been mutual. It didn't seem like Laurie was a fan of Galvin's, either—which really spoke well of Galvin's character—even though he was doing his level best to be a good sport. Her mother exclusively liked bad boys.

Over the years, she'd tried to understand how her mother had turned out the way she had, but she wasn't objective enough to diagnose her with anything.

"I'm not sure why you care, Mother." Laurie hated when Jessica told people they were mother and daughter. She thought that she looked young enough that they could be sisters. And they might—if not for Laurie's pack-a-day smoking habit. "It's not like you ever stay in L.A. long enough to form an educated opinion about me and any of my boyfriends."

Laurie snorted. "You've only ever had one." She motioned at Galvin. "This one's better, but he's way too good-looking for you. He'll definitely cheat."

Jessica's stomach tightened even more. She felt hot and sweaty and like she was about to throw up everywhere. Her mother was always making snide comments about her looks. When she was younger, it was all about how she should show some skin if she wanted boys to like her. Now, it was all about how she should wear more makeup and stop dressing like an old lady. Maybe her mother wouldn't have come here, insulting Jessica and generally making herself a nuisance until Jessica gave her enough money to go away for six months, if she'd cut her out of her life.

But Jessica suspected that Laurie just wouldn't listen.

Laurie ignored the fact that neither Jessica nor Galvin responded to her insults. "How did you two meet?"

"We've actually known each other since college," Galvin said. His voice was tight, and there was a tic in his jaw that Jessica had only noticed when he was sitting in traffic on the 405. Her mother was definitely as irritating as traffic on the way to LAX, so that seemed appropriate. She wished there was a way to tell him that getting angry at Laurie would only make things worse. The only way to manage her mother was to ignore her antics and pay her off.

"Mom, you were telling me that *you* just broke up with *your* boyfriend?" Jessica said. Laurie loved to talk about herself. Recounting her own dramas was her favorite pastime.

Laurie threw the rest of her drink back, and Galvin's eyes opened wide—with either shock or admiration—she wasn't sure which. "I don't know why you didn't come and visit me and Reg in Tucson over Christmas."

"Well, you didn't invite me. Considering that I'm biracial and your boyfriend was in a motorcycle gang known for virulent white supremacy, I figured that I'd skip it and spend the holidays with Luke's family." Jessica had often wondered how her parents had ever gotten together. Laurie had always claimed "not to see color" unless her current boyfriend happened to hate Black and brown people. Laurie became whatever her current situation required of her, so she hadn't defended Jessica against any of her numerous racist boyfriends' shitty comments and slurs.

"You shouldn't believe everything you read." Laurie had asked Jessica to keep an open mind about Reggie, the latest in her collection of violent losers. "Reg was truly a sweetie, and he was really looking forward to meeting you."

Jessica sniffed. "I'm sure, but it sounds like you broke up."

Laurie waved her hand dismissively. "Not really, just a little, temporary disagreement. I just came here because I missed you."

Jessica just nodded. They needed to move this along. When she'd said that thing about Reg being a racist, she'd felt the tension in Galvin's body ratchet up from across the room. She liked that it made him so mad and that she could tell what he was feeling without words. Luke had always ignored her mother's hijinks and then complained about her after she left. He'd never once even looked like he would jump in and defend Jessica from one of Laurie's sneak attacks.

"I just came because you posted about this one on Instagram." Laurie pointed a narrowed gaze at Galvin, and Jessica immediately understood what was going on here. Her mother knew that she would never post about her relationship on social media and hadn't known that Luke had walked out on her. Of course she would be curious as to why Jessica was talking about a relationship on Instagram right after she'd launched a book. And Laurie's comment on the book was, "Men are men and I love men being men. Why would I want to change them?"

So Laurie was here to investigate and see what she could extract from the situation.

"What do you want, Laurie?" Jessica asked. Then she looked over at Galvin—for what she wasn't sure—but the look of steely resolve on his face gave her the kind of reassurance she hadn't known that she needed. She was glad that she'd asked him to come over today, even though it was probably revealing too much about herself and the way she grew up right now.

"Well, I know you got a big check the day the book came out—"

Laurie must have done enough research to know how much money she'd made from her book advance and how book advances were paid out. And the last time she had visited had been right after she'd signed her book deal and posted the announcement on her private social media.

Jessica's shoulders drooped and she put her forehead against the table. She hadn't cut her mother completely out of her life yet because she'd always hoped that she would change—even a little bit. But Laurie was always going to be working whatever angle would keep her flush with cigarettes and cheap booze. Jessica would be frustrated with a client who refused to set boundaries around this kind of behavior, and it made her feel weak and stupid. But setting boundaries would infuriate Laurie. She would blow up her phone, post nasty things about her on social media, and show up with one of her shitty boyfriends so that he could feel sorry for her because her daughter was so mean to her.

Sometimes just giving in was easier than dealing with one of her mother's tantrums. Because even though she was a truly awful parent, Jessica still loved her. Even though Laurie had had a lot of truly terrible relationships, it was her way of using the skills she had at her disposal to feed and clothe her daughter. Even though her mother struggled to take herself and her life seriously, the perfect, fun, spontaneous adventures they'd had while Jessica was growing up lingered in her psyche.

Jessica had done everything in her power to be nothing like her mother as an adult, but they'd been a team from the time that Jessica was a toddler. She'd never quite been able to completely shake that mindset. The connection had turned toxic and hurt her more than any other relationship she'd ever had in her life. But it was still there, and Jessica couldn't let it go.

Before she could open her mouth and her checkbook, yet again, Galvin spoke. "Laurie, do you have a place to stay in town?"

"I usually stay with Jessica." Her mother sounded defensive, and Jessica was about to warn him off, but he wasn't looking at her. He was totally focused on Laurie in this intense way that she'd never seen out of him. It was clearly sort of freaking her mother out. "I don't see how that's any of your business."

"Well, I really care about Jessica, and your presence here is upsetting her, so it's definitely my business." Galvin's words shocked her a little. Galvin had told her how he found her beautiful and how much he admired her, but he'd never said he cared about her. "I think that you should either get a hotel for the night—on me—or Jessica is going to come stay with me tonight."

"Young man, this is family business." Laurie rarely raised her voice, and never around a man, so it was shocking to hear her yelling at Galvin. "I think you should leave."

"I asked him to come over, Laurie." Jessica decided to drop the "Mother" thing for the moment. This exchange was volatile enough on its own.

"Why?" Laurie stood up with her cocktail glass and headed back to the liquor cabinet. "It's pretty clear to me that he's some gigolo that you hired to cover up the fact that you can't keep a man."

"At least I know when they're not worth keeping." Jessica's mean side came out sometimes when her mother got like this. "And at least I'd never try to blackmail my own kid."

Laurie stomped her foot. "It's not blackmail, when it's family."

"Enough, Laurie." Jessica started when Galvin spoke. He stood up and walked toward her mother. "Where's your bag? You're going to leave right now. I'm going to call a car and check you into the Chateau Marmont for the night. Put as much booze and food as you want on your tab. Then, tomorrow at noon, another car is going to pick you up and take you to LAX. Let me know how much it will cost to change back your flight so you can crawl back into whatever hole you crawled out of to traumatize your daughter today sooner rather than later."

Her mother was stunned into silence. So was Jessica. She'd never been able to stand up to her mother—at least not in a lasting way. It was shocking, but it felt great. Jessica wasn't sure what to say. It had probably been a mistake to ask Galvin to come over, but he'd fixed it—temporarily or not.

"And you're not going to say anything to anyone about the duration of my relationship with Jessica. Because it's none of your business. By some miracle, she ended up kind, compassionate, smart, and responsible. Just from sitting here today, I don't think that had anything to do with you." He was wrong there, but Jessica didn't want to correct him. She didn't have the courage to kick her mother out. She should probably feel like he was overstepping a boundary, but no one had ever stood up for her like he was. The way she'd built her life as an adult had everything to do with how much she didn't want to be her mother. But it still felt nice to have someone recognize how different they were. "And maybe wait for her to call you and invite you before you show up next time?"

Laurie didn't speak, but she put down her glass and walked toward the door, where she'd dropped her bags when she came in.

"Are we understood, Laurie?"

Her mother stopped short and turned to Galvin. "I'm leaving, aren't I?"

"You're very welcome for the hotel and flight change." Galvin was really turning the screws. Jessica would never have the balls to dress down her mother like this, but her mother would never comply with her. But Galvin was a man—a big, strong, handsome, charming man. And her mother was so accustomed to following the whims of a man, she couldn't turn off that conditioning on a dime. This might be the only time in history that Jessica was grateful for the patriarchy.

"Thank you, Galvin," her mother said, though everyone knew that she really meant, "Fuck off into space."

Galvin ignored it and tapped on his phone for a few moments. "I wish I could say it was a pleasure to meet you. Your car will be outside in a few minutes. You'd better go."

Her mother didn't meet her gaze as she walked out.

CHAPTER SIXTEEN

GALVIN WAS A little nervous to look at Jessica after her mother left, but he couldn't avoid it forever. He knew that he'd overstepped, but her mother had pissed him off. Jessica hadn't even seemed like herself when her mother was here. It was as though she'd shrunk into the smallest version of herself, and he couldn't stand it.

He slowly turned and faced her. To his surprise, she didn't look pissed. And, to his delight, she looked like herself again. She was always beautiful to him, but the way she looked at him now stole whatever words he'd planned to use to reassure her in that moment.

"I'm sorry about her," she said.

Why was she apologizing for her malevolent floozy of a mother? He wanted to tell her that he admired her for surviving a childhood with that woman. He wanted to gather her up in his arms and hold her until he was sure she was okay. It was unfamiliar, and he'd never felt so enmeshed in a relationship before. "No need."

"Well, I'm sorry you needed to spend thousands of dollars to get rid of her. My way probably would have been cheaper."

"But it would have cost you more in the long run. She would have kept coming back." He'd used the voice he generally only deployed on contractors who tried to cheat him on materials.

"She'll come back anyway. She always does." Jessica flopped onto her couch, and he sat right next to her.

He might not really have the right to give her forehead kisses and reassurance, but that didn't change the fact that he wanted to. He would give her whatever she needed. "What do you need?"

Jessica was leaning back so her head was resting on the back of the couch, and she was staring at the ceiling. She sighed and turned to him. "I don't need anything."

He didn't believe her. He knew that she was trying to be strong. "Did Luke just let her talk to you that way?"

Jessica nodded, and Galvin added that to the long list of reasons he hated that guy. Wasn't that one of the main reasons that people did long-term relationships? To have someone around who would always take your side against people outside of the relationship? Galvin wasn't even her real boyfriend. He was just her fuck buddy with PR benefits, but he knew that she'd really been in a tight spot if she'd invited him into that shit show.

"Where's your dad in all this?" She hadn't shared much about her upbringing, and he totally understood why after today. But he wanted to know every bit of her story.

She shrugged. "We never met. And I don't know who he was. Laurie said that he died, but I'm pretty sure that was a lie just like everything else."

"So it was just the two of you until you went to college?" He couldn't believe that she'd survived that. And it explained why she was so tightly controlled. She'd had to be, growing up around the utter chaos of that woman.

"Most of the time she had a shitty boyfriend." The way she said that made his stomach drop. He wondered if any of the shitty boyfriends had put their shitty paws on Jessica. It made him want to hunt them down and rip them limb from limb.

Galvin was an easygoing guy. No one would ever guess that he was capable of feeling the depths of rage he felt just thinking about something bad happening to her. He barely recognized himself. But he didn't let most people get close enough to arouse his own instinct to protect.

But Jessica was right there. He didn't think she knew it, but there was no way he was letting her go after this PR relationship ended. He just couldn't do it.

"I think you need a hot bath and a decent meal," he said.

Jessica shook her head. "You've done enough for me today. I feel like I could sleep for about a thousand years."

"Sleep for a thousand years at my house, then." He really needed her to say yes. He couldn't let her stay here, alone. And a change of scenery would do them both good. "You know my place is cozier than yours is, and I have all the stuff to make you pasta carbonara. I also ordered some desserts from that place you love on Fairfax."

"Did my mother warn you that she was coming to town so you could stock up on comfort food?" she asked with a slight smile. His company might not be all that appealing, but he knew her well enough that she wouldn't turn down carbs on carbs.

"And I have wine that will wash away the taste of that antifreeze your mother was drinking."

"You're going to think this is wild, but she hates good vodka. She started bringing Popov along with her when she showed up, so I started stocking it. That way, she couldn't make fun of me for being too fancy for her. I don't even like vodka that much. That was more of a Luke thing."

Nothing about that woman would surprise him, but he added it to the list of reasons he disliked Laurie. "We're going to dump it out before we leave."

"What makes you think that I'm going to go along with your plan?" She smiled when she said it, but he was willing to do some convincing. He put his hand around her jaw and pulled her close. He kissed her forehead like he'd been wanting to since Laurie walked out. Then he kissed the spot behind her ear that would make her melt against him. Then he touched his mouth to hers.

"If you come with me, I'll have you for dessert." He bit her bottom lip lightly, to drive home his point. If he had his way, he would consume her right here, right now. But the ghost of her mother lingered in this place, and he didn't like the idea of fucking her in the bed that she'd shared with Luke. He didn't want to think about how she'd shared a life with someone else and realized that he didn't know what he was doing right now.

On one hand, it surprised him how easy it had been to be there for her and support her. But it was so hard to not be sure if he should. He didn't want to fuck up. So he kissed her again, and hoped what he had to offer was enough for her.

TRUE TO HIS word, he'd poured out the handle of cheap vodka that she'd always kept at the house—at Luke's suggestion—while she packed an overnight bag. She was still processing what had happened with her mother today, and she knew there would be fallout. But she felt remarkably safe and calm now.

She hadn't been lying to him or minimizing anything when she'd told him that she didn't need anything. He'd made that the truth when he'd kicked her mother out of her house. She knew that her mother would come back. She would always come back. Whenever Jessica felt weak or tired, her mother came back. There would be hell to pay.

But she was safe from her for now.

And she and Galvin were going to have a sleepover. They hadn't done that before. When this fake-dating scheme had started, she hadn't imagined it. But something had shifted when he stood up to that bully at her book signing. It had started to feel real. It had all been dates and heavy petting, and he hadn't even let her make him come. It was starting to get weird, and she was going to put her foot down tonight.

She could guess that he was afraid that his usual post-nut anxiety would rear its ugly head and he'd do a runner. But she didn't think it would happen now. They were connected by something more than just sex—it had started out as friendship and now it was feeling like something more. It wasn't partnership, yet. But it had that potential. She would never say as much to him because that would definitely scare him. But she knew it in her bones.

Jessica wasn't sure what she was expecting from Galvin's house. They'd mostly hung out in public places or her condo. He hadn't invited her in the one time she'd picked him up for a date. But she definitely wasn't expecting something quite as warm and cozy as this.

He lived in her actual dream home. It was right down the

street from the place that she'd wanted to buy with Luke, and it was probably designed by the same architect. The exterior was painted a bright white and trimmed in dark wood. As he led her up the front walk, he pointed out that the water features used rainwater collection and irrigated the garden while mitigating runoff.

She was impressed with all of that. She liked the environment as much as the next girl. But she had a brief, internal freak-out when she walked into his house. It was genuinely cozy. Totally neat, but utterly lived in. The furniture was coordinated, but it didn't match. There were both family pictures and art pieces on the few walls that weren't taken up by built-in bookcases.

Before she could stop herself, she rudely walked around the perimeter of the open living space, surveying the books. Predictably, he had lots of big books about art and architecture, but he had eclectic taste in fiction—sci-fi and fantasy, mysteries and thrillers, and even a few romance titles. She was particularly impressed that his shelves weren't totally dominated by dead white men.

"Did an interior designer pick out your books?" It seemed impossible that he would have had time to read all of these books with his reputation for being a man-about-town.

Galvin scoffed. "Nope. I read them all."

On closer inspection, the spines on the paperbacks were mostly wrinkled, so she knew he was telling the truth. The more she found out about him, the less and less his carefree, playboy image made sense. He had depth. But looking at him, he seemed a little bit embarrassed that she was seeing inside his inner sanctum. "Eclectic collection."

He shrugged. "I spent a lot of time alone as a kid, and books were always good company."

Something else they had in common. Wherever she and her mother moved while she was growing up, she made sure to get a library card. More than once, on the way out of town, she'd had to beg her mother to swing by the drop box to return the books. "Me too."

He stood there staring at her. There was something naked and vulnerable about his gaze that entranced her. She didn't get too much of it, because he turned and said, "I'm going to run you a bath."

She followed him.

GALVIN HAD NEVER invited one of his girlfriends over to his house. Somehow, even though he'd dated half the city, it had never come up. But he'd always been with women who were so far up their own ass that they didn't notice that their relationship was superficial. They were so used to people being obsessed with them and relinquishing their own personalities that they didn't really get into his thoughts or feelings.

And he'd always been fine with that. He'd chosen his romantic partners for precisely that reason, all his life. Until he'd shot up in height and filled out before college, no one had noticed him romantically. All of a sudden, people looked at him differently—hungrily—and he wasn't sure what to do with that. Eventually, he'd put up a wall of charming cad who no one would take seriously as a barrier between him and other people.

Over time, that wall had taken over, and he'd thought that was who he was. His personal boundaries were the only thing he had between himself and being consumed. But he didn't feel the need for those boundaries with Jessica. Somehow, their PR relationship was already more real than any of the other relationships he'd been in.

The fact that he'd allowed her into his home was huge for him. But he still couldn't tell her how huge because that would be too vulnerable—her knowing how close he felt to her.

Instead, he led her to his bathroom. It had the original tiling around the sink from when the house was built, but he'd turned the back half into a wet room, with a shower and bath. He started the water and grabbed his robe off the back of the door. He liked the idea of her wearing something of his. Again, he'd always been annoyed when girlfriends had tried to wear any of his clothes, because he knew he'd never see it again. But he liked the idea of Jessica wearing his robe, in his house, drinking his wine in his bathtub.

And yeah, part of the appeal of that whole scenario would be that she was naked. But there was more to it than that. The room filled with steam, and he put in a few drops of the bath stuff that matched his cologne. She would smell like him. Something about that made a possessive thing rise in his chest, as though he was marking her.

He brought the robe to her when she lingered in the doorway. She looked up at him through her lashes. "You're not going to stay?"

"If I stay, I'll end up having to mop up the floor." He would get one look of her delicious body, all wet and glistening under the perfect lighting that he'd installed himself, and they would end up taking a bath together.

He kissed her on the forehead—he couldn't seem to stop doing that—and said, "I'm going to go start dinner, and I'll bring you some wine in a few minutes."

CHAPTER SEVENTEEN

JESSICA WOULD MOST certainly go out of her mind—in a very clinical sense—if Galvin didn't fuck her tonight.

She knew he was attracted to her. They'd been intimate a number of times. And, even though she'd finished, he hadn't taken things any further. It was going to give her a complex. She was out of practice in flirting, and she wasn't sure what else to do.

It was on the verge of stressing her out, even though she was sitting in bathwater that smelled like him in his perfect bathroom in her dream house. When he came back in, he'd changed into a T-shirt and jeans, his feet bare. He held a giant glass of red wine in his hand. Before handing it to her, he placed a bamboo table over the bath. All this to make her comfortable and happy.

The one thing that she wished he'd do but didn't was look at her. She was not a "naked person." She felt fine about her body. It met societal standards of thinness, and somehow she'd never got caught up in diet culture because she'd never had the impulse to be noticed for her appearance. But she wanted Galvin to see her. She wanted him to think she was sexy and desirable.

"There you go." He put the wine down and turned to leave.

"Stay." She hadn't meant for that to sound like an order, but it had. "Keep me company."

He pointed with his thumb to the bathroom door like he was trying to leave a party. "I should really start dinner."

"I'm not in any danger of turning hangry in the next five minutes." She wrinkled up her nose at him. "I really need your company right now more than food."

"Okay." He didn't seem to want to stay.

"What is going on with you?" she asked.

He shrugged. "What do you mean?"

Jessica sighed. One thing about being in a relationship for so long was that she'd gotten out of the practice of articulating her thoughts. She and Luke had known each other so well that they didn't have to sit down and have conversations about little moods. Each little mood had practically been shorthand. And, honestly, she missed that.

Maybe she needed to embrace the weirdness and awkwardness of getting to know someone new.

"You seem really uncomfortable with me here," he said. "Do you want me to leave?"

When she shook her head, he sat down on the floor next to the tub with his knees pulled toward his chest. He rested his forehead on his folded hands between his knees. He waited so long to speak that she almost got up out of the tub.

"I don't want to make you uncomfortable," he finally said.

Jessica was confused. Despite the fact that she was worried

about making him uneasy, she'd never been more comfortable in her life. They'd been dating—even though it was sort of fake and sort of not—for weeks now. She was more comfortable with him than she had been with a few of her therapists in college.

"I'm not uncomfortable. Why would you worry about that?"

He lifted his head and looked at her. She loved his eyes. Even though the whole package of him was lovely, he could seduce someone with his eyes alone without even trying. "I want you, Jessica."

"I'm more than okay with that, Galvin." She took a sip of her wine and hoped that he wouldn't notice that her hands were shaking. Because then he might leave the room without them actually making any progress. "I want you, too."

"How much I want you scares me," he said. "I've never felt like this before, and I am so afraid that I will screw it up that I feel like I can't do anything. I don't want to try any of my usual moves on you, because it feels wrong. Dating and sex were always just for fun before. But the stakes are higher here."

"I'm not going to make a video disparaging your prowess in the bedroom. You've made me come enough times that I could honestly serve as a character witness for your abilities at this point."

He laughed softly. "You're so amazing."

"I'm not. I'm just me."

"But that's amazing to me." He looked up at the ceiling. "Your mother is the worst person I've ever met in my life. She would actually try to extort money from her own daughter—"

"And you kicked her out of my house. You did something that I've never been able to do." Jessica reached out a free hand and put it on his knee. It would leave a wet mark on his jeans, but she needed to touch him. "And I know you weren't doing it to protect yourself. You were just thinking about my feelings. You're a more caring person than I think you know."

"I care about you." He shook his head. "I think all of my past relationships have been about my own ego, feeling good in the moment, or networking." He said the last word like it was dirty, and she supposed it was. "All of my relationships have been transactional until this point, and I feel so fucked up right now because I can't control what I feel for you."

His words heated her to the very core. "That's not a bad thing."

"I want to devour you. I feel almost animalistic. When your mother threatened you, I wanted to shove her out your door physically. I'm not that guy. I've never even gotten in a fistfight."

Jessica looked down at his hands. They were big and strong, but she knew how gentle they could be. When he'd confronted her mother, she'd felt the anger coming off of him. Now that her nervous system was regulated again, and she'd washed off the layer of scum she felt every time she was around Laurie, she could reflect on how hot it was that he'd had her back.

"I know that you felt angry, but I have never felt so safe and cherished," she said.

"Really?"

"When I'm around my mother, I feel like I'm drowning. She's like an undertow of a person, and every time it feels like she's sucking me in. When you told her to leave and stay away from me, it was like a lifeguard pulling me out and giving me CPR."

"Why do you still talk to her?"

Jessica laughed and took her hand off his knee. She took a sip of wine and looked at her toes. She needed a pedicure. "I know that she's never going to be the mother I needed her to be. But I'm the only person she has in her life. If I stop talking to her, she'll be all alone. And I guess I feel like the occasional sensation of drowning is better than the guilt I would feel for leaving her on her own."

"I'm not the person to talk about the consequences of one's actions, but maybe she needs to be left alone to deal with hers."

"Maybe you're right." She didn't feel guilty right now, when she wasn't the one who had actually established the boundary, but she doubted whether she would keep it up. "Can we talk more about how you want me?"

He chuckled and flashed a charming grin. It wasn't fake, more flirty. And she liked that so much. It meant that they were on the road to fun stuff like sex, instead of heavy stuff, like talking about her mother. "Yes, let's."

He took her wineglass from her hand and took a sip. She watched his lips against the glass and the way his throat flexed as he swallowed. She was in tune with every move that he made.

"Why haven't you made a move?" She hoped she didn't sound as butt hurt about it as she felt.

Galvin leaned forward until their faces were just a few inches apart. "I've been making moves, but I don't want to screw things up."

"You're not going to screw things up, Galvin." She wasn't sure that this was true, but she felt like he needed to hear it.

"I don't want to lose you."

She let those words sink in and feel good. He wanted her. He didn't want to lose her. He was taking things slowly. He was taking care of her. "You're doing all the right things if you don't want to lose me."

"But if we go all the way, and I freak out, what happens then?"

Jessica shrugged. "We talk about it, and you stop freaking out. Or I give you some space."

"That easy?" He sounded incredulous.

"Maybe not easy, but definitely worth it," Jessica said. She got the feeling that no one had ever tried very hard with Galvin, that he didn't truly feel like he was worth putting work and faith into. "You're worth it to me. Am I worth it to you?"

He dropped his head. "Of course you're worth it to me. If you weren't, I wouldn't be scared, and I definitely wouldn't be admitting to being scared."

"Then, I think we're good to go."

The smile on his face then wasn't his charming smile—it was predatory. "Do you want dinner first?"

She didn't want to wait another second to be with him. "I think I'd like to start with dessert."

GALVIN HADN'T BEEN so nervous about sexual intercourse since his first time, freshman year in college. Back then, he'd hardly been able to believe that anyone would be into him. Now, he was shocked that a woman like Jessica—someone who knew him and needed more than just a well-lit picture at a good angle—was into him.

But when she'd said that he was worth the risk, something had broken open inside him. He didn't want to hold anything back, and he was willing to take a chance on everything going to shit for the opportunity to feel close to her.

He held up his bathrobe when she stood, and she said, "You're already trying to get me dressed again?"

"No, but I want every part of you but one to be dry when you're on my sheets." He tried to make that sound sexy, but it wasn't that sexy to be concerned about his duvet, was it. He was already screwing this up.

"I really like that you think about these things." She surprised him.

"You do?" It was interesting that anal-retentive tendencies about his stuff would be something that she liked about him. The way she saw things intrigued him.

"Yeah. One of my patients last week came in and spent her whole session talking about all the stuff around her apartment her shitty boyfriend had ruined. Like, he got drunk and pushed all of her furniture up against one wall. Messed up all the rugs."

Galvin shuddered. "At least I know that I'm doing one thing right."

He rubbed her skin under the robe and was pretty sure she was all dried off. She turned in his arms. He brushed a few tendrils of hair behind her ear. Her lips parted and she tilted her head, awaiting his kiss. But he let her anticipate it for a long moment. He'd converted to her belief that sometimes waiting was nice.

She made a soft, pleading noise as he wetted his lips with his tongue. "Now who's having a hard time waiting?"

"Me," she said as she curled her hands in the fabric of his shirt and pulled his face down to hers.

The kiss was incendiary where he'd expected it to be sweet. Her desire for him was an undeniable thing that she didn't bother to temper. And that woke up a predator inside him. He backed her into his bedroom and didn't stop until the back of her thighs hit the edge of his bed. She gasped when he pulled the belt on the robe away, and then she shimmied out of it until it pooled on the floor around her.

He'd kept his gaze on her face while they were talking during her bath, but now his gaze went directly to her nipples. They were a plump reddish brown, like late summer fruit. And he knew they were so sweet that he couldn't resist dipping his head and taking a taste.

Jessica clawed her way to the hem of his shirt and pulled it up and over his head as he let her nipple slip out of his mouth to pay attention to the other one. But he never got to because she pulled his head up to kiss him on the mouth again, leaving him to explore the terrain of her curves with his hands.

He moaned into her mouth. Everywhere she touched him was on fire. She undid the buttons on his jeans, and he almost sighed with relief. He felt as though he'd been continually hard for weeks, no amount of jacking off a substitute for her touch.

He pushed his jeans down his thighs, and they dropped to the floor. Jessica helped him out of his boxer briefs and gripped his dick in her palm like she was greedy for it.

She looked up at him with a devilish gleam in her eyes. "Condoms?"

"Bedside drawer." He inclined his head toward his nightstand. He'd put them there a few days ago, not thinking about it too hard. But really, he'd hoped they'd end up here. She turned and crawled across the bed, and he took the opportunity to admire the curve of her ass.

She turned over her shoulder and winked at him. “This is a very, very nice duvet.”

He knelt on the bed and slapped her ass. She startled, and her flesh jiggled. “Hurry up.”

“Oh, so now you’re in a hurry?” Still, her hands shook as she pulled the box of condoms out of the drawer and struggled with the plastic overwrap.

He took the package from her hands and ripped it open. Then, he pulled a condom out and threw it on the other side of the bed. They had more ground to cover before they would need that.

CHAPTER EIGHTEEN

GALVIN WAS ALMOST too beautiful to take in. She was particularly obsessed with the swirls of dark hair across his chest. She had sort of assumed that he didn't have as much chest hair as he did. He was so refined and well put together that it felt incongruous. But he was a lot more complicated than he wanted people to think he was.

He also had a really nice cock, and she was kind of sorry that she hadn't gotten to experience it until now. Because even though Galvin was making strides when it came to his ability to open up and be vulnerable, she knew this relationship probably had an expiration date. Maybe he *would* freak out after they had sex. Maybe they'd date for over a decade, and he'd leave her—just like Luke. She'd just gotten out of a big relationship and needed time to process. The lust she was feeling for Galvin was likely just an attractive distraction from the pain that would inevitably come.

He certainly didn't seem to be in a rush. His mouth moved

across her collarbones and lingered over the whole curve of each of her breasts. When she brought up her hand to cradle his face, he turned his head and kissed the palm. His fingers ghosted over the skin stretched across her rib cage as his tongue dipped into her navel. It tickled, and the sensation could have broken the moment with anyone else. But he followed it with a bite to the skin directly below.

He spread her thighs and kissed the tender skin near the center of her. Every time he touched her, her body reacted like it was the first time. She knew it was just her nervous system reacting to the newness of him, the uncertainty of the situation. If they were totally clear with each other about what was happening here, then she wouldn't be this drawn to him and how he touched her. It wouldn't be so magical. If it ever became her daily bread, she would grow tired of it, and they would grow tired of each other. The sex would become a thing that was nice to have, but not necessarily essential.

But right now, she felt as though she would die if he didn't continue to touch her, if he didn't pleasure her with his mouth. She wondered how he was holding off on plunging inside her. He hadn't been lying or exaggerating when he'd said that he wanted her. Even though she was in the habit of doubting herself these days, she knew that was certain.

He knew where to lick and suck and how to use his fingers and angle her hips toward his mouth to make her come at lightning speed. She cried out and shook, and her skin was covered by a fine sheen of sweat by the time he crawled over her body and grabbed the condom package.

She watched him roll it over his cock, and the lurid sight made her hungry for more. Already. He was like a buffet after a day during which she hadn't had time to eat. He'd made sure she wouldn't gorge herself by taking things slow over the past few weeks, but she was beyond the point of starving.

"You still want this?" he asked, as though her panting for his cock wasn't a clear indication.

"Gimme." For a woman who had always carefully plotted out her next move in every aspect of her life, her overwhelming greed for him was a totally new experience. It was as though she'd broken the seal on a desire for sensual indulgence, and she couldn't quite get the cap back on, no matter what. Even if getting close to him would eventually lead to heartbreak, she didn't care. Hell, she was supposedly heartbroken right now, and she was going to cling to any morsels of joy left on the table of life.

She lifted up her knees and offered herself to him, but he stopped again, and just looked at her. It might have felt uncomfortable if the deep desire on his face wasn't there. She might have wanted to cover parts of herself up if she wasn't sure that he was savoring her rather than thinking about what he wished was different.

"I need it, Galvin." She saw the moment that her pleas penetrated, and his control snapped.

"What do you need, pretty girl?" he asked in the most carnal-sounding voice imaginable as he placed one palm next to her ear and used his other hand to line his cock up with her entrance. "Do you need this inside you? Can you not get enough with my mouth and fingers?"

"Yes. Yes. I need more." She didn't even sound like herself anymore. She didn't know who this woman was—the one that he'd unleashed just by being himself. She wondered at the pieces of herself that she'd let go missing over all those years with Luke.

It wasn't that it was all bad, but she'd never realized how much of herself she'd locked away in order to make Luke happy. She'd instinctively known which emotions and ideas were acceptable to him. Everything else she'd tucked away until it was as though it didn't exist.

But Galvin didn't have any of that artifice when it came to her. She'd been too tired to hold it up anymore when they'd met.

When he pressed his body inside hers, all thoughts of who she'd had to be for her previous relationship slipped away. They were no longer relevant. The only thing that mattered was what she was feeling in exactly that moment. And it was likely the same for him. He groaned in pleasure as he bottomed out, his pelvic bone against her clit.

"Okay?"

Instead of answering him, she drew her legs up and wrapped them around his hips, trying to pull him closer—though that was likely impossible in the moment. She wrapped her hands around his waist, hoping it might prompt him to move. She needed him to move.

"I love it." She shouldn't even be uttering that particular l-word in this room, right now, with him. This didn't have anything to do with love. This was merely chemistry—conjured up by two particular people with histories that made them susceptible to each other.

This was a rebound for her, and he had something to prove with her. She should be making that her daily affirmation and possibly tattooing it on her palm, but she couldn't seem to care a whole lot when he finally did move.

"Touch yourself," he said. "You need to come again, and I'm not going to last very long."

"I won't. I can't." They'd hooked up enough that he should know better by now. She was pretty much one and done. Him fucking her felt absolutely amazing, but she wasn't going to have another orgasm.

"I think you can do anything you want to, pretty girl." She shouldn't like him calling her that. She hadn't been a girl for a very long time. But she did. "The only question is whether you want to come again all over my cock."

She did very much, and it seemed important to him, too. Maybe it was in service of his ego, but if his ego got her a second orgasm, she could live with it. So, she snaked one hand between them and touched her clit. He pinned it there with her hips and directed her movements with his pelvis.

It probably said something fucked up about her that she enjoyed him using diminutives and treating her like she was a puppet, and her pleasure was all in service of his. But she did. Right now, they existed outside of space and any rules of propriety. She didn't care that she'd never liked that before. She liked it with him.

He was right, he wasn't going to last long, but being filled by him and stimulating herself broke her open once again. Her body arched into his a few seconds before he stiffened on top of her and emptied himself into the condom.

He rolled away and disposed of the condom in the bathroom while she was still lying on top of his bed, the sweat on her skin rapidly cooling underneath the ceiling fan. When he leaned on the doorframe between the en suite and his bedroom and looked at her, she shivered.

"Are you cold?"

She didn't know how to answer his question because she didn't know what she was. "Maybe."

His brow furrowed, and she couldn't have that, him being confused about what she felt. She motioned for him to come over. "Are you okay?"

He pulled the covers back and on the other side of the bed and tucked her underneath them with what seemed like zero effort. So, he obviously wasn't feeling as boneless and lethargic as she was.

She was braced for him to tuck her in and then try to get some space, but he surprised her by scooting in next to her. After warning herself that this was just a fling pretending to be a relationship for the internet, she hadn't allowed herself to expect a postcoital cuddle. And even if she had expected it, she couldn't have predicted how much she would need it.

"You're not going to tell me to put my pants on and get out?" She knew she was being insecure, and he would probably be repulsed by that. But she didn't want to miss something and overstay her welcome.

But he took it in stride, and chuckled. "I'd tell you to put the rest of your clothes on first." He squeezed her shoulder to tell her that he was just joking. "I don't want to let you go just yet, even though I promised to feed you."

He kissed her on the temple, and then they snoozed.

CHAPTER NINETEEN

"YOU HAVE GOT to be fucking kidding me."

Jessica looked around the restaurant to make sure that no one was staring at them after Kelly's exclamation. It was the Wednesday after the Saturday debacle with her mother and the cataclysmic sex with Galvin, and she was having lunch to debrief with her two best friends.

"Shhhhhh. There are children here." Barbie had grown up in a very conservative family and was already uncomfortable after Jessica had detailed Galvin's money sex moves to them over antipasti. Yelling the f-word in a crowded restaurant had put her over the edge.

Kelly just sat back in her chair and shook her head. "He did not have those kinds of moves in college." It was a little bit weird that Galvin had hooked up with one of her best friends, but that was over a decade ago, they couldn't let it stay weird. Even in a city the size of L.A., there were only so many men worth sleeping with. If you tossed one back, you couldn't exactly expect all of your friends to leave him in the sea. "He was eager to please and eager to learn, but it sounds like you guys set the bed on fire."

"And then he made you pasta carbonara and you ate in bed while watching murder documentaries?" Barbie was the one shaking her head this time. "The fucking dream."

Jessica nodded. "With a really nice Barolo."

"Kind of makes you wish that he was your real boyfriend, doesn't it?" She didn't know how Kelly had just read her mind. She was going to have to work harder on keeping her face neutral going forward.

"I know it's really foolish." Jessica shrugged and took a drink of sparkling water. "He's not looking for a commitment, and I'm just getting over my relationship with Luke."

Kelly snorted. "Look at the therapist who preaches all about self-awareness and emotional honesty lying to herself again."

"I'm not lying to myself. Luke walked out less than a month ago." Jessica shook her head and put a piece of prosciutto in her mouth. "This thing with Galvin isn't serious. It can't be. It's not even a real relationship."

She said that last part quietly, so no one in the restaurant would hear her. It was strange to be a quasi-public figure in the city. She had a book out and had done some kind-of-famous podcasts and local news spots. Her social media posts with Galvin had garnered more followers and attention than she'd ever dreamed of. A few people had even recognized her when she went in to pick up her lunchtime coffee order. But L.A. was a city that ran on gossip. The stuff about major celebrities went further, but the habit of gossiping was deeply ingrained in every aspect of how the town worked. And Galvin was a little bit famous in a different way than her—he'd had an actually famous romantic partner—so he was actually sort of as famous as them now.

Jessica had never wanted to be famous. She'd just wanted to use her expertise and experience to help people. But it seemed that goal was becoming jumbled up with the one to save face after Luke dumped her unceremoniously and figure out her future. She shouldn't be adding in variables that would only confuse things further, like whether or not she could or should be in a real relationship with Galvin Baker.

"I swear to God, you guys. The sex is amazing, but it's not going to last."

Barbie scrunched up her face. Kelly looked at her and said, "No. We are not going to talk about that."

"Talk about what?" Jessica hated both secrets and surprises. Growing up, they had never meant anything good. And her nervous system had not gotten the memo that they could sometimes result in something good. But this secret—whatever it was—definitely wasn't something good.

"It's not relevant," Kelly said.

Barbie pursed her lips. "I think we should tell her. They had sex, and now we have to tell her."

There was a tense standoff between the two of them, and Jessica's gaze ping-ponged between her friends, as though she could deduce something useful just by looking at them.

"You have to tell me now. I'll never sleep again, if you don't tell me right now."

Kelly shrugged and motioned for Barbie to proceed. "Fine. Go ahead."

Barbie gave her a compassionate look that bordered on pitying. "Jessica—"

She was being way too hesitant. "Just lay it on me."

"We were talking and remembering college, because it's so wild that you're dating—even if it's not a conventional sort of relationship—someone we all knew. And we remembered something."

"What do you fucking remember?" She shouldn't be swearing at her friend, but her habit of pussyfooting around difficult topics was distinctly not helpful at the moment.

"Well, back in college, Galvin hated Luke."

Jessica was relieved. That wasn't much of a secret at all. "He still hates him."

"But do you remember why?" Kelly was much more forthright about things.

Jessica shook her head. "I didn't go to as many parties as the two of you, so I didn't know as much gossip."

"They, like, got in a big fight. Galvin almost broke Luke's jaw, and he had to petition not to get kicked out of the fraternity."

Jessica for sure didn't condone violence, but this had happened when they were in their early twenties. They were a lot older now. And he hadn't reacted violently to her mother, even though he'd been really angry. It wasn't like he had anger issues now. "I agree with Kelly, this isn't relevant to how Galvin is now. It's old news."

Kelly sighed, probably pissed she had to spell this out. "Barbie thinks that it was over a girl, and that Galvin is only dating you now so that he can get back at Luke."

That made her stomach sink just a little. When they were

together, their relationship felt real. Even though it was probably only temporary, he seemed really interested in her. But he did tense up whenever she mentioned Luke, and he'd never articulated why he hated the guy. Up until recently, Galvin's entire romantic life had been all about ego and conquest. Maybe someone interfering with one of his liaisons would prompt him to pretend to be in a relationship with her just to get back at Luke at a time when he was toxic on the dating market, but it honestly felt like a bit of a stretch.

What she was more upset about at the moment was that her friends thought she was so naïve that she would fall for a guy who was only using her for revenge. She was smart enough to see that he was probably treating her as some sort of romantic and sexual rehab facility before he was rereleased into the wilds of dating C-list actresses and West Coast models, but she didn't think he was using her to stick it to Luke.

"I haven't even heard from Luke since he moved out."

"You haven't?" Barbie gasped and covered Jessica's hand with hers. Jessica had only been reaching over for more ham. "Are you okay?"

"I'm fine, Barbie," Jessica said in her most authoritative tone. "I'm getting railed by a guy with magic fingers and a magic dick to match. Believe me, if a woman chose a casual relationship with Luke over a casual relationship with Galvin, she wasn't fit to be making her own decisions anyway."

Barbie pulled her hand back, freeing Jessica to procure more charcuterie.

"That good?" Kelly asked.

Jessica nodded as she spread some goat cheese with figs over bread. "That good."

The rest of lunch was less focused on her love life and more focused on how Barbie had a day full of starlets to make up for an awards show and didn't know how she would manage it.

As Jessica was leaving lunch, she saw messages from Galvin and Abby. The first one made her smile, and the second one made her anxious. She decided to call Abby back first.

"What the fuck is wrong with you, not answering your phone?" was the first thing Abby said to her. "I've been trying to get ahold of you for an hour."

"You're the second person to ask what's wrong with me today, and I'm getting a little tired of it. I was just eating lunch."

"You can't eat with your phone in your hand like everyone else?"

"I was telling Barbie and Kelly how things were going with Galvin—"

"I don't fucking care about that." Abby cut her off.

"It was your idea."

"Yes, it was and it worked," Abby said, in a more singsong voice. "I was calling to tell you that you made the *New York Times* Best Sellers list!"

Jessica was sure she hadn't heard what she'd just heard. "No."

"Yes."

"But how?" This had always been the goal, but she'd lost sight of that the moment she'd walked in her condo just as Luke was getting his shit and leaving. And then she'd gotten caught up in Galvin and their fake relationship. She'd just lost sight for a few weeks of what that fake relationship was supposed to give her.

It was supposed to give her this.

She'd thought she'd feel triumphant, free. She'd thought

she'd finally feel like she was out of Luke's shadow, and she was sure she wouldn't feel like a little girl who didn't have control of her life anymore.

And some of that was true. She felt more free than she had her whole life; she'd thought about Luke so rarely in the past few weeks that she was starting to think that he'd done her a favor by leaving, and she now wasn't worried about her mother showing up unannounced and fucking up her life.

But it wasn't because of anything that she'd done. It was all because of Galvin. It should make it all feel cheaper, especially given that no one but some of the stubborn hope that lived inside her believed that she and Galvin could make a go of things. She knew better than to put her faith in a relationship like the one they had. They'd only slept together once, and they hadn't even talked about whether they should continue seeing each other after the PR relationship ceased to serve a purpose.

There was another reason that she wasn't as excited about this as she should be. Part of the reason they were dating for public consumption was to raise the profile of her book. Every time she'd posted about him, her publisher had reported a bump in the sales figures. Galvin was a big part of her success. And now that her book had the highest profile there was, how long could they last?

"Are you listening to me?" Abby's question shocked her out of her spiral. She knew better than to place any credence in the longevity of her PR relationship, but she needed to listen to her friend and publicist.

"I'm sorry. I'm just so surprised. I thought this would happen after the first week or not at all."

"I did tell you that sometimes writers with smaller platforms take some time to build up momentum." Abby had told her this, but her lifelong tendency to look on the catastrophic side had prevented her from thinking that it was true.

"That you did, but I just had no idea that sales had popped this much." She should have been paying closer attention to her sales figures than to Galvin Baker.

"You don't sound excited. Why don't you sound excited?"

Jessica hesitated before answering. She couldn't very well say that she was feeling maudlin because she'd gotten high on her own supply of PR dick.

"I am really excited. Just surprised." She put her head on the steering wheel, grateful that this wasn't a video call. She hated lying to her friends.

"Okay, so I'm going to set up some morning show press, and that feature writer who wrote that wild profile on Mimi Jameson last month for *Vanity Fair* is doing a piece called 'The New Toxic Bachelors,' and she wants to interview you next week." Abby had been busy while Jessica wasn't answering her phone.

"She wants to interview me as an expert on toxic bachelors?"

"Yeah, it's the perfect fit." Abby paused. "She also saw that you were dating Galvin and wanted to press on that angle. But I think I shut that down."

The sinking feeling in her belly was back. "She wants to include Galvin in the article? As one of the bad guys?"

Jessica didn't know how to explain to Abby that Galvin had really never been one of the bad guys. He had always had a good heart, but he'd done a lot of shitty things to people to protect it. Despite the fact that she'd written the book for men who were having problems dating women and didn't know why, she didn't see Galvin in those pages anymore. He had complex reasons for trying to keep things casual for most of his life, and she suspected that he was trying to change. Even if they didn't make a go of it. Which they wouldn't. She had to stop thinking that.

"I need to think about this. I'm not sure Galvin will be okay with it."

"You're making decisions together now?" Abby asked, sounding surprised that Jessica would consider Galvin at all in her press strategy. Jessica knew that Abby wouldn't approve of her having a real-life relationship with Galvin—she really didn't like the guy—but wouldn't it be better to just be honest and deal with the consequences?

"I don't want to put him in that position, Abby. I care about him as a person."

"Oh, fuck no." Abby was so emphatic that Jessica might have agreed with her if she didn't have her wits about her. That kind of power was a great thing to have in a publicist until they used it against you.

"It's not really any of your business—"

"None of my business?! It was my whole idea!" Abby exclaimed. Jessica hoped Abby was someplace private. "I can't believe you would fall for that guy."

"I haven't fallen for him. We're just seeing where things go."

"Fucking Luke."

Jessica could feel Abby getting more and more worked up through the phone. "Luke doesn't have anything to do with this."

"Doesn't he? If he hadn't walked out on you like a little bitch, then you wouldn't have run into Galvin, and this wouldn't be happening. I swear to God that I will kill you myself if you fall in love with that guy."

"That's a little harsh, and that's not where this is going. I can guarantee you." Jessica could not guarantee that, not even a little bit, but she was focused on calming Abby down at the moment.

"Okay. Use him for sex, then. I hope it's not as bad as Kennedy said it was."

"It's not." She wasn't going to tell Abby how good it was. She would have a hard time doing that without sounding like a Disney Princess, and that wouldn't help her case for being able to avoid falling for him.

And she really had to get control of her own thoughts about the thing. It would be stupid to fall in love with Galvin—just not for the reasons that Abby stated.

Galvin does not want a commitment.

Galvin has never wanted a girlfriend.

Galvin does not do anything long-term.

And one thing she absolutely knew for sure in her bones—purchased in hard lessons about hoping her mother would change and watching clients saunter down paths to self-destruction despite her best efforts—was that she could not change what people wanted. Hell, she'd learned a refinement on that lesson recently—she couldn't even assume that her long-term boyfriend loved her and wanted to be with her when he'd said nothing about wanting to leave.

None of her good reasons for not getting further involved with Galvin were going to change what she was going to do. She'd thought she was better than this, but all she could do was hope that her pride wouldn't set her up for a giant fall.

"Just be careful, Jess. I don't want to see this guy humiliate you," Abby said. She seemed to have calmed down, but Jessica thought that she'd probably just taken on that distress as her own.

"I'm being careful."

"I'll try to steer the feature writer so she doesn't prod too deeply into the real aspect of your relationship. Do you think you can kind of gloss over it if you're actually feeling schmoopy and in love with him?"

"I'll do what I can."

"I trust you."

Too bad Jessica didn't trust herself.

CHAPTER TWENTY

GALVIN FELT BAD enough about subjecting Jessica to his parents at this Architecture Society dinner, and it didn't help that she'd barely spoken three words and hadn't met his eyes since he'd picked her up at her condo.

"You look really pretty tonight." He'd already said that, but she'd just made a faint humming sound. This time, she just nodded. "Are you upset with me?"

They hadn't been able to hang out since the morning after the night at his house. He'd never had a more perfect Sunday than the one she spent in his bed, on his kitchen counter, and later on his couch. He hadn't wanted her to leave, but he also hadn't wanted to scare her by begging her to stay forever.

And he'd thought she felt the same way about their time together. Everything she'd done and said had pointed in that direction before she'd left. And they'd talked on the phone and via text since then. Until Wednesday.

"Did something happen on Wednesday?"

She gasped, and he figured that he was right.

"Tell me." It had to be something awful, or she wouldn't be acting like this. His Jessica was clear-eyed and forthright. She had problems and pushed through them. She didn't react to a bump in the road by shutting down and shutting out the people who cared about her. Unless this was bigger than a bump in the road or she didn't count him among the people who cared about her?

"I hit the *Times* bestseller list," she said, as though it wasn't the biggest deal in the world and the thing she'd been working for.

"That's a good thing, right?" He was so confused, and that was one thing he'd never experienced with Jessica. He'd spent a lot of time over the past five days thinking about all the reasons why he wasn't ready to run away from Jessica. Apparently, she was figuring out strategies to push him away.

"It is." Finally, she spoke. "It's just that there's going to be more attention on the both of us now, and I don't know that it's the kind of attention that will help you."

One thing that he'd learned over the month he'd been dating Jessica was that he didn't give as much of a fuck about what people thought about him as he'd thought. Sure, he might need to work harder to prove his chops professionally if he wasn't dating influencers and starlets who would promote him and pass his name around. But that would be worth it if he could be with Jessica.

He just wasn't sure he could be with her.

"Are you breaking up with me?"

Jessica sighed. "No. I don't—I don't want that."

"Well, then. What is it?" He chuckled, even though nothing

about this was at all humorous. "You're supposed to be the great communicator."

She looked at him then. "I'm not as good at a lot of things as I thought I was."

"You're good at everything you try. But a relationship with someone who has a personality is new for you, and you have to try kind of hard. That's okay. You're getting the hang of it."

She scowled at his condescending tone, but at least he got a reaction. Her sort of blankness had really scared him.

"There's this feature writer who is doing an article. She wants to talk to me about her topic, and I'm afraid that you're going to come up."

"I'm your PR boyfriend. Of course I'm going to come up." He was still confused by her reaction to all of this good news. "Are you having a hard time with all the attention?"

She shrugged. "Kind of. I had to move around some standing appointments next week so I could be on some of the national morning shows."

He reached over and grabbed her thigh. She didn't tense up or tell him to take his hand off her, so he left it there. "This is all great news. Tell me why it has you so upset. I just want to help."

"The article is called 'The New Toxic Bachelors,' and Abby is worried that you'll get smeared. One of the reasons that the writer wants to talk to me—besides the bestselling book with the wild title—is that I'm dating you." Jessica sounded wrecked, as though she'd been worrying about this since she heard the news.

Galvin had been humiliated on Instagram and on a couple of dumb gossip blogs and podcasts, but this was a feature in one of the few glossy publications left. This would do great things for

Jessica's book sales, and it would probably get her a contract for a new book. But she was more worried about how it would affect him. He didn't know what being in love felt like—not as an adult—but he was worried that the warm feelings he was having over her attempts to protect him might be it.

"Listen, even if they do, I'm not sure that a few hundred thousand more people thinking that I'm utter trash in bed is going to make a difference. I've done and said things in relationships that I regret, but I'm not in those relationships anymore. I need you to do what's right for you and not worry about me."

They pulled up to the valet stand, and his anxieties about being around his parents came up. Those overpowered any concerns he had about Jessica's newfound notoriety making his life more difficult.

"I just don't want you to see me as a liability." He didn't unlock the doors right away, because Jessica still seemed on the verge of bolting. The idea of never seeing her again made him feel like someone had taken a vegetable peeler to the surface of his heart. It was a raw and open wound that he felt just thinking about the possibility of her walking away from him.

He'd avoided this kind of base vulnerability for decades. He hadn't wanted it, and he'd pushed back at anyone who got too close for a long time. But he wouldn't give up the taste of Jessica's delicious kisses or the way she looked at him over her morning coffee for feeling like his heart was intact inside his chest.

His life had been busy, but empty. The debacle with Kennedy had forced him to stop and look around. And Jessica had made him realize that there was something in the world that he wanted more than proving his parents wrong about his choices.

There was a kind of fulfillment to be found when there was someone who had your back.

And it couldn't have been anyone other than Jessica. Maybe because they'd started out as friends, and she didn't believe all the stories swirling around him. Maybe because she was trained to see the things behind what people said about themselves. Or maybe it was just because she was his perfect complement.

He wanted to say so much to her in this moment, but he had a feeling that spilling the full depth of his feelings for her now would cause her to run away.

"Let's just get through dinner—"

"I'm so sorry that I'm laying all of this on you when you're winning an award. And your parents." Jessica's face crumpled, and she seemed like she was on the verge of tears.

"Do you want me to take you home?" The valet tapped on his window, and he turned away from Jessica to give him a dirty look. Before, he would have gotten out of the car and called his date an Uber without even thinking about it, but he felt fierce about Jessica. He didn't want her to leave unless she needed that. And then he would leave with her. "These awards are just self-congratulatory paperweights, and I don't like spending time with my parents all that much."

"At least we have that in common," she said on a bit of a laugh. "I want to see you recognized for your work, and I'm curious about your parents," Jessica said. "It's the least I can do after how you helped with my mom."

"You don't owe me anything, Jessica." He was a better person, and he wanted to be a better person, just by being around her. She didn't have any illusions about who he was or what mistakes he'd made. But she liked what she saw from him enough to give him the time of day anyway. He'd never be able to repay her for that. "I care about you, and I wasn't going to watch her treat you that way."

She looked at him then, with glossy eyes. He'd never seen something more beautiful in his life. And she held his raw, peeled heart in her hands even though he wasn't ready to tell her that. He couldn't breathe until she told him whether she was still in this with him. He didn't even care about the dinner. If she didn't want to go in, his mother would insult him and tell him that he was just as useless to talk to as his father. If she did go in, his father would say something offensive within the first few lines of conversation. And then they would watch his parents pick at each other until they were nothing but bones for the rest of the night.

It would be miserable, but it would be bearable if Jessica was next to him.

"We can leave right now." The valet tapped on his window again, and several cars behind them laid on their horns. "Just say the word."

"Let's go in. Let's be brave," she said. "After all, they can't be worse than my mother."

JESSICA WAS A mature adult who could admit when she was wrong. However, she'd rarely been quite as wrong as when she'd predicted that Galvin's parents couldn't be worse than her mother. There were two of them, for starters. And where her mother was outwardly mean and transparently always looking for an angle, Galvin's parents looked like loving parents. At least on the outside.

They were waiting in the foyer of the hotel where the awards ceremony was being held. It was clear that Galvin had never had a chance of not being breathtakingly handsome. His father was tall and broad shouldered, with the same thick, dark hair—down to the cowlick at the front. His mother was so thin that she looked brittle, and Galvin had gotten his penetrating gaze and green eyes from her.

They both smiled at them, and they didn't look loathsome and mean until they got close. Jessica didn't believe in woo-woo stuff. Everything people interpreted as "vibes" came from brain chemicals and instincts that had kept their ancestors alive when they had to run from saber-toothed tigers on the savanna. But, if she did believe in vibes, the Bakers had some of the worst she'd ever experienced.

When Mr. "Call me Gil" Baker and Mrs. "Aren't you lovely?" Baker shook her hand in turn, cold fingers crawled down her spine. Neither of them hugged their son or congratulated him on his award. And she didn't like the look in Gil's eye when he looked her up and down. And when Mrs. Baker looked Galvin up and down and deemed his Brioni suit unacceptable with a quick purse to her lips, Jessica wanted to fight her.

Even though Galvin had tried to warn her, she'd been caught off guard. But once she met the two of them, none of her worries about what the future might hold mattered. The only thing on her mind was making sure that Galvin's parents couldn't do any more damage.

For his part, he didn't seem to be affected by them. Maybe he was accustomed to how dismissive and contemptuous his parents were. By all accounts, Jessica should be, too. But when it was Galvin, it made her angry. She wondered if this matched up to his experience of her mother. And maybe his depth of caring for her had prompted his defense of her.

Jessica wanted to call them both on their attitude, but they turned and went into the ballroom and just expected Galvin and Jessica to follow. Jessica shot a look at Galvin's face, which betrayed nothing. But then he put his arm around her waist, and it felt like he was holding on for dear life.

She was so glad that she hadn't left him to deal with this alone. Or had him leave with her. She knew people like his parents, and they would probably criticize him for leaving an awards dinner with their last breath. They were petty, small people who only cared about how their son made them look—whether or not he was happy. No wonder Galvin had chased partners that wouldn't get too close but would raise his profile.

"It's going to be okay," she said, even though she didn't know if that was true.

Galvin cracked a smile, and that felt like a win until she realized it was his "I don't feel anything" smile. "It won't, but I'm glad you're here anyway."

CHAPTER TWENTY-ONE

"I DON'T KNOW WHY he builds those silly little houses." Galvin's father was trying to explain, for the fourth or fifth time that night, why commercial architecture was the future. "People shouldn't even be building single-family homes anymore. They're not environmentally friendly or sustainable."

"I think Galvin's homes are beautiful. As humans, we need art. It's not as important as food or water, but we wouldn't be human without it." Jessica had said the same thing three or four times. After the third, Galvin had leaned over and whispered "Don't bother" in her ear. But he wasn't at the table now. He was giving a speech and talking about the marriage of utility and beauty and the vision that had inspired the movie star's home that he was winning an award for—an award for smart environmental design.

It was hard to pay attention to what Galvin was saying through the blind rage his parents were invoking. When Mr. Baker tried rephrasing his insults, yet again, Jessica gave him a sharp look and put her finger to her lips.

She could have been mistaken, but Mrs. Baker might have cracked a smile at someone shushing her husband. So, she was just a bitch all around.

Instead of stewing more on how awful Galvin's parents were, she let herself look at him. He was funny, charming, and exuded a kind of self-confidence and competence that was hard-won. He wore the hell out of a suit, but he still blushed a little bit under the attention of a ballroom full of his colleagues.

They'd shown pictures on the big screen of his designs. She'd seen them before, but they were really remarkable when they were blown up so large it was almost like being in the house. She'd known he was talented. Even with all the connections in the world, it wasn't like architecture was easy.

"He should have gone to Syracuse, like us. But he just had to stay close to home so he could star-fuck." Jessica changed her assessment of his mother. She wasn't just a bitch. She was dead inside.

This time, Jessica didn't try to defend Galvin's choices to his parents. She could see now that it was a complete waste of time. And the more she tried to defend him the more they found things to complain about. They were a lost cause.

At least they weren't saying these things to his face. But from the way Galvin had reacted to them—almost like he put on a costume as soon as he set eyes on them—she knew he had to have heard all of these things multiple times before.

Instead of telling his parents off, making it clear that she hoped one of their giant buildings collapsed while they were the only people inside, she took a long sip of champagne. At least his parents' quagmires served better hooch. And she was glad she was there for him, because when he looked out into the crowd, he could bypass looking for approval from either of his dickhead parents and see her. She approved of him. She cared about him. She saw him. Hell, she might love him. Even though it was the wrong thing to do.

She was past worrying that he only felt like home to her because she'd only ever had home in instability. Years of therapy and training in giving therapy had gotten her past that. She was beginning to think that people slotted themselves into roles in dating as a sort of armor, and you couldn't always tell what was underneath. It certainly felt like Galvin's suit of armor had fallen to the wayside, but she would survive if it hadn't, and she was being a fool.

Luckily, they didn't have to spend too much more time with his parents after the dinner and awards. They got up as soon as the dancing started, leaving Jessica and Galvin alone at the table.

He was like a different person as soon as they left, and Jessica was finally able to relax. "We can leave if you want," he said.

Jessica shook her head. "It's your night, and you deserve to celebrate." She lifted her glass. "To the best architect in L.A."

He smiled back at her, and it warmed her to her toes. She couldn't help the flood of heat in her veins every time he looked at her like that—desire in every line of his face. She almost couldn't believe that she'd compared his appearance to his parents. The materials might be the same, but they were completely different on him. Like his home and the residences he designed, there was warmth and care in every line.

"I think you might be the best thing that ever happened to me," he said.

A bit of cold wiggled its way into her core then. "I'm afraid that being with me might only expose you to more bad publicity." She couldn't get over feeling that an arrangement that might have served both of them at the beginning might just ruin his reputation.

"I need you to stop thinking about that." He took a sip of his champagne and waited until she took a sip of hers. "What can I do to take your mind off it?"

When he'd picked her up that night, she'd planned on telling him that it was a bad idea for them to continue seeing each other, because of the particular shade of spotlight her bestseller status had brought. She'd also assumed that he wouldn't want to have sex with her after she told him that. But the way he looked at her—like he was thinking about how her mouth would feel wrapped around his cock—and the way he leaned in close enough to kiss the spot at the base of her neck that he knew drove her crazy, told her that he was definitely thinking he could take her mind off their troubles with sex.

She wasn't sure that it was healthy to not finish this conversation. They were both skating very close to the edge of something dangerous, and she should be clinging to some semblance of common sense. But the way he made her feel rendered that impossible.

"You're incorrigible. And your parents are around here somewhere." Maybe that would have the effect of a cold shower.

"I don't care if they see me boost you up on this table and eat my dessert right here." He was so filthy that it should have made her blush and shy away. She'd certainly never even fantasized about someone saying something like that to her, but it felt right coming from him. It felt like the truth, and it reflected how she felt about him, too.

He wouldn't put her at risk of public indecency charges, but the fact that he wanted her so much and didn't care who knew was heady.

"I don't think that's necessary, Mr. Baker."

He straightened so that his mouth wasn't millimeters from her throat and took her hand, tracing circles in the palm. She wondered at the fact that this was even more arousing than getting close to heavy petting in public. "I think the only thing that's necessary is me and you and a flat surface as soon as possible."

The heady way he touched her was making her forget that this was temporary. That was really the problem, wasn't it? They couldn't just get lost in their sexual connection and stay there. "You're really hard to resist." It just slipped out.

His touch paused, and Jessica was mortified. "Why would you resist me?" he asked. "You're trying to break up with me already?"

When he kissed her behind her ear, it made it difficult to think clearly. "In the car—"

"That's why you were so quiet." He stopped then. "And I just rolled over and didn't listen to you. I begged you to come in here with me, and you obliged because you're a good person. You just think my usefulness has come to an end." There was hurt in his voice.

"No, that's not it—"

He dropped her hand then, and she was desperate to have him touching her and saying inappropriate things to her again.

"I get it. Now that this reporter is poking around, you're worried that you won't be able to keep up the facade of actually caring about me."

"Galvin, shut your mouth and listen."

JESSICA HAD NEVER used her stern, therapist voice with him before. It was a little bit shocking, so he shut his mouth. He'd known something was bothering her tonight, but he hadn't thought she was going to break things off with him.

He really should have been expecting it. Once her book had gotten the attention it deserved, he wouldn't be useful to her anymore. And now he was a liability—an embarrassment. Just like he was to his parents. He scanned the room for them just so he wouldn't have to look at Jessica right now. She would see way too much on his face. She always saw too much. And he'd thought she'd genuinely liked what she was starting to see.

But he was wrong.

This should be easier. He'd been broken up with plenty of times—for not calling when he said he would, for refusing to propose after six months, for refusing to uproot his whole life and move to a commune—but he'd never been broken up with because it wouldn't look good for them to be seen together. It reminded him way too much of how he'd felt when no one in his life seemed to like him very much—not his parents, most of his teachers, or even some of his classmates.

And Jessica was the first person he'd been open and vulnerable with in his adult life. This was a disaster.

"Listen to me," Jessica said.

He didn't want to, but he did it anyway on the off chance

that she was going to tell him that breaking up with him was a bad attempt at a joke.

"I was worried about you. I know you only agreed to date me because people wouldn't believe in my ability to give advice about relationships if I wasn't in one. And now, it's so risky with all this attention for us to be fake-dating."

"It's not fake for me anymore." He couldn't stop being honest with her now. It didn't feel right.

Jessica didn't look shocked. And her gaze didn't fill with anything as humiliating as pity. He saw something that he was choosing to interpret as hope. "It's not fake for me, either. That's why it feels so dangerous."

"It feels dangerous to be with me?" He hadn't done anything but try to make her feel safe once he realized he had real feelings for her.

"Much more dangerous than being with Luke," she said. He wished he could disappear that man's name from existence—just snap his fingers and make all the Lukes vanish into the ether. "But it's my mind lying to me. I know you don't want to hurt me, and that makes me so afraid. I'm afraid to mess it up. I'm afraid to let myself care too much, in case this is all a dream and I'm going to wake up tomorrow and all this is gone."

"Dinner and dancing with my parents is not the stuff of dreams, Jessica."

She laughed. "No, but watching you up there was. You're so good at what you do, and all the attention after you broke things off with Kennedy was a distraction. I don't want to be another distraction."

Losing Jessica would be a distraction. He wasn't sure when it had happened, but she was the first person he'd called when he'd gotten the news that he was going to win this award. He'd won, like, five, but he'd never felt the urge to call one of his girlfriends about any of them.

Instead of spending any more time trying to convince her that he was actually serious about her, despite everything he'd ever said about not being capable of being serious, he stood up and held out his hand. "Come on. I have to show you something."

"Here?" She looked around. "Where? You're *not* going to have some sort of dance-off to prove your devotion."

He laughed. She was always making him laugh, and he wondered if anyone had ever told her how funny she was. Probably, but he would be sure to tell her more. "No, but note for next time."

"That wasn't a suggestion," she said. He pulled her through the tables and toward the exit of the ballroom. "We aren't going to stay and celebrate your night?"

He squeezed her hand and pulled her faster. She probably had to run in heels, but the only other option was flipping her over his shoulder and running, and that would probably embarrass her. "Just come with me."

"Yes, sir," she said with her trademark sarcasm. He wondered if she would be into it if he took her over his knee when she talked to him like that—not because he didn't like her giving him sass, but because he really did.

She didn't say anything else when he took her to the bank of elevators in the lobby. He'd had the idea to do this as soon as he saw where the event was going to be held.

"We got a room?" she asked, a little bewildered. "Or are we going to commit some lewd acts in the elevator?"

As soon as the door closed, he said, "Again, note for next time on the lewd acts. But we're going to go upstairs to the penthouse suite and have the romantic evening that I'd planned to surprise you with before you said you were going to break up with me."

She looked at the ornate decorations in the elevator and whistled. "I should probably try to break up with you more often."

"Can we stop joking about you breaking up with me? I'm trying to be romantic here, and it's harshing my mellow."

"Well, your parents really harsh all mellow of any room they enter, so I think we're even."

"What's your clinical opinion about my parents?" He was sure she had one. Part of him wished that he hadn't invited her to join him tonight. But he wanted to see her, and he wanted to celebrate with her.

"You don't want to know." So it was bad.

"I'm sorry." He wouldn't do this again, even if he convinced her to stay with him.

She grabbed his hand again as the elevator climbed floors. "There's nothing to apologize for. I understand more than anyone."

"You do, and that's why you shouldn't have to put up with them."

The elevator arrived at their floor, and she didn't let his hand go. This had seemed like a good idea when he'd booked the room. But now, after she'd admitted to thinking about ending things, that scraped-raw feeling was back. He hadn't had the urge to cut and run after they'd had sex, but he had it now that he didn't know where they stood. He had it under control, but it was there all the same.

"I don't want you to break up with me," he said. He didn't.

But he wasn't ready to tell her that he could see himself committing to her now, either.

"Obviously, I don't want to break up with you, either."

"Then I still don't understand why you were going to do it." He opened the door to one of the four suites on the top floor, but she didn't walk in before him.

"Because I don't want your past dissected in the press. I don't want you to resent me."

"I could never resent you." He moved toward her.

She put her hand on his chest. "You say that now, but I saw how you felt after Kennedy made the video. You were wrecked."

He felt as though steam might come out of his ears, because his gears were grinding so hard trying to figure out how to convince her. Only one option was crystal clear—showing her.

"I'm not sure what I can do to reassure you that I'm in this." He put his hand over hers, holding it there. "All I know is that you're the only person I want to be with most of the time. The difference between whatever this reporter is going to say about me and what Kennedy did say about me is that I no longer care if I can't pick a random girl up at a bar or a party to amuse myself for the night."

She opened her mouth to speak, but he gave her a stern look and she shut it. Her fingers fluttered against his chest, and he wondered if the thought of him with another girl made her wish she had the dexterity to snap his sternum and rip his heart out. He got a similar compulsion when he thought about how she'd wasted so much time with Luke, but it was Luke's heart that he wanted to crush in his palm.

"I don't want to be with anyone else but you."

Her face softened, and he knew he was getting through. He flipped her hand in his and pulled her through the door. Before she could say anything, he crouched in the entryway and undid the fastenings on her shoes. She'd told him that she rarely wore heels, and he knew they had to be killing her. She'd worn them for him, and he loved that.

When her shoes were off, he stayed on his knees and backed her up against the door with his torso. She might have expected him to push her skirt up and eat her right there, but right now he just needed to get close. He wrapped his arms around her waist and rested his head against her stomach.

Her fingertips fluttered in the air for a few moments before coming to rest against his head. She lightly dug her fingernails into his scalp, and he nearly melted in pleasure. She might not have a long list of lovers, but she'd noticed that it made gooseflesh pop all over his skin when she did that and so she did it all the time. God, she drove him crazy. At the same time, touching her, being with her, gave him a kind of peace he'd never known he could feel.

He couldn't lose her.

He didn't know how long they were like that. And he didn't know what it meant. To an outsider, it might look like he'd thrown himself at her feet and was begging her to stay with him. And maybe that was what it was. He just hoped that he wasn't an anchor holding her down. She'd spent much too long in the shadow of an asshole, and she deserved to fly.

He looked up at her face and found her staring at him. Without thinking, he ran one hand up her thigh. Her dress had a deep slit, and it was almost like an open door to the center of her. He might not be sure of his merits as a partner in life, but he knew she liked what he had to offer her in terms of pleasure.

When her dress was out of the way, he pressed an open-mouthed kiss to the front of her panties. She gasped and her fingernails dug a little more insistently into his scalp. That was all the prompting he needed to reach around her hips and pull her panties down until they fell to the floor on their own. He made her lift one foot so she could spread her legs.

He felt like a pervert whenever he was about to taste her because he was addicted to the taste and smell of her arousal on him. If he wasn't hard already, his reaction to the smell of her was always instantaneous. He savored her, taking his time as he parted the center of her and used his tongue and fingers to make her moan and pull his hair. She looked down at him, their gazes locked for a long time. He wanted her to see how much he loved this, how much he worshipped her body. He wanted to prove that he was a better choice than the safe ones she'd made her whole life.

Being with him might not make sense for an authority on loving and healthy relationships, but he wanted to prove her wrong. Sometimes the only way to prove the rule was to be the exception.

Her breath caught when he sucked on her clit. He knew it wouldn't take long for her to come then. She looked away from him, and he let her that time. The next time he made her come, though, he would hold her jaw so she couldn't look away. She needed to see while he was inside her how much she absolutely decimated everything inside him that would make him run.

Her body bucked against the door, and she let go of his hair to pull his whole head to the core of her when she came. She was just as undone by him as he was by her. He couldn't believe that she was actually going to end this.

He stayed kneeling at her feet, wiped his face, and took her in. Somehow the curls of her hair had gotten mussed—probably when she was thrashing at the door. The skin on her chest was flushed, and her breasts jiggled as she took in ragged breaths.

She'd worn a red sequin dress that seemed very out of character but affected him as though he was a bull in the ring. Even though the night had been weird—they didn't seem to have any nights that weren't weird—he'd focused on her and that red dress all night.

"That was [illegible]"

"Delicious." Her gaze snapped back to him when he said that, and her blush deepened. She got so flustered when he said dirty things to her that he would have to do it more. "It makes me never want to get off my knees for you."

She grabbed at the back collar of his shirt and pulled him up until he was standing. "You shouldn't say those things to me."

"Why not?" He pulled the rest of her hair out of its updo, and carefully pulled the strands over her shoulders so it wouldn't get caught in the door. They had a whole room for a whole night, but he was going to have her on every flat surface at least twice before they were done.

"It makes me think of how good you are at this, and how you got good at this . . ."

He didn't want her thinking about any of his other lovers. They were all in the past. And besides, not many of them had been like this. There was that old saying that sex was like pizza—always a little good, even if it was bad—and it was sort of true. But he felt as though he'd been eating greasy takeout for decades and all of a sudden had access to slices from Sicily. He could never go back to the stuff he'd eaten before.

"It's not always this good."

She snorted a little. "That's good. I've started to feel a little guilty about encouraging my clients to seek out more than chemistry."

"Even when you have chemistry—and we do—it's not always like this."

Her brow furrowed and he kissed her forehead. She took the opportunity to work the knot on his tie loose. He loved the feel of her small, efficient fingers taking him apart.

"It would have killed me if I felt this way about every woman I've had sex with. You're an addiction, Jessica Gallagher. It's a good thing you never gave me the time of day in college."

"Why's that?" She'd pushed his jacket over his shoulders and was working on the buttons of his shirt now. Once she got his pants off, he would be incapable of explaining why he was glad she'd looked right through him when they were younger.

"I would have wanted to do nothing but eat your sweet pussy, all day, every day. I never would have finished grad school."

"Neither would I."

"I would have been gone for you."

SHIRTLESS GALVIN BAKER never would have been in love with her in college. She never would have allowed that, and she knew that his sweet words were part of his whole appeal. But they were so sweet that she couldn't believe they were real. A big part of her wanted to believe that what they had between them was more than just transcendent sexual chemistry. He'd certainly seemed upset when she'd let it slip that she planned to break things off tonight.

And she hadn't planned to be quite so severe about it. She'd been trying to give him the option. She knew they would end eventually—rebound relationships that started out as fake dating didn't have staying power outside of fairy tales and romance novels. But she didn't want him to look back and feel resentful of her for keeping him on the hook for too long.

But he'd said he didn't care about his reputation, and there was no PR value to him getting a hotel room for the two of them that night. Maybe he just wanted to have a few drinks at the awards dinner—with his parents, it would be warranted—without worrying about driving, but he didn't need to get a penthouse for that. And if he didn't want to spend any more time with her, he certainly could have put her in a cab.

Why was she having such a problem taking him at his word? He'd never lied to her, and there was no reason to believe that he would start now. But she'd taken Luke at his word for a decade and a half, and he'd disappeared on her. She'd trusted him with the most precious parts of herself, and it hadn't mattered in the end. All the trust and love she'd poured into that relationship didn't matter in the end. He'd thrown it away like it was worthless. Like she was worthless.

And now she couldn't believe Galvin when he said he cared about her more than what she'd promised to do for him.

"Unless you're not that into me—"

She'd been silent for so long that he was doubting that she wanted to be here with him. And that wasn't the truth. She wanted to be here with him, but part of her was still living in the past. And she couldn't tell him why she was reticent to believe him. He'd never liked Luke, and she'd noticed him wincing whenever she mentioned him. She didn't want to bring her ex into this room, even though he was lurking in the general vicinity.

Instead of dragging Luke into the room, she said, "I'm into you, but I don't know if I'm good for you."

He ran his hand through his hair in frustration, making it stick out in all sorts of directions. She wanted to walk over to him and smooth it for him, but she wasn't sure she could without falling into that bed with him. It would be better if she left now instead of deepening their connection with more sex. The more she allowed herself to touch him, the harder it would be to stop.

"You're the best thing for me. The human equivalent of milk." He walked toward her. "You do a body good."

She couldn't help herself. That made her smile. He made her smile without even trying. She could really fall in love with him. And wouldn't that be a total disaster?

"We should take a minute to think about this." There was zero passion or belief behind those words. She wanted nothing more than to fall into him and forget that anything else existed outside of this room.

"Every time I give you time to think about this, you try to run away from me. You keep trying to minimize what we have together." He rubbed a hand across his face. When he met her gaze again, he actually looked pissed at her. "I don't think you understand how rare it is to have what we have. I've never felt like this with anyone else. The possibility of negative PR is not a good enough reason to give this up. I'm not giving you up."

Him saying that broke something inside her. She would worry about what everyone thought of her and them tomorrow. Right now, she walked back across the room, lifted up on her toes, and covered his mouth with hers. His lips still held the faint taste of her and lit her up as she wrapped her arms around his neck. He grabbed her hips and pulled her close to his groin. She squirmed against him, and he growled into her mouth.

Before she'd gotten to know him, she never would have expected him to be such an intense lover. When it was just the two of them, the witty and urbane mask he showed to the rest of the world completely fell away, and he was almost a different person. He was growly and feral at the same time he was sensual and slow. Maybe it was only this way between the two of them and he'd kept the mask on with past lovers, but she couldn't imagine giving him notes on the way he made her feel and the things he did to her body—much less making a video disparaging him in public.

Even though he hadn't come yet, he didn't rush her. He kept kissing her while he danced his fingers down her lower back to her zipper. He lowered it slowly, stroking her skin as he revealed each hint of skin.

"You're so soft, but you have this spine of steel," he said. "You don't have to hold the weight of the world. I know you want to protect me but losing you would be worse than anything."

She placed a kiss on his bare throat and moved her fingers to his belt. "I wanted to protect you the way you protected me from my terrible mother."

He moved away from her enough so she could get his pants and boxer briefs off and then sat down to get his shoes off. He looked up at her to find her staring at his cock. Her skin flushed even more. "Dress off."

He couldn't ever know how she reacted to him taking charge in the bedroom. She never would have asked that from another lover. The first few guys she'd slept with had been in college—they'd been boys really. And Luke didn't want to take charge of anything in the realm of their relationship. Something that had made him attractive to her—the ability to steer her life and his—had made her respect him less in the end. He hadn't felt like a partner, even when it came to sex. And she wouldn't have thought that she liked being ordered around.

But when it came to Galvin, she liked it a whole lot. She shimmied out of her dress. It didn't allow for a bra, so she was totally naked.

He surprised her by pulling her close and kissing her belly and the underside of her breasts. "Are you sure we shouldn't get down to business?" She pointed at his dick. "That must be painful."

He chuckled against her skin, and it sent a shiver through her whole body. "It's a sweet kind of pain."

"Still, I think we should—"

In the middle of her sentence, he wrapped his hands around her waist and flipped her so she was sprawled below him on the bed. She laughed, but it was breathless and mixed with a moan. "We should what?"

While he waited for her to answer, he took both of her hands in one of his and pinned them above her head. He nuzzled her face and kissed her at random intervals. They were fully adults, and she'd never had sex like this—she'd never felt like she was worth savoring.

"We should do whatever you want to do."

He pulled back and wolfishly smiled at her. "That's the right answer." But then he got up and found his pants, which only momentarily confused her before he pulled a condom out of his pocket. "There are more in the bathroom."

He rolled it on, and she was enthralled with watching him. She liked the way he moved—as though he was totally confident in his body. She might have even licked her lips. Her admiration was definitely all over her face, because he said, "You like what you see."

"Shut up." He didn't need to point out how gone she was for his physical form. Anyone who saw him naked would be impressed at how his genetics and exercise mixed to make him strong and graceful, even though he was big enough to have to duck his head in doorways in old buildings.

He prowled back to her when the condom was on, but he didn't just get on top of her and start pounding away. From what her clients said, that was the modus operandi of most really good-looking guys who slept with a lot of people. They weren't interested in connecting because there would always be another partner available.

"How did you get so good at this?" It wasn't the right question to be asking right now. If she'd kept her mouth shut, she'd probably be about three-quarters of the way to a second orgasm.

"You're great for my ego." He shrugged, and it was attractive because it was incongruous with his confident demeanor. He was more complex than he seemed to be on first glance, and she was glad she'd finally gotten the chance to see it. "But you and I are a unique mix, and it's so good because we want it to be, and it just is."

She grabbed his face and pulled it down to hers. "Right answer."

He moaned into her mouth when she wrapped her legs around him and rubbed her center against his erection. That snapped his control, just as she'd planned. He lined up his dick with her entrance and filled her up. Both of them stilled for a long moment. She never wanted to forget this moment. Despite his pretty words, she knew that this would end eventually. She would have to squirrel away the memories of this for when it did.

She memorized his face as he drove inside her, and he must have noticed that she was looking at him very intently. He slowed down and said, "Touch yourself."

When she didn't immediately comply—when did he get so bossy?—he stopped moving altogether. "What's wrong?"

"Nothing was wrong until you stopped."

"You weren't there with me. You were thinking so hard that I could see the wheels turning in your head."

"I was just looking at you."

"And if you have the capacity to just look at me, you're obviously not as into this as you should be." He sounded irritated, but he was still hard, so he couldn't be that irritated.

"I refuse to argue with you while you're inside me."

"Then don't argue and touch yourself."

At this point, it was easier to just do what she was told than to argue any more, so she snaked her fingers in between them and rubbed her clit. His sweaty torso brushed the back of her hand as he started to move again.

"Happy now?"

"I'll be happy when you're too blissed out to sass me."

She liked when he talked to her like that, and she was too into him to question it. It was like sex with him shut off the part of her brain that housed feminism. And even though she was climbing toward another climax, she still tried to imprint on her mind the look of him wrecked by them together.

CHAPTER TWENTY-TWO

"A LOT OF THE advice in your book is really harsh, starting with the title. Is that because you hate men?" Jessica didn't hate men, but she was certainly starting to hate this reporter. When they'd sat down at the bar on the roof of the Standard, she'd gotten a good vibe from this woman. There was something sharp and wary about her gaze that told Jessica that she had a story to tell. She always loved when she had a client with that kind of wary gaze. It meant that there were going to be layers to get through before they got to the good stuff. A challenge.

But Jessica had failed to take into account the fact that she was the person being interviewed, which wasn't anything like therapy, but it made her feel like she was in therapy. With a really ferocious therapist who had no interest in holding space for her to process anything.

"I don't hate men. I have a lot of male clients and there are a lot of men in my life that I love. I wrote the book because I want them to live happy lives and have the best possible experiences in romantic partnerships."

"But you think men need to be told that 'women are people, too'? That seems really elementary." The reporter had closely studied her book, which she appreciated. It was better than the people who took one look at the title and decided she was a misandrist who'd written a joke book. That had actually been in an email from an angry men's rights activist.

"If you take a look at the way we've set up our society, women, nonbinary people, anyone with a marginalized sexuality, racial background, or disability is essentially part of an underclass. And, in my experience, a lot of straight men don't treat the women they date like people at all. They treat potential romantic partners like consumer products and endlessly compare one to the other like they were deciding which boat to buy."

"You certainly sound like you hate men."

"If I hated men, I wouldn't have written a book encouraging them to be better. I actually think men are harmed as much as anyone else by the way that society treats them."

"How exactly does society treat them poorly? They have most of the money and the power, and they use it to oppress everyone else, and then they act like they are doing women a favor when they deign to date them.

"They have the audacity to impose arbitrary standards on how women should look, talk, and think. And they never even take a minute to think about whether or not they add anything to the lives of the women they expect to be perfect."

Jessica didn't rush to respond when the reporter stopped talking. She looked at the woman for a beat. There was definitely a story there, but she wasn't here to hear it. "I think that men are confused. I think everyone is very confused about what we're supposed to be doing in the dating space. And it's almost impossible to assume good intent from anyone involved because dating apps have gamified the whole process.

"It can certainly feel like you're just shopping for a partner because the interface and algorithms are virtually the same across social media and dating apps. You have to first think about the incentives of dating app companies—it's certainly not to help everyone who wants a partner find a partner so they can delete the app."

The reporter looked incredulous. "You're blaming the dating apps for how men treat women in the dating space?"

Jessica shook her head and wished that this was a written interview. She could articulate herself better in writing when the person she was conversing with couldn't attack her. If this woman were a client, this was where she would sit silently for several moments.

"I think blame is unproductive. Accountability and awareness are important. It's useless to be angry at a corporation in a capitalist society for doing what it does, but it's important to be aware of what dating apps are doing and temper expectations accordingly."

The reporter, Logan, sat back and looked at her notes for a moment. It finally gave Jessica a chance to breathe. She took a sip of her water and wished she'd ordered a cocktail.

That wish was compounded when her interrogation resumed. "So, you're dating Galvin Baker—the architect." Hearing his name made her heart pick up speed, but the reporter said it like it was an accusation.

"Yes. Galvin is my boyfriend." She didn't even feel like she was lying about it this time, but she didn't elaborate because she wasn't sure where the reporter was going with this.

"You're aware of his previous relationship with Kennedy Mower?" The reporter said that like it was a piece of incriminating evidence on a legal procedural show. She felt as though the woman was waiting for her to break down on the stand with some sort of tearful apology for daring to date a man who'd had a messy breakup with an influencer.

"Yes."

"Would you like to elaborate?"

Jessica decided to play dumb and wait for the reporter to ask the question that she really wanted to ask.

The reporter sighed and asked, "Are any of the allegations that Kennedy made in the video true?"

"Allegations? It's not like she accused him of doing anything criminal, and this is what I'm talking about. I think that even guys who may have been bad boyfriends can be good boyfriends if they have some additional insight into how others perceive their actions."

Logan looked pleased to have provoked a response, and that should have stopped Jessica from continuing. It didn't. "There's more than one side to the story in most relationships. Galvin is a really good man who had his own reasons for ending that relationship. In my experience, he's kind, considerate, and fabulous in bed."

That stunned the reporter into silence. Jessica wished she hadn't said that last part, not because it wasn't true, but because it wasn't really appropriate or within the scope of the article. Jesus. Abby was going to kill her.

"What I meant—"

The reporter held up a hand. "It's perfectly clear what you meant. Do you think you might be a little biased because of your new relationship?"

"Everyone's biased about relationships. Everyone has biases about everything. It's when we try to deny or aren't aware of our biases that they become a problem. Of course I'm partial to a man that I'm dating, but he's not on trial for anything."

"If you're going to start railing about cancel culture," the reporter sneered, "you can save your breath."

Jessica knew that this was part of her job. Abby would be disappointed in her, would probably fire her as a client, and definitely wouldn't bail her out if she got in a catfight with this woman, defending Galvin's honor. But still, she considered flipping a table or throwing a drink for a split second longer than anyone who knew her would ever imagine.

Abby would also be disappointed when she walked out of this interview, but Jessica wasn't going to sit through this. The way this woman spoke to her was completely out of line. The only thing keeping her in her seat was the possibility that this woman would take out her anger on Galvin.

And she might regret defending him in the future. That was a distinct possibility. He could be putting on a whole show for her right now, pretending to be a great boyfriend to lull her into a sense of security before dumping her mercilessly. That could very well be the truth. And she could look very foolish—even more foolish than she would if people realized that her boyfriend of fifteen years had walked out on her.

But she was approaching the point in caring for Galvin that she didn't care about how it looked. That part of her—the part of her that was sure she knew better than the hundreds of other girls he'd dated—was the one that answered.

"I don't know what will happen with my relationship, and I'm not going to go into the specifics." The reporter raised her eyebrows, indicating that Jessica had given her plenty of specifics. "I wrote this book to encourage men to start treating women like they are people and not like a collection of warm, wet holes. That's really the bare minimum, and that's what I'm prepared to speak to today."

"So you're getting more than the bare minimum personally."

"Yes. Definitely."

GALVIN WAS LEAVING Erewhon with a green juice that probably cost more than a car payment on a Ford Focus when he ran into Kennedy. He was on his way to a site visit with his landscape engineer and building engineer, so he did not have time for this.

"Galvin. Baker." Kennedy always said his first name and his surname as though they were complete sentences, with a distinct vocal fry that had made her famous. It had always kind of bothered him. Especially now, when he heard other people do it, so he knew that they followed Kennedy and had probably seen the video.

Still, he turned around and smiled, because he didn't want any more smoke from Kennedy or her minions. "Kennedy. Mower. How the hell are you?"

She looked him up and down, and he did the same. She'd changed her hair color from a dark brown to a mix of blond and brown. She wore sunglasses that showed his reflection but hid her dead eyes. Why had he ever dated someone with dead eyes? And she smelled like a mix of the expensive self-tanner she used to streak all over his sheets and cigarette smoke from the nasty habit she hid from television viewers and her millions of social media followers.

"I'm good, but it seems like you're doing even better." Kennedy sounded like she resented the fact that he hadn't disappeared off the face of the earth in shame after she'd attempted to humiliate him.

"Yeah, I've pulled up okay." He didn't want to talk about his relationship with Jessica. Even though it had started out fake, it was real now. He felt the need to guard it, because he knew that Jessica was private with her feelings and emotions. It was part of his job as her boyfriend to guard that for her.

"You're, like, dating someone normal." Kennedy also said "normal" like it was a bad thing. "She's, like, old and a doctor?"

"She's a therapist, and she's my age." He was sort of taking the bait, but he didn't like it when Kennedy said disparaging things about other women. It was ugly and spoke to her insecurity. Seriously, why had he ever dated her? It was time to change the subject. "You look well."

She kind of turned and preened so he could see her from more angles. "Don't I?" Complimenting her appearance was always the one way to distract her. It was like a shiny thing with a squirrel, except it was her own ego. "Do you want to get lunch?"

Months ago, before he'd run into Jessica and started their fake relationship, Galvin might have jumped at the chance to rehabilitate his reputation by renewing his affair with Kennedy. And he thought she was definitely getting at that with her coy hair flip and the way she leaned toward him. But she only wanted his attention because it was clear that he'd moved on.

He should have blocked her social media. But that might have made her mad and provoked her. It was better that she could see he was doing well and then make a few jabs at him out in public. Still, he tried to seem disappointed that they couldn't "catch up" when he said, "I have some meetings, but maybe some other time."

Kennedy frowned. "That's too bad. I want to apologize for all the mean things I said." She stepped closer to him and put her hand on his chest. It felt way too intimate, and he wanted to remove it. But he also didn't want her making another angry video. That would both affect his reputation again and probably put his nascent relationship at risk. He felt like he was trying to avoid getting bitten by a pretty but poisonous snake right now.

He knew that Kennedy was more complicated than that, but her real life and public image were enmeshed in a way that made her view all interactions as transactional. And she was a master manipulator in getting those transactions to work in her favor. His first mistake with her had been to worry more about her feelings getting hurt than her ego. The ego was the really dangerous element in the whole deal. If she perceived him as blowing her off, she could go after him. That would suck, but he would be fine. People would view that as her being bitter that he'd found happiness despite her best efforts.

What he was really afraid of was her going after Jessica. She'd hit the bestseller list, but he didn't want anything to interfere with her career. Even if he had to put up with shenanigans from Kennedy, he would do it to keep Jessica safe and happy.

The idea that he might not be able to do that stopped him in his tracks. His past would always exist. If Kennedy wasn't coming around to stir up trouble, it could be any one of his previous girlfriends. He'd never felt shame about the number of women he'd dated and the possibility that he'd treated them poorly before. He'd always felt that it was just part of the dating game, and people who didn't want to play should just stay on the sidelines.

Because his parents' relationship was purely business, that was how he'd grown up to see relationships. Hell, that was why he hadn't balked at dating Jessica to earn herself clout and himself redemption.

But all that was before he'd fallen in love.

He'd never been with anyone who made him want to be a better version of himself. He'd never looked back on the things he'd done and felt the need to protect someone else from that. Sure, after Kennedy's video, he'd realized that his way of doing the business of dating was no longer working—that he'd have to make more convincing sounds about wanting something real. But that had all been in order to gain something.

"You look weird." While he'd been standing there, feeling like his whole adult life had been a mistake, Kennedy had continued her appraisal of him.

"I do?" He probably looked like he was about to be sick, because he felt like it. His skin was clammy, and his stomach was in knots. He looked down at his half-full green juice. If he did hurl, it would get ugly.

"Yeah, like, I was going to put a selfie of the two of us smiling in my stories, just to show that it's all, like, water under the bridge or whatever. But you look like you're sort of constipated and that doesn't go with my aesthetic."

There was a lot that Galvin could say to that. First, he didn't want to seem like a chump by showing up in her stories a few months after she'd tried to blackball his dick. Second, he looked constipated because he'd just realized that his entire dating life had been about his image rather than his growth for almost two decades. Third, he thought she might want to look at the fact that she'd commodified every aspect of her existence, which only revealed that she was just as vacant as he'd been.

But he didn't say any of that. It would only piss her off. She'd make another video, probably targeting Jessica because that was how Kennedy rolled. And then he'd lose his only chance at redemption—he couldn't see living a full life without Jessica. If he lost her, he'd just revert to being a calculating fuckboy until he was too old to sustain it. And then he'd be alone.

"Listen, it was great to see you, but I have to run to a meeting." Then he gave her a look up and down and winked at her, even though he wasn't feeling winky. "You look great. Take care of yourself."

When she moved closer to hug him, he grabbed her by the elbow to keep her at a distance. He kissed her on the cheek, though. Just so he wouldn't offend her.

"Take. Care. Of. Yourself." This time, each of her one-word sentences sounded bewildered.

When Galvin got in his car, he wanted to call Jessica and tell her everything that had happened. But he held off. She was in session, and she wouldn't respect him if he called for reassurance that he was no longer the same asshole who had dumped Kennedy Mower.

CHAPTER TWENTY-THREE

"WHY ARE WE doing this again?" Jessica asked. "Neither of us are college reunion people."

They'd first RSVP'd yes to the event because it seemed like a way to convince the social media world that they were in a real relationship. But now that they were in a real relationship, they didn't need to prove that they were in one. Sort of counterintuitive, but it worked for her.

"Because it'll be fun to see people we haven't seen for years," Galvin said. He seemed excited about going, which was weird.

"We both see the people we like to see from college, already." Jessica had kept up with her friends from school, and Galvin was colleagues with a number of their classmates. She really didn't see the point in making small talk with a bunch of virtual strangers. Plus, once anyone found out she was a therapist, she was going to be listening to a lot of gnarly problems she didn't want to know about.

Because of that last thing, she put a stack of cards for a

therapy referral service in her bag. She was all booked up with patients at the moment, and she wouldn't want to see anyone she knew in a personal capacity professionally.

"I'm not going to let anyone corner you and demand your opinion on whether or not they should divorce their cheating husband." Galvin straightened his tie and turned away from the mirror in his bedroom.

"Honestly, if anyone asks, I'll just give them Alex's number, anyway."

She'd been staying at his place most nights of the week. It was moving too fast, they'd only been sleeping together a few weeks, but she couldn't stand being away from him. His presence made her feel giddy and light and she was addicted to waking up in his arms. She was also addicted to fucking him, but she knew that would fade. She was truly worried about how much she craved the sound of his voice at the end of the day.

It was so different from anything she'd ever experienced before. She'd come to the realization that her relationship with Luke had only lasted as long as it did because he was so busy. She'd actually found him very annoying a lot of the time. She'd convinced herself that it was normal to feel that kind of contempt when you were with someone long-term, but she wasn't so sure anymore.

Galvin did annoying things—his neatness was so compulsive that he lined up her shoes in the entryway so that they pointed in the same direction as his shoes. Every time she passed them on the way to the bathroom from the living room, she knocked them off-kilter just so. She supposed that she was annoying, too.

But she wouldn't have moved the shoes when she was with Luke. She would have seethed for years about it and eventually purchased a shoe rack so the shoes could go in the closet, and it wouldn't bother him to see them out of alignment.

With Galvin, she could have fun with the petty annoyances that came up. Like his apparent excitement about going to their college reunion. It was times like this that she wished that she could believably seduce someone out of doing something. Galvin might have thought she was pretty the night that they'd run into each other, but fucking hadn't been in the air. Jessica just didn't exude that kind of energy—on purpose. She'd never wanted a line of slavering perverts following her wherever she went, like her mother had. But it would be really convenient to whip Galvin into a sex-crazed frenzy long enough for him to forget going to the reunion.

"Is this about seeing Luke?" Galvin asked.

Jessica hadn't even allowed herself to think about that. Of course, part of it was about Galvin. Jessica still wasn't clear on exactly why Galvin hated Luke, and she'd been so preoccupied with the book going well and the waiting for the other shoe to drop when that reporter published her article that she hadn't really dwelled on Luke and Galvin's blood feud.

"Is Luke why you want to go? I don't think he'll show up at this thing. He doesn't do much outside of work." She wasn't sure who she was trying to convince. Even though she hadn't thought about Luke, the idea of seeing him still made her feel raw on the inside. Him walking out the door had stripped something away from her—the idea that she could still make good choices and had some semblance of control over her life.

If she saw him, and it was painful, she'd have to think a lot more about whether she was truly over him. And whether her current relationship with Galvin was just a Band-Aid.

"Why would I want to see Luke?" Galvin sauntered over to her sitting on the bed in his bathrobe. She was slow-walking their departure, and she hadn't gotten dressed yet. "Are you going to wear that?" He pointed to the little black dress that she'd hung on the front of his closet.

Getting desperate, she pulled open one side of his bathrobe so that he could see the black lace bra she wore underneath. "I was kind of hoping that I could convince you not to go, and I wouldn't have to."

His face went a little slack, but the side of his mouth slid up. She started breathing a little faster when his gaze dipped to her breast. He walked until his knees hit the side of the bed, and then he braced his hands on either side of her hips. She breathed the freshly showered scent of him in and lifted her face so that she could nuzzle the side of his neck. Maybe she could seduce him to get her way. It wasn't ethical, but it was more than fair. They would both have a good night if they stayed home. They would both have a better night.

"You're being a very bad girl," he drawled. She was getting to him.

She raised her hand and cupped the side of his face. He hadn't shaved for a second time today, and the stubble felt rough across her palm. She wanted it to redden the skin of her belly and breasts and between her thighs. Now that she was touching him, it wasn't about getting him to forget going to the stupid college reunion. It was about the drugged feeling she had whenever he touched her. It was about the way she burned to be with him, even though they'd had sex the night before and this morning. It was about how she didn't want to burst the little bubble they'd made for themselves in the weeks since their relationship had become real.

He obliged her and kissed her, but it wasn't the kind of kiss that was going to lead to his very fine shirt being torn off and thrown on the floor. It was sexy, but slow.

"Please . . ."

She didn't have any qualms about begging him for what she wanted when it came to sex because she knew that he wasn't going to hold her needs against her. There was a lightness to their relationship that worked in concert with the intensity. She knew so much about relationship dynamics and longitudinal studies about what made relationships satisfying that she'd forgotten that there was a certain element of magic to it.

She'd been so caught up in trying to help her clients with unhealthy relationship patterns getting to something that simply wasn't toxic, that she'd forgotten why they all chased the high of being really into someone. There truly was nothing like it.

But then he stopped kissing her and rested his forehead against hers. "Why don't you want to go, really?"

She took a deep breath. "Now that it's real between us, I don't want anyone to say anything to you that will make you doubt us. We're not a marketing ploy anymore."

"Oh." He drew back and stood, crossing his arms over his chest. She shouldn't have said that. "You're ashamed to be seen with me?"

"No, it's not that." She didn't know how to explain her reticence in a way that he wouldn't take offense to. They really hadn't had to work hard at communicating with their words yet, so she didn't know where all the land mines were. But she could only do the best she could. If they were going to make a go of this relationship—and she really wanted to—she was going to have to figure out how to communicate with him eventually. So much between them felt really easy, and he was worth the effort.

"I never talked about my relationship with Luke when I was doing press before the book came out for a reason."

"Because he's a douchebag, and I'm thinking that you don't want to talk about our relationship because you think that I'm a douchebag but in a different way." He looked frustrated and upset. She wanted to make him feel better, but she knew that impulse wasn't necessarily healthy if it came at the cost of her own boundaries.

"I care about you so much that I don't want what we have to get ruined by other people interfering." She knew her friends would have a lot to say about the two of them being together. It was one thing to know that he'd dated most of her friends, but it would be quite another to see him interact with them now. Was she afraid of feeling jealous? Maybe. But it wasn't only that.

He sat on the bed next to her, and it was kind of a relief not to have him staring at her as she tried to explain her reticence. "I don't want our classmates to make me start questioning things between us."

"If your friends can do that, then maybe what we have isn't strong enough." He sounded so defeated, and she hated causing him pain. But he'd never stuck around in a relationship long enough to have tough discussions about deep-seated fears and feelings before.

"I want it to be." Maybe she was being reactive. And maybe the fact that he was so overwhelmingly handsome was playing on her fears and insecurities about whether someone like him would actually ever choose to be with someone like her. "I guess I'm just afraid that you'll see me next to all of the other women you dated in college and decide that I'm not good enough."

She could feel his body still and the air around them seemed cooler to her. He turned, and his gaze bored a hole through her. Like the Terminator. "What are you talking about?"

"No one ever notices me. You never noticed me until I was the only one around to listen to you talk about your ex's stupid video." She hadn't meant to say all that, but it must have been lingering below the surface. Maybe she needed to call her therapist in the morning and schedule an emergency session.

He didn't touch her, but he moved closer. "I noticed you, but you were never going to be a fling for me. I think I knew that, even back then. You could see right through me, and it's sort of terrifying."

"Just what a girl loves to hear."

"You were terrifying because I didn't want anyone to see through the careful facade I was creating so that no one could ever hurt me again." That was pretty insightful for someone who hadn't been in therapy that long. "But I totally noticed that you were hot. The fact that you also didn't buy my brand of bullshit was really fascinating. But I wasn't ready for you."

"I thought that if I chose the safest, most boring person to be in a relationship, I'd never have the sorts of problems that my mom had in her love life—or the kinds of problems that I see in my practice. But I was wrong. And being with you feels so risky. You are my first relationship where I feel like there's anything on the line, and I'm coming to realize that I have no idea what I'm doing."

He took her hand and squeezed it. "Neither of us knows what we're doing, but we're both happy. Isn't that what matters?"

That was what mattered. But she couldn't shake the feeling in the pit of her stomach that they shouldn't go to their college reunion together. Her life's work required her to guide people in looking back on their past to forge a better future, but she didn't want to look back on her own. That made her a coward, and the one thing that she wanted to take from her mother was her bravery. She never would have spent years in a relationship that wasn't going anywhere. She would have left.

"It is what matters." She knew she didn't sound like she believed her own words.

"We can stay home if you want." But he sounded disappointed. No matter what she said about her amorphous feelings about not going to their reunion, she knew for a fact that he would believe that she was embarrassed to be dating him.

Because that wasn't the truth—she couldn't believe that he'd chosen to be with her, and her reluctance wasn't logical or clearly defined. She wasn't going to hurt him. "No, we'll go."

"If you want to leave for any reason, just let me know and we'll be gone."

Jessica smiled at him. "Do I need a safe word?"

Heat spread in her stomach when he grinned at her. "No, but we can explore other activities that might require a safe word when we get home."

JESSICA WAS RIGHT. He was not a reunion guy. Even though he'd never moved out of town, he didn't even go to alumni football games. Once he'd collected his diploma, he hadn't looked back. But he'd never left the self he'd created behind. He'd continued using sex and the kind of woman he could convince to date him as salves for his ego.

He couldn't go back until he felt like he'd built something in his life that he could be proud of. And he knew it was small and petty, but he hoped Luke was going to be there. He wanted to see the look on the other man's face when Galvin walked into the Alumni Club with Jessica.

Jessica's reluctance to attend with him was the only thing that gave him pause. And—even though they were past that—it had resurrected his worry that Jessica saw him as just the rebound guy. As they walked up to the table where they were handing out name cards, her shoulders were hunched, and her steps were tentative. He was tempted to turn them both around and leave, until two of her friends spotted them.

Two women—one willowy blonde and one athletic brunette—approached them. They both looked familiar, and he had a flash of making out with the blonde at a keg party sophomore year. He thought her name was Kelly or Kelsey, but then he remembered that Jessica was close with a Kelly.

Kelly ignored him, but the brunette looked him up and down, narrowing her gaze when it met his. She was skeptical of their relationship, and that lined up with what Jessica had told him about Barbie.

He put on his most genuine and self-effacing smile, hoping to disarm her. But her posture didn't soften, and she pursed her lips a little more.

"You look stunning, Jessica," Kelly said, before facing Galvin.

"If you hurt her, I will disembowel you—surgically." That's right. Kelly went to medical school.

Jessica grabbed his hand and said, "Can we please lay off the threats?"

"Not unless and until we're sure that he's no longer a creeper who can't sustain an erection." Barbie said that loudly, parroting Kennedy's words from the infamous video. If she'd seen it, then a good number of the people here had seen it. Before attending, he'd been worried about Jessica being embarrassed by him. He'd practiced a few smooth retorts in anticipation of digs from people who had seen the video. But none of them came out now.

This could be bad. Very bad.

"Barbara St. Vincent." Jessica used her friend's full name—which sounded like it had been pulled from a 1980s soap opera—in an admonishing tone. "You're going to be nice to my boyfriend, or we're going to leave."

His sense of impending doom eased when Jessica defended him to her friend, and he liked the way the word "boyfriend" sounded coming out of her mouth. He hoped that he would never take that for granted.

"I can't even give him a little bit of shit?" Barbara asked, disappointed.

Jessica shook her head. "No. It's weird enough that you both hooked up with him in college. I won't have you speculating about his level of dick game while I'm trying to keep my eyes akimbo for my ex-boyfriend."

Galvin didn't remember hooking up with Barbie. He usually remembered his hookups. He wracked his brain trying to come up with a sliver of memory, until Barbie laughed. "Listen, I think I just kissed him that one time because he was bad at suck and blow." When Jessica looked at her quizzically, she continued, "You know the game where you suck on a playing card and then someone sucks it off of your mouth? Of course you don't."

Kelly and Barbie laughed, and Jessica gave them a sharp look. "Can we go five minutes without talking about sucking or blowing?"

Her friends stopped laughing, but Kelly looked at Jessica seriously and said, "Well, you haven't been available for brunches or lunches or yoga classes in forever because you've been busy actually sucking and blowing. You're going to have to let us fit this in somewhere."

"Can we go to brunch next weekend and try to get through this nightmare?" Jessica still sounded strained.

"We can leave," Galvin said as Jessica's friends opened their mouths to argue against Jessica's characterization of the evening as a nightmare. "Seriously. I'm sorry I pushed you into coming."

If her friends weren't going to be nicer to her, then they weren't going to stay. Jessica had eaten shit for too long dating Luke—at least, that was how Galvin saw it—to eat shit from her supposed friends.

"We're sorry," Barbie said. "We know you don't like to talk about sex in public, and we're just being salty because you're getting reliably laid."

"You were never like this when I was with Luke."

Kelly snorted. "That's because we never thought of him as a reliable lay—more like a reliable bore."

"Apology accepted, as long as it comes with a glass of whatever boxed wine they are serving at the bar."

They walked into the ballroom that they were using for the reunion proper. There was a DJ on the back wall, playing a song that would have been popular during their time at the school, and there were several middle-aged guys testing the integrity of their knee cartilage and pant seams as they tried to "get low."

"I hope there's some wine left here," Jessica said with a look of disgust on her face as she surveyed the crowd. He realized then that she hadn't wanted to come here tonight because this was very silly. The whole idea of spending several hours making small talk with people they might have known fifteen years ago was sort of wild. With social media, you could see so much about people's lives without actually having to come into contact with them.

This kind of thing was for people who had peaked in college. Jessica certainly hadn't—she'd only gotten better with age. He might have, but he hoped he was turning it around.

"I'm on the committee, so I made sure they ordered plenty," Kelly said. "Plus, I think that whole morass is courtesy of Fireball."

Galvin's stomach turned just thinking about that beverage. He'd once ghosted a girl after she'd come to bed smelling of the stuff. He'd lost a whole night of sleep nauseous from it, and it seemed like a weird thing to tell her bothered him. She'd never contacted him again, either.

They went to the bar and got drinks. Galvin had come here for nostalgia and got a vodka soda.

CHAPTER TWENTY-FOUR

JESSICA THOUGHT SHE was fully prepared to run into Luke. She thought she was over their breakup. It made sense. They hadn't been in love in a long time, and maybe they never had been. She knew she wasn't going to be able to sidestep the pain forever, but she thought she'd be able to process it on her own time, after her rebound relationship with Galvin fizzled out.

But now that she and Galvin were really trying to move forward, she thought she might be able to avoid the kind of searing pain and ruthless self-examination that she would have put herself through absent Galvin's presence in her life completely.

She should have known better.

It wasn't seeing Luke that she couldn't have possibly braced herself for. It was seeing him with someone else—a very pregnant someone else.

Barbie, Galvin, and Kelly were complaining about the cheap vodka available at the open bar. Jessica murmured her agreement and sipped her wine. Cheap vodka reminded her of her mother, but the scent didn't make the hair on the back of her neck stand up the way it did before Galvin threw Laurie out of her house. But her friends actually had something to agree with Galvin about, and they were no longer interrogating him, so she wasn't going to interject.

She scanned the room, looking for other people who had been in her sorority or classes or study groups, when her scan stopped on Luke. He'd been so familiar to her not so long ago, but it was a bit of a shock to the system to see him now.

He looked as though he'd actually made an effort—changed out of his scrubs and actually put on a suit. It fit, and so he'd actually had something tailored for once. When they'd first met, she'd thought it was charming that he cared so little for his own appearance. He was all substance and no style. She'd always thought that meant that he was deep and only cared about what was on the inside. Maybe he just didn't care what she'd thought of what he looked like.

It took her a beat to notice the woman on his arm, and the first thing she noticed was her broad smile. It was almost too wide—like a cartoon—and it didn't feel like a genuine smile. It reminded Jessica of her third grade teacher. Mrs. Heffenslag had always had a smile on her face, but it would get even wider when she was meting out punishments for behavioral infractions. She'd had a smile on her face as she'd smashed Jessica's hands in her desk for reaching in for her favorite pink pen.

Jessica didn't know why she remembered that moment right now, when she was looking at the woman who was clearly her replacement. But maybe she felt like she was being punished for reaching for something for herself. And, of course, she'd wondered if Luke had met someone else before leaving her, but he'd denied it. She'd believed him, and she'd put it out of her mind and then distracted herself with Galvin.

She felt stupid for believing him now, especially when she noticed that the woman had a very prominent baby bump. Her hand rested there protectively, and that was what made the ache in Jessica's chest start up. She didn't do anything—she just stared at the two of them, reading their body language as though it would give her any explanation for how this had happened.

Luke put his hand on the woman's lower back, lowered his mouth to her temple, and kissed her before whispering something in her ear that made her smile even wider. And that was a real smile.

They'd had a whole life together. For the first decade, she'd thought about when they would get married and when they would have a baby. But Luke had kept putting it off—after he finished his residency, and then after he completed his fellowship; after she completed a PhD program became after her book was published. They would always talk about it "later," and then later never came. She'd contented herself with the life they had. She'd thought she had everything she wanted.

Apparently, Luke had decided he could only find happiness with someone else.

She looked very young. When she smiled, the skin didn't even crinkle around her eyes. And it could just be the pregnancy, but her face had a fullness that spoke to youth. While they were together, Jessica had never been jealous of any of the women who hit on Luke. He'd never paid them any attention, and so she'd never had any reason to have the pit in her stomach she had now.

Luke was a lot of things—lazy at home, a workaholic, distracted, unkempt—but she'd never once worried that he was cheating on her until he moved out. Now she felt so fucking stupid. Her mind was a storm, and she felt like everyone else in that room—including the man she'd shown up with—had completely disappeared. The air was thick, and it was hard to pull it into her lungs. It didn't even feel like she had a body at that moment—just her brain floating in a soup of her own jealousy, guilt, and regret.

She jumped when Galvin put his arm around her waist, and she didn't lean into him like she'd developed the habit of doing.

"What's wrong?" he asked, but she couldn't bring herself to speak. She couldn't stop staring at the more put-together version of Luke across the room with a very pregnant woman who wasn't her talking to their classmates as though they weren't deliberately tearing her heart out.

She wanted to grab a bottle of the cheap vodka from the bartender and make a Molotov cocktail. Mentally, she was doing just that. Instead of doing that in reality, all of the big emotions were making it hard to think, hard to breathe, impossible to speak.

But she registered when Galvin saw Luke and his date. He stiffened and said, "Fuck."

Then, he physically turned Jessica's body to face him. He cupped her face in his hands so that she had to meet his gaze. All she wanted was to look away in that very moment. She wanted to go home and huddle under her covers and chew on the image of Luke with this woman for a whole day.

"Are you okay?" He could obviously tell that she was very much not okay, but she couldn't make the words to respond. Cold sweat ran down her back, and her ribs felt too small to hold her lungs. She opened her mouth, but nothing came out. The urge to flee overwhelmed her.

Instead of responding to Galvin's question, she shook her head and escaped his grasp. She found Luke and the woman in the crowd again, just in time to see them approaching.

"I can't believe it," Galvin said, echoing the sentiment that characterized how all of her cells felt in that moment. "Do you want to go?"

She did, but she knew that she wasn't going to get answers if she left. Luke hadn't answered his phone after a few logistical calls postbreakup, and setting up an appointment to have a video conference, like they had a few times when he was on call for a whole week, seemed inappropriate.

And now she realized that he probably hadn't been on call as much as he'd claimed to be. All the times that he hadn't wanted to have sex with her because he was "tired" on date night came rushing back to her. It wasn't just that their relationship wasn't working. It wasn't just that she'd been living with the consequences of choosing someone safe who didn't excite her. She'd chosen someone who did the same thing that every single one of her mother's boyfriends had done. It was just a little classed up because he was a surgeon instead of a bartender.

"Fuck," she said. Galvin squeezed her hand. She was glad she wasn't alone, but then she noticed Luke noticing Galvin and the sneer on his face. Before she could examine it, a wave of embarrassment came over her and she dropped Galvin's hand.

She instantly regretted it when her whole body went cold. Instead of reaching back out, she wrapped her arms around her own waist. It wasn't a power pose that would exude confidence and the impression of not being bothered by seeing the man she'd thought she'd spend her whole life with standing in front of her with a woman who he'd clearly gotten pregnant when they were still together.

Luke didn't even have the decency to seem ashamed of himself. Yeah—Brené Brown, whatever, shame is toxic, yada yada yada—this was the kind of thing that deserved shame. You didn't do this to someone you'd spent your whole life with if there wasn't something seriously flawed within you as a person.

"You look well, Jessica."

She was pretty sure she looked like horseshit that had been trampled over by more horses. At least the woman's smile had dimmed when Luke said her name. He hadn't lied to her and told her he was single when he was fucking her. She knew who Jessica was, and she'd fucked Luke anyway. Tramp.

It wasn't a charitable thought, and cheating was always the cheater's fault, but Jessica fucking hated this woman and would have been fantasizing about doing her bodily harm if she wasn't pregnant. Now she knew how Laurie had racked up all of those vandalism charges. For the first time in her life, Jessica could envision herself keying a car or letting some air out of this woman's tires—but, like, all her tires, so she couldn't drive, not just one so she would crash.

"Who is this?" Jessica's words were demanding, she knew that. But she didn't have the capacity for pleasantries at the moment. She was a few seconds from doing a murder, so she needed to get the information she needed and get out of here.

Galvin had receded into the background, and he was probably mad at her for getting so upset about her ex, but she'd have to deal with that later. Her emotional capacity was tapped out trying not to punch her ex-boyfriend in his perfect nose.

"This is Kari," Luke said. "My fiancée."

"Fuck you." Jessica had always gone out of her way to be respectful to Luke, even when they had disagreements. Her statement just then seemed to shock Luke. "How long?"

"How long, what?" Luke was really going to make her ask him the question.

"How long were you fucking her while you were living with me?" She put a real emphasis on the curse word that time, and if she cared whether the people around them heard them having a disagreement, she would have been embarrassed. "Was it months or years?"

"I don't see why that matters now." Luke looked around, and Kari's smile completely disappeared; she looked visibly uncomfortable.

Jessica threw back the rest of her glass of wine and looked at her. "Bet you wish you could have a drink right now, don't you?" Knocking Luke out of his arrogant wheelhouse had given Jessica a charge. She wanted him back on his heels right now.

"It matters because you came here tonight with a woman who wasn't me. Now, I can't say for sure that you knew I'd be in attendance, but it sure seems like you wanted me to find out that you'd knocked up some other woman while we were still together by seeing you here or through mutual friends who would see you here."

Luke stepped closer to her, but he must have seen the murder in her gaze and backed off. "I was going to tell you."

"Again, fuck off."

He gave her a look and opened his hands to show her that he wasn't threatening. "After everything we've been through, you shouldn't talk to me like that."

"After everything we've been through, you shouldn't have gotten another woman pregnant while we were still together."

She noticed then that Galvin had pulled Kari to the side. She didn't know if she wanted to punch him in the face or thank him. But she didn't want Kari to hear what she had to say to Luke, and Galvin had probably moved the woman away just in case Jessica decided to start chucking floral centerpieces at Luke's head.

"I didn't want you to find out like this." Luke was still trying to defend himself.

"How did you want me to find out?" She did not have the patience for this, and she could tell that Luke was surprised by how she was talking to him. She'd never spoken to him this way when they were together. "I'm sure you thought I'd be hiding in our half-empty condo, still licking my wounds because you walked away. I was always there waiting for you, so why wouldn't that be the case even after you walked away with the life we'd always planned for?"

"I know you haven't been waiting around." He nodded his head at Galvin. "I saw you cavorting with that guy all over your Instagram, and I knew you'd moved on. I questioned your judgment, sure, but I didn't think that you'd get upset about seeing that I had done it, too."

Jessica put her hand on her hip and gritted her teeth to keep from braining Luke with her wineglass. "You're right. I have moved on. But I waited till *after* you left to do so. You clearly didn't."

"We weren't happy together for a long time, and I knew that we weren't going to end up married with children."

"See, the problem is that you never told me that until you

were walking out the door. And I don't know if you would ever have walked out the door had you not gotten another woman pregnant." She was close to shrieking at that point, and several people were staring at them. Out of her peripheral vision, she could see Barbie and Kelly at a nearby table. They always had her back, and she knew they would prevent her from doing anything that would get her arrested, if necessary.

"I wasn't sure I was going to leave until I left. We had so many years together—"

"So you were thinking about abandoning your child?" When he opened his mouth to answer, she continued, "Does Kari know that?"

Luke's shoulders dropped, and she could tell he was growing weary of trying to defend himself. Good, there was nothing that he could say that would make what he'd done defensible. "I didn't think you'd care. I didn't think there was enough spark left in our relationship that you would care one way or the other."

"I don't care that you left me. I care that you lied to me and betrayed me. I care that you wasted so many years of my life when I could have found someone else and gotten what I needed from them. Was I just convenient to have around?"

She thought back to all the times that she'd tried to be the perfect daughter so that her mother wouldn't have to hunt for a new boyfriend to take care of them—clipping coupons, signing herself up for free lunch and free breakfast at school so that her mom could have the whole box of Pop-Tarts to herself. Maybe she was so used to making things work on their own that she'd sought out a partner who would need exactly that kind of care from her as an adult. She hadn't ever really been in love with Luke; he'd just given her something familiar.

Fuck.

"I don't want to make a scene. I honestly thought that you'd moved on," Luke said. "It's beyond me why you'd ever move on with that guy, but I'm guessing by the way that you're reacting to seeing me that you deliberately sought out someone who I hated."

"Shut the fuck up, Luke." Four f-bombs in one argument with Luke was kind of a record. "I didn't pick Galvin out because you hated him. I picked him because he's been there for me every moment I needed him to be, from the second we ran into each other. He takes care of me in the way that I need, and that's something I've never had. He makes me have fun, even when I don't want to. And he's tall. I like that he's tall, and I'm not constantly making myself smaller so that he doesn't feel like less."

She didn't have to say that last part. Luke was sensitive about his height, and she knew that. But it felt really good to dig in the knife in the only way she knew how.

"He also turned you into a bitch." As soon as Luke said that, Barbie and Kelly stood up and moved to Jessica's side. Surprisingly, Jessica didn't feel like dealing out physical violence. As soon as she'd realized that her relationship with Luke was just the continuation of a pattern and not some grand, lost romance, some of her anger toward him slipped away. Not all of it, but enough for her to realize that it wouldn't be worth an arrest record just to make him hurt.

"You don't get to call me that."

Luke stopped talking and paled, and that was when she noticed that Galvin had walked back over. Had he heard what Luke had called her? Was she going to have to bail him out of jail?

She chanced a look in his direction, and his face was twisted into a brand of anger that she'd never seen from him—not when her mother had been acting out at her house and not when his father had made digs about his chosen specialty all night. He was almost unrecognizable.

"You heard her," Galvin said, his voice so cold that the ballroom dropped in temperature by about ten degrees. "You don't get to call her that. And if I had anything to say about it, you wouldn't get to call her anything."

Luke's lips thinned into a line that made him look mean. And old. Luke had never been blindingly handsome, but now that she didn't believe she was in love with him, he looked less than handsome. He looked as boring as he truly was.

Jessica turned to Kari and tried to muster up a genuine smile. She probably looked deranged when she said, "Best wishes with this one." Then, she turned to Galvin and said, "We need to leave now."

CHAPTER TWENTY-FIVE

JESSICA DIDN'T SAY anything during the car ride back to his house. At first, Galvin was afraid she was going to tell the driver to drop her off at her condo, but she'd stayed silent. She also didn't sit in the seat next to him or reach out for his hand. He had no idea what she was thinking about what had just happened.

He had guesses, of course. He knew how he'd felt when someone had stolen his first girlfriend and he'd been the last to know. When he'd finally found out, it had also been public and embarrassing. But he'd been nineteen. It wasn't as though he and Caitlyn had built a life together. Still, he'd felt as though his heart had been beaten flat by a meat tenderizer but was still trying to beat in his chest.

Before tonight, it had seemed as though Jessica had taken the breakup in stride. He felt as though he'd given her a soft place to fall. Until tonight, he hadn't worried that he was just a rebound for a long time. After all, their relationship had been so easy, almost from the start. That meant that he was fixed, and one breakup fifteen years ago didn't mean that he didn't know how to love. He knew that now.

But Jessica seemed to be wrecked by her confrontation with Luke. He'd seen the pained look on her face when she saw Luke's very pregnant girlfriend and known that she wasn't as over the breakup as he'd thought she was. Did that mean she didn't love him after all?

She hadn't said the words. He knew that she cared about him, but that didn't mean that she saw him as a permanent fixture in her life. If she was still this upset about Luke's betrayal, maybe that meant that she didn't have the kind of strong feelings for him that he had for her?

He couldn't let that happen.

But, as they drove down the 10 toward his house, the lights of the city flashing in front of them as they stared out of opposite windows, he wasn't sure how to stop it. If Jessica wanted a baby, he would give her one.

That thought shocked him. He'd never thought about having children very much. None of his previous relationships was going to lead there. Even with Caitlyn, it was so far off that they'd never even really talked about it. But he could picture it with Jessica. They wouldn't be like any of their parents. Jessica was so conscientious that he'd have to make sure she didn't slip into anxiety and paranoia, and he liked the thought of allowing a kid to decide their own path in life. He liked the idea of a small person with Jessica's empathy and his smile walking through the world.

Now that he thought about it, he would do anything to have it. But first he needed to know if he was more than a rebound fling, and this was just a rough night.

When they got to his driveway, Jessica popped out of the car and made it to the stoop before he did. She had her arms wrapped around her waist and didn't meet his gaze. He opened the door and she followed him in. He threw his keys in the bowl by the door and kicked his shoes off.

He walked around behind her and took her coat, hanging it on the hook that she'd designated as hers by the door. A few hours ago, she'd been utterly at home here. Now, it felt like everything was different. What he wouldn't give to turn back the clock by about three hours and stay here fucking her instead. It was stupid that he had wanted to show her off to people who had never mattered in his life.

She let him take her hand, and he pulled her into the living room. She sat on the couch and he poured them both a scotch from a really good bottle he'd gotten from James Fahereghty when he'd finished his house.

He took the glasses over to the couch, and Jessica took down her whole glass in one gulp. Didn't even cough, though he knew for a fact it was peaty as hell. Then, she held out the glass and said, "Another."

Ever the dutiful boyfriend—he was still the boyfriend for now—he got up and filled her glass again. She didn't take down this one right away.

"Do you want to talk about it? Or we could not talk about it?" Her face was impassive, which worried him. She was never this quiet or muted for long. "I think we should talk about it."

"Why did you hate Luke all along?" That was the last question in the world he thought she'd ask. It didn't matter why he hated Luke. Luke had always been a shitty guy. But they needed to be talking about their relationship, and not her ex.

"He's not the guy he presents himself as, and that's always bothered me." There, that was diplomatic enough. That worked, didn't it?

"What do you mean by that?" She gave him a quizzical look, sort of like how he imagined she looked in session as a therapist, but drunker. "Like, did he do anything specific that made you realize that he was a fraud? I know he's a fraud now. I can't believe he was cheating on me. How did I never suspect?"

She was spiraling, and he had to get this under control. "You've been broken up for *months*. I thought you were over it."

Jessica's eyes got really big and round, and he realized that he'd made a huge mistake in making this about him and their relationship. He was really falling down on the boyfriend job, and he didn't know what to do.

"Why are you making this about you right now?" Jessica stood up and put her hands on her hips. "This is about my life and my feelings."

She might as well have had steam coming out of her ears.

"I thought I was part of your life now." Galvin was quiet, feigning a calm he did not feel. "I need to understand why you're so upset about this."

"Me being upset about this has nothing to do with you." Jessica started pacing and wrapped her arms around herself. She looked up to the ceiling and mouthed something he couldn't make out. He felt as though he was losing control of the situation, but all he could do was sit there and wring his hands through the urge to kiss her and remind her that what she had with Luke was in the past and he was her present.

At this moment, he had no idea if he was going to be her future.

"Maybe you were just surprised, okay?"

"I shouldn't have been." Jessica shook her head, still pacing a hole into his antique carpet. "I asked him the day he moved out, but I assumed he was being honest with me."

Jessica looked wrecked. "Do you think he was cheating on me the whole time?"

And this time, he really didn't have an answer for her. If he had to guess, then Luke had probably cheated on her for most of their relationship. But he didn't have any proof and telling her that would only hurt her feelings. She didn't deserve to have her feelings hurt any more tonight. He wanted to reach for her and take away the thoughts spinning in her brain, but he knew she wouldn't go for that.

"I don't know."

She was silent for a long moment, taking sips of her drink. He didn't want to speak and intrude on her thoughts. Well, he did, but he didn't dare. He was afraid of saying the wrong thing, and he wasn't sure that he could get through to her in the moment.

Jessica laughed ruefully and turned away from him. Anger stuck a knife in his gut. Sure, seeing Luke had to be upsetting for her, but she was with Galvin now. The only reason that she would be this upset about seeing Luke and figuring out that he'd been cheating on her was if she still had feelings for him.

"Are you still in love with him?" He didn't mean to say it, and he felt himself flush with a mixture of anger and embarrassment.

Jessica grimaced at him. "No! What are you talking about?"

"You're so upset right now, that I just thought—"

"You thought what?" She put down her drink and put her

hands on her hips, staring him down. Her cheeks were pink, and her gaze felt as though sparks flew toward him.

"You're so upset about Luke that it's making me question what you feel for me."

"Well, you're so up your own fucking ass that you can't be there for me. I can't believe you." He winced, but she ignored the impact of what she'd said. She turned around and ran her fingers through her hair. "Of course I'm upset that my boyfriend of over a decade cheated on me and got another woman pregnant."

"Why does it matter if he's with someone else?" Galvin sighed. "I thought we were happy."

Jessica growled. "This has absolutely nothing to do with you."

Everything about her had everything to do with Galvin. If she couldn't see that—

"If you're such a little boy that you can't understand why I'm big mad about this, regardless of how I feel about you, then I'm not sure what we're doing together."

"Don't say that. I shouldn't have said that." He wanted everything to slow down. "Let me try again."

"I can't do that tonight. I'm done."

He could tell from the look on her face that she meant she was done with him. He didn't know if that was just for tonight or forever, but she wasn't going to hear anything he said. "I respect that. I just—"

She put her hand up and turned away from him. She walked over to the entryway and found her coat and bag. She dug out her phone. "I'm going to call a car and get out of here."

"I'll call you tomorrow." He couldn't accept that this was the end. They didn't have that much time in together, but surely they had more to talk about. He'd never thought he would feel this way again. After his first girlfriend had cheated on him, he'd gotten ripped and started paying more attention to his appearance. He'd taken on the persona of a guy who never got dumped, who could fuck any woman he wanted, the guy who only had to wink and smile to take a girl home. He'd become an assassin sort of lover.

And it had worked, until it didn't. Until he'd fallen in love with Jessica. Now he felt just as powerless.

"Don't." Then she walked out the door with his beating heart ripped out of his chest.

JESSICA HELD BACK her tears until she got in the car. It was touch-and-go for a few minutes, when she thought it would take fifteen minutes for the car to show up, but the app changed drivers and she was able to hold out for seven.

The driver took one look at her face and didn't try to make small talk. Jessica was able to bury her face in her hands and let out the rough sobs that she'd been holding in. Luke had cheated on her and gotten another woman pregnant. Instead of telling her, he'd walked out the door letting her believe that she hadn't been working hard enough at maintaining their relationship.

And the man she dated after him didn't even understand why she was upset. Instead of giving her a hug and letting her be upset, he was only interested in what her anger said about him.

If a client came into her office with this story, she'd empathize, and she'd encourage them to feel their way through the emotions, but not to make up a story about what this meant about them. But Jessica couldn't help but ask herself what this meant about her. There was a primal part of her psyche that told her she was unlovable because no one had ever managed to love her. Her conscious mind knew that it wasn't true—even true love wasn't always forever, and people who loved you could never do it flawlessly. Maybe Luke had actually loved her. Maybe he didn't know how to end their relationship after so long and had sabotaged it instead. People got hurt more when their partner was trying not to hurt them.

Someday, she'd probably be able to forgive Luke for what he'd done. It might take decades, but she could probably manage to avoid slashing his tires until that happened. They'd had good stuff in their relationship before he'd turned it to shit. And she knew that it had probably been time for things to end long before they did.

She might have even been able to put it behind her faster if not for Galvin's behavior. She wondered at her ability to be so wrong about him. From the moment they'd met, she'd felt seen by him. He seemed to get her. But the fact that he wanted to make her drama about him tonight made her question everything. He'd worried that he was just a rebound, but that was about him repairing his reputation and self-concept. It wasn't about how he felt for her—he just wanted to prove he could be a decent boyfriend.

Other than sadness and hurt, she was angry at herself. She'd let herself fall so hard so fast for Galvin. And it had been so easy. He'd been so easy to be around, and when they were together she felt like she was fully on fire with a kind of chemistry she'd never felt before.

The idea of never seeing him again made her feel so empty. Her chest was hollow, and her head was starting to hurt from all the crying. It hadn't hurt this bad when Luke walked out. At that point, not knowing the whole story, she'd felt a sort of relief. They hadn't been connecting, and he'd called it quits because she never would have. It was almost as simple and clean as a breakup after that long could have been. But now, this sinking feeling that she was inadequate and had never been enough for him permeated her bones.

Luke was having a baby with someone else, and Galvin had somehow made it all about himself. She couldn't pick the right man no matter what, and everything she'd written in her book was a lie.

There was no right way to pick a partner. And trying to convince men to treat women better for their own happiness was a fool's errand. Maybe her mother had the right idea. She skipped along through the world, using and discarding men for her own pleasure and financial gain. Sometimes she got attached and breakups got emotionally thorny, but that would end as soon as she met the next guy. And sure, growing up without any sense of stability or nurturing hadn't been great for Jessica, but maybe stability wasn't always a choice.

Jessica had tried to make every right decision, but look at her now. A half-empty condo, a bestselling book, and a broken heart.

It took her a few moments to realize that the car had stopped in front of her condo. Reminding herself to leave the driver—bless him—a big tip, she got out of the car and walked back into her half-empty life.

CHAPTER TWENTY-SIX

A WEEK LATER, JESSICA had only left her condo for work. Galvin had called her the next day as promised, and she hadn't answered. She was a combination of angry about how he'd treated the situation and embarrassed about how much she'd freaked out. He'd called every day, but she just wasn't ready to deal with him and her feelings for him.

And eventually, he'd stop calling.

Instead of facing her issues, as soon as she'd returned each day, she unhooked her bra and pulled it through the sleeve of the simple sheath dress she had in every neutral shade and threw it on her bed. Having an underwire sticking to her ribs even long enough to completely undress and pull on sweats was too much discomfort to endure on top of the raw feeling she had over every inch of her skin after the events of Saturday night.

She also knew that she was fucking it up as a therapist at the moment. She was empty, but she didn't really have any useful insights for anyone now that she realized that she didn't know anything. She'd even gotten teary with a client who was excited about a promising date. She thought she'd covered until the client had given her a sympathetic look and asked if she was okay during the session. She'd never had the mask slip off quite so decisively before.

But it was Saturday now, and she had her day free. She didn't have to get out of bed, though she really should get up and clean the condo and wash the sheets. They still sort of smelled like Galvin from the last time he was here. And, if she did laundry, she would have to wash and return the T-shirt and boxer shorts that he'd left here. She'd been wearing them to bed.

It was absolutely pathetic. She'd never borrowed any of Luke's clothes—partially because it made her feel weird that they were almost too tight for her. But Galvin's were roomy and very expensive. Wearing his clothes gave her a little bit of the feeling she had when she was wrapped in his arms. She wanted to keep as much of that as she could for however long she could.

It boggled her mind that she was more upset about Galvin's callous behavior than she was about Luke's infidelity. After all, that had involved a lot more lies over a longer period of time. Galvin had become so integrated into her life, and they'd become so intimate over such a short period of time—of course it was going to hurt to lose that abruptly. But Luke had been pulling away, bit by bit, over years and years. It was so gradual that she hadn't noticed it. By the time he'd finally left, there was little difference to her life before and after—just the missing furniture.

She should get up and shop for furniture. Even though she was probably going to sell the condo and move somewhere more suited to her tastes, she should probably furnish it to get it sold faster.

But thinking about furnishings and interiors would make her want Galvin's opinion, and she couldn't have that anymore. He would definitely answer her calls, but she couldn't trust herself not to fall into his arms again. And that wasn't healthy. He was a rebound, and she would be better off putting their relationship in the past.

About a hundred times a day, Jessica turned over every moment they'd spent together in her mind. She would pick them up and examine them from every side, trying to figure out whether he had ever been authentic in his affections. It had certainly felt like he wanted to be with her, but she couldn't know.

The next time a client came in after having fallen for a narcissist, Jessica would be able to empathize and relate, but she couldn't shake the self-recriminations that she should have known better.

She was pulled out of her meditation on all the ways that she'd been a fool by the lock of her front door clicking. Luke didn't have a key anymore, and Galvin never had one, so it could only be Barbie or Kelly. They had been texting her since last Sunday, but she hadn't had the energy to answer. Outside of work, she'd only been able to lie in bed and watch reruns of ID Channel shows that she'd already seen.

She was shocked when Abby walked into her bedroom. It was Saturday, so she wasn't wearing her customary suit, and it was kind of strange to see her in workout clothes. They were friendly, but they didn't have a relationship like that.

"When your friends called and said that they were worried about you, I didn't believe them." Abby looked horrified, and Jessica could only guess at what she looked like in that moment. The hair had to be greasy—she hadn't washed it since Wednesday. And she couldn't recall whether she'd washed off her makeup the night before. Probably not. That felt like too much effort, even now.

"How did they know to call you?" She was surprised neither of them had shown up until she remembered that Barbie was on location for a film in Toronto this month, and Kelly had a week full of being on call. She wondered if Kelly would be able to get any information about Luke and Kari via the hospital grapevine. She didn't care—well, maybe a little—but that was more curiosity than anything else.

Abby shrugged. "My information is on your book website."

"And Kelly gave you the key?"

"No, I demanded it as soon as she called. I wanted to make sure that you were going to be ready to go on Monday."

"What's Monday? It's only Saturday." The only ease Jessica felt at the moment was that she wasn't going to have to face the world for at least thirty-six more hours.

"You're going to be on *The Viewpoint* on Monday."

Panic rose in Jessica's throat. "No, I'm not."

"Oh yes, you are." Abby smiled, but it was not a pleased, happy, or nice smile. It was diabolical, and Jessica had never been on the receiving end. She imagined that anyone faced with Abby's visage in this state rolled over and did whatever she wanted them to do, but Jessica couldn't even work up fear of the consequences of failing to comply with Abby's demands.

"I can't go on a talk show." Jessica searched for the words to make Abby understand that her life was falling apart, and she had no business telling anyone else how to live their lives. "I don't understand men."

Abby rolled her eyes. "No one understands straight men.

Even straight men don't understand straight men. If they knew themselves and what was best for them, we wouldn't have a fifty percent divorce rate and such a steep decline in fertility that lawmakers are continually clawing back women's rights. Which just makes us want to fuck them less. God, they're stupid."

"Didn't Kelly or Barbie tell you what happened?" Jessica really didn't want to go into the whole Luke thing, because that would force her to go into the Galvin of it all. And she really lacked the energy for that.

"No, they just said that the reunion hadn't gone as planned, and neither of them could reach you." Abby's fierce expression softened a little. "Why, what happened at the reunion? It has to be something big to turn you from perfectly pressed to rabid raccoon chic."

"Luke brought his very pregnant new fiancée to the reunion." It was sort of like ripping off a Band-Aid, painful to say, but over quickly. "And then Galvin freaked out because I was freaking out, and I think we might have broken up. Maybe. Probably."

The "I eat nails for breakfast" look was back, but Jessica didn't think it was at her. And then it was almost as though Abby was making advanced mathematical calculations in her brain and couldn't engage with the outside world for a few moments. Maybe this was all too much for her to cover up with the television people and the publishing people. They were probably going to rescind the offer to write another book and expose her as a fraud. She would be a laughingstock. All her clients would discontinue working with her, and she'd end up living in her mother's trailer.

"That shithead. I thought he was more than a stupid, fucking pretty boy. I guess I was wrong." Abby's insults stopped Jessica's spiral. "And I could strangle Luke in his sleep."

"They're both shitheads. But Luke is going to be a father, and I would feel bad if he died and left his fiancée to raise the kid."

"She was very pregnant, so she was clearly fucking him when you were together. Single parenthood would serve her right, and we might even be doing her a favor. Luke is the king of the shitheads." Abby had a point. Luke was more of a liability than a help when it came to domestic labor. "But I was talking about Galvin. I knew he was a fuckboy, but the way he looked at you. I thought he had changed—"

Abby had experience with disappointing men—she'd just been through an acrimonious divorce with a very famous and powerful man. She didn't like to talk about it, and that said enough to Jessica—Abby wasn't the sort of woman to avoid a subject unless it was truly taboo. Maybe that was why the book had resonated so much with her, and she'd wanted to work with Jessica.

"I think my book is just bullshit." Jessica had been thinking that her tone had been way too harsh, and she'd been way too prescriptive, the longer she was dating Galvin. And now she didn't know what to think. The only thing she knew was that going on television and selling that book was going to be nigh on impossible in her current state.

"Shut up. It's not bullshit. If you could see some of the DMs and emails that my assistant has been sifting through since the release, you would not say that. Men who hadn't been able to get a date in a decade saying that they have set up appointments with therapists or drinks dates with the woman of their dreams, girlfriends who are getting flowers and help with the laundry the first time in their entire relationships, a couple of proposals, even."

Jessica was surprised. She'd refused to look at reviews for the book, because she expected them all to be bad. Whenever a woman dared to challenge long-standing ways of relating, there was bound to be backlash. She'd expected people to call her stupid and ugly and go on about doing their business the same way they always had.

"Maybe it's not total bullshit. It's academically sound, supported by the literature. But I just don't have the confidence to appear on national television and pretend to know what the fuck I'm talking about."

"Because Galvin hurt your feelings? Because his ego made him screw up?"

"It's not just that. It was fun while it lasted, but it was a rebound. It had to end at some point."

"You know that I think straight men are dumb, but I think you're blowing one fight out of proportion. And, if it was so good, why did it have to end? I mean, I'll trust your judgment if you think he's an asshole—"

"He's not an asshole—at least I never thought he was until a week ago. I fell for my own story that he was just misunderstood." Jessica snorted at her own stupidity. "I fell for the old line of thinking that I could fix or change a man just because he made my pussy really happy."

"Who hasn't?" Abby was typing something out on her phone, but she was still engaged in the conversation. "If anything, this makes you more relatable if it goes public, and I can work with that."

"But I thought it was a disaster if it went public that I can't make a relationship work."

"It might have taken some massaging, but I really thought you could use some good dick after spending over a decade with the other shithead."

Jessica really missed the good dick. And the talented hands. And the way he smelled when he got out of the shower. She missed running her fingers through the hair on Galvin's chest. She missed everything about him, and he had called every day. Did she really have to give him up?

"You're not going to start crying, are you? My hourly fee doubles if I have to deal with tears."

"I have a lot to cry about." She'd cried more in the past week than in the months since Luke had moved out. She was bereft, and she hadn't let herself care enough about another person to be bereft when they disappeared in a long time—maybe ever.

"Yes, but you have to stop crying so that we can control the puffiness for your national television appearance on Monday."

"I'm not flying to New York. You can't make me get on the plane."

Abby gave her a look that told her she would not hesitate to call in a group of mercenaries to kidnap her to New York if that was what it came to.

"What do I do if they ask about Galvin?" Jessica wasn't comfortable lying in general. Lying on TV made her want to break out in hives.

"Be vague, like you have in all of the other interviews." Abby said it like it would be easy. Maybe for her it was not a big deal to slap down questions about her personal life—she'd gone through a very public divorce not too long ago—but Jessica hadn't wanted to date for publicity at all. "It's not like either of you are major public figures. He doesn't have multiple TikTok accounts claiming to be his wife popping up on the daily."

There was a hint of bitterness to her tone, but Jessica couldn't explore that right now. Even though she was desperate to get out of this, she knew that this was what she'd wanted all along. She'd wanted her book to be huge because she knew it would help people. Even though she wasn't sure whether she was right about anything anymore, she knew there was some value in the insights she'd gotten through clients.

Jessica sighed, though she wasn't quite ready to throw back the covers yet. "What time is my flight?"

ABBY HAD SENT him a text with a link to a plane ticket. Her message—If you want your girl back, you will show up. A car will take you to the hotel—was all it took for him to pack a bag. To say he'd been completely miserable for the past week was an understatement. He'd been busy on a project, but every moment that wasn't devoted to getting his client to agree to the materials that would keep them in budget had been occupied by thoughts of Jessica. And she hadn't called him back.

He missed talking to her on the way home and asking what she wanted to eat. It made the traffic much more tolerable. She always had a clear idea of what she wanted, and she never threw the answer back to him. One of the things he liked most about her was that he'd never wondered where he stood with her. If she was unhappy with him, she told him. If he inadvertently violated a boundary that she wanted to keep, she made it clear. Her clear sense of who she was and what she wanted made it all the more intoxicating when she gave up her iron control to him in bed or let him surprise her anyplace else.

Her trust in him made him look at himself in a whole new way. He'd always felt like a feckless boy in relationships before. He'd always dated women who deferred to his tastes, but he realized now why they were all probably frustrated with him most of the time. With Jessica, he didn't feel like she was trying to wedge herself into his life. He felt like they were two individual puzzle pieces that fit together. But they were both full pictures on their own.

But he'd ruined all that by making her feelings about him. He might never stop kicking himself for it. By the time Saturday and Abby's cryptic text rolled around, he hadn't slept more than four hours a night all week. He knew he looked like shit, and he definitely felt like shit. He wanted nothing more than to sit in his backyard with a big glass of scotch and his own thoughts.

Fuck, he was becoming his dad.

But there was something he wanted more than to become a miserable bastard with a pickled liver—he wanted Jessica back. She'd been clear that she didn't want to talk to him. And he couldn't really blame her. He had really been a jerk the night of the reunion. He hadn't known how to support her. He wouldn't blame her if she made another Instagram live video about him, detailing all the ways that he truly was a cad.

But Abby's text had sparked enough hope in him that Jessica was at least a little miserable without him. He knew enough about Jessica's publicist to know that she wasn't a romantic—she'd walked away from her marriage without a second glance—but she was fiercely protective of her clients. If she was reaching out to Galvin, then it was for Jessica's ultimate benefit.

He didn't dare hope that Jessica had requested his presence. She hadn't reached out to him all week, which told him that she wasn't ready to talk. She was big mad and had every right to be. And Galvin wasn't sure what to do or how to repair their relationship. He had never tried to fix a fuckup this big before. He was out of his depth. He'd texted her multiple things and had all manner of gifts in online shopping carts, but it all felt hollow. He'd even thought about sending his favorite decorator to her apartment to pick out new furniture, but that might make things worse. He was sort of paralyzed.

It was ironic that all the years he'd spent trying to avoid getting too deep into a relationship because of that first heartbreak were what kept him from building the skills necessary to prevent this one.

He was a fucking idiot, and he'd berated himself every moment since she walked out the door. But he knew that hating himself wasn't going to get him back into Jessica's good graces—he wasn't sure what would, but he was willing to trust Abby right now.

Abby had put him at the back of the plane, which made sense. He deserved row 30, with the airplane toilet smell and getting hit with the drinks cart so many times that he limped off the plane. He just felt lucky that she'd ordered him a decent car and booked him into the Carlyle.

When he got to the hotel room, he found an itinerary on the bed. When he saw what had been planned for him, his stomach dropped. Jessica would hate this. She couldn't actually know about it. She would never agree to it.

Immediately, he called Abby. "Does she know that I'm going to be here?"

"Of course not." He could practically hear her rolling her eyes over the phone. "I never would have gotten her out of bed had she known that you were going to be there."

"I'm absolutely not going to show up on set." Jessica would cut him out of her life, permanently, without a second thought.

"I figured that you might say that, and I'm disappointed but not surprised."

"And you flew me here anyway? Thanks for the aisle seat in the back of the plane, by the way. I'm in a great mood and don't need a ninety minute massage at all."

"You fucked up, and I thought the groveling should start the minute you began your journey of redemption." Abby sighed. "Listen, you have a dope hotel suite and about thirty-six hours to figure out how you're going to win her back. I teed up the grand gesture of you showing up in her greenroom and making amends so that she doesn't fuck up her whole career when she goes on live television, but you know her better than I do."

"You're worried about her screwing up?" The Jessica he knew would be able to stay totally cool and professional no matter what the circumstances. The only times he'd ever seen her thrown out of her zone was when her mother showed up unannounced and when she ran into Luke and his fiancée.

"She was in bed at three p.m. and hadn't washed her hair in, like, a week. When I walked into her condo, there was just a pile of dirty bras next to the door."

None of that seemed like Jessica at all. Galvin panicked. He knew how important it was to Jessica to have her book be successful. If their breakup was putting her at risk of losing that, he had to do something. It was a gamble for him to show up unannounced. He didn't know if she would forgive him, or if it would upset her so much that it would throw her off her game.

But if she was bedridden over him, it meant that her feelings for him had actually been real. If that was the case, it meant that he had a chance to win her back—for real this time, with not a single lie between them.

"If I show up, I'm not going to be on the show," he said. He wasn't going to litigate his past in the public eye anymore. Besides, it didn't matter anymore anyway. If he couldn't be with Jessica, he didn't much care whether he ever got laid again. And his career was going well enough that he didn't have to worry too much about bad publicity.

"I mean, it would be really cute if you gave her an on-air testimonial, but fine." Abby then gave him all the details about where to show up and when to surprise Jessica.

CHAPTER TWENTY-SEVEN

JESSICA WOULD NEVER get used to "glam," and she would never figure out how to get the kind of volume in her hair that the studio's hairstylist had managed. She looked like a Real Housewife, and it was kind of freaking her out. She might have more credibility as a therapist if she'd shown up in her dirty sweats and smeared makeup rather than someone who looked likely to flip a table or throw a drink.

"What do you think?" the hairstylist asked when she turned off the very loud curling iron brush thingy that almost seemed sentient as it wrapped her hair around.

Jessica practiced her professional, composed smile with the woman in the mirror. "It looks great. Thank you." She was sincere—the woman had put in a monumental effort to ensure that she didn't look like a total sad sack—and it had sort of worked. She wondered what her Housewife tagline would be.

She was contemplating whether she would say something like, "I'm not all talk, and I'm going to shrink these other bitches down to size," when she thought she saw Galvin pass by the open door in the mirror.

No, absolutely not. It couldn't be him. He'd called every day this week. But how did he know that she was in New York? Then it dawned on her, the only person who knew that she was in New York was Abby. Abby wouldn't have called him, would she? True, she'd ambushed Jessica at her apartment and practically forced her onto the plane. And she'd looked very concerned for Jessica's mental health the whole time. But mashing her together with Galvin like they were a wayward Barbie and Ken set, in a high-pressure situation like her first appearance on national television, didn't seem like an Abby move.

But Abby didn't believe in dicking around when it came to anything—including emotions.

And then he was standing right there behind her, looking at her in the mirror. She was almost too stunned to meet his gaze.

"You're here." She was at the point of shock that she could only state things that were obviously true. But she was overwhelmed by this particular truth. She knew he was real because she could smell the soap he used along with the flowers he held in his hands—peonies. She'd once told him they were her favorite, and he remembered.

"I'm sorry." He looked truly contrite. She'd seen him angry, flirty, sex addled, focused on work, frustrated, and sad. But she'd never seen him look as though he'd truly lost something important to him.

The sadness she saw in his eyes was totally new. It made her want to reach out and comfort him. Even though he'd fumbled their first argument. After all, she'd messed it up, too.

"I know." She wouldn't let herself forgive him right now.

She'd forgiven her mother countless times, and Laurie had used that forgiveness as a weapon against her. She'd taken that forgiveness and treated it like it was a debt that Jessica owed her. But Jessica now realized that forgiveness should have been a gift she'd given herself along with boundaries to keep her heart safe in the future.

If she and Galvin had a future, he had to learn from this. He couldn't be a dillweed again. And he had to understand that her anger at Luke had nothing to do with how she felt about him.

"It's true we have some stuff to work through, but I know how much this means to you. I don't want you to think that I fucked up because of anything you did. You know what you're doing. You're brilliant, and what happened between us has no impact on what your book has to offer—what you have to offer."

"I know that, Galvin." She wouldn't reveal to him how kind but unnecessary it was for him to show up and tell her all these things. And she didn't want to let him know how much it touched her that he'd flown here to do it. He could have apologized later, when she returned to L.A. But she didn't have that kind of charity in her at the moment. It would be smart for her to guard her heart a little now and then. "I'm a professional grown-up, and I can do my job without you checking on my feelings."

She immediately felt guilty for snapping at him, but she didn't apologize or backtrack. She didn't even wince.

"I guess I deserve that."

"No, you don't."

"No, I don't." He shook his head and looked down at his shoes. "Do you want me to leave?" He pointed at the door, and she considered whether she did want him to leave. The moment she asked herself the question, she knew the answer.

GALVIN WAITED FOR her to kick him out of the greenroom. He probably shouldn't have shown up at all, but once he'd arrived in the city, he couldn't stay away. And seeing her now, even though she was nearly unrecognizable in the amount of makeup the studio had applied, he was just happy to be in the same room.

He didn't want to ruin what should be a great day for her, so he would leave if she asked him to. But he hoped that she would let him stay and maybe take her out to lunch after the segment. If he plied her with soft cheeses, she might put him out of his misery. They might still have a shot in hell of making this work.

She didn't get the chance to answer him, though. A production assistant stuck their head in the door and said, "Thirty seconds."

Jessica popped up and smoothed the black dress she wore. She looked dynamite, as always. He wanted her, like he would forever. She didn't look at him as she left the room, but she did say, "Stay."

CHAPTER TWENTY-EIGHT

"PLEASE WELCOME JESSICA Gallagher, author of *Ten Things Not to Do If You Ever Want to See a Naked Girl Again*." This was a bad idea. It was among the worst ideas that Abby had come up with. More like one of the worst ideas in the history of bad ideas. And having Galvin show up right before she came out was an even worse idea. Seeing him had knocked her off the tenuous balance that she'd found on the way to New York.

Still, she put her most placid smile on and walked out to the table. She was a little intimidated, because she knew that some of the panelists were inclined to disagree with her. But she tried to set that aside. Once she was seated, the audience sounds died down.

"So, why write a dating book for straight men. Are they the ones coming to you for advice?"

It was just like every other first question in every other media interview. She could answer this. "This is definitely a generalization, but it's the women in heterosexual partnerships who are often seeking the advice and trying to make things work. Society tells them that their value increases when they are attached to a man. I don't believe that, but I think that men are late to figuring out that their lives are better inside of a committed partnership or attachment of some kind. And that attachment is often stronger if they're with someone they view as an equal."

"Is that the reason for the provocative title?"

Perfect. Another question about the book rather than her own relationship status. "My editor thought that a provocative title was the best way to get the book into the right hands, and she was totally correct. But the book is more about finding out what it takes to build a life with someone rather than just how to get them to have sex with you."

"Your current boyfriend would seem to be the expert on the second thing."

Jessica had been lulled into a sense of security by the first few questions. She hoped her surprise at the host asking about Galvin didn't show on her face. And she hoped that her smile looked polite rather than like the smile of a woman contemplating violence. "My current boyfriend does have a reputation." The audience laughed. Apparently, there was crossover between *Kopying Kennedy* and *The Viewpoint*. "But I'm not here to discuss my relationship."

"Doesn't your ability to make a relationship work go to your credibility?" Jessica had forgotten that this host was formerly a prosecutor. "Besides, you seem to have whipped him into shape in record time."

"I'm not sure what you mean by that."

"You made him live by your rules."

"I haven't made him do anything." Jessica was incensed now.

"My book might have a cheeky title and seem prescriptive with a list of rules, but what I'm really trying to get at is that a lot of straight men don't even really view women as people. I'm trying to meet people where they are and give them tools to change their outlook on romantic relationships. So that they can be more satisfying for everyone involved."

"I think it's pretty severe to say that men don't view women as people." The conservative host was always going to have a problem with that.

"From my practice, I can tell you that the young women I see view dating as one of the most dehumanizing activities that they participate in."

"How so?"

Happy to be on more neutral ground with the questioning, Jessica gave this other host a genuine smile. "Well, if you sat where I sit every day, you would hear about men on dating apps and even podcasts making lists of things they want and won't accept from the women they're dating that read like laundry lists. They seem to want some sort of sentient blow-up doll to slot into their lives instead of partnership. And it's not working for them, so they're not getting into relationships, which frustrates the men, who then join online affinity groups and end up indoctrinated with extreme misogyny and often racist behavior.

"We're all suffering because we're not communicating with each other and being present with one another on a human level."

One of the other hosts nodded. "So you're saying that the straights are not okay?"

The audience laughed, and Jessica nodded. "No. No, we are not."

The hosts threw to commercial, and Jessica got offstage as soon as possible. When she got back to the greenroom, Galvin wrapped her in a hug. She hesitated, for just a moment. As she was talking about dating in general onstage, she'd realized something. Even though Galvin had fucked up once, he'd treated her with the utmost care at every other time. The truth was that there was nothing he could have done that night that would have helped. She'd needed to process and hadn't told Galvin what she needed. She was just as much at fault here.

She let herself fully surrender to Galvin's embrace. It felt so good. He smelled so good. He was home. She'd thought she'd found home in another person before, but she hadn't. She'd always been changing herself to fit the picture of who Luke had wanted. Galvin was the first person in her life who cared about what she wanted.

"I'm sorry that I freaked out in front of you," she said into his jacket. "It really wasn't about you."

He pulled back. "It was, a little bit."

"I'm serious." She balled up the lapel of his jacket in her fist. "If we're going to make this work long-term, we have to be honest with each other and we have to listen to each other. I shouldn't have made such a big deal over Luke cheating on me in front of you, and I should have been able to listen to why it upset you that I was so upset."

"I shouldn't have gotten up my own ass. I wasn't there for you in the way that you needed, and I thought you got so upset about Luke because I wasn't important to you." He brushed her hair out of her face and over her ear. "I panicked. Because I love you."

"You love me?" Her eyes got big again.

He smiled and kissed her forehead. "I love you."

She let the words settle into her mind. Galvin Baker loved her. She loved him, too. He wasn't the person she'd pictured spending her life with, but she couldn't imagine sharing it with anyone else but him.

"I love you, too."

He laughed. "You sound confused by that."

"That's probably because I am confused by the fact that I love you."

"I mean, it's not like a scary diagnosis."

"Yes, it is."

He released her and took a few steps back. "You're in love with me, but you're scared of being in love with me?"

Jessica moved toward him and grabbed his hand. "No." He visibly relaxed. "I just know that this time, I don't just think I'm in love. I know it, down to my very bones. It's part of me. And no matter what happens, a part of me will always love you."

"I'm scared, too. And I don't know how to do this."

Jessica laughed a little. "I don't know how to do this, either, and I'm supposed to be the expert."

He took her back into his arms. "Then, I think the only thing to do is figure it out together."

"Like partners." Jessica had finally found what she was looking for, and it may not have come in the package she'd expected, but it felt right.

"And lovers." He ran his nose up the side of her neck. "We can't forget that."

As per usual, his touch made her lose her mind a little. He made her lose her past and he took her heart.

"I promise not to freak out again."

"I don't need you to make that promise." She pulled his head up and kissed him, hungrily and deeply. It lasted a long time, long enough for the taping to end and production staff to flood the halls with noise. When one of them came in the door, they broke their kiss. Then, her stomach growled.

"Time for lunch," he said. "What do you want?"

"Surprise me."

ACKNOWLEDGMENTS

First off, I need to thank my longtime therapist, Julie. You wouldn't be reading this book without her encouragement of me. Over the decade and change we worked together, I learned so much about myself and how my mind works. I wrote and published twelve books, partially thanks to her suggesting that I use my wild imagination for something other than destroying my real-life romantic relationships. (I should note that Julie is nothing like Jessica, and she would never write a pop-psychology dating book.)

I also want to thank the readers that see themselves in the pages of my books, especially the more unlikable heroines. Meeting you in person and hearing from you keeps me writing and creating relatable characters. I want to thank everyone who is or has been part of the team that brings my books to life—Kristine, Mary, Courtney, and all of the copyeditors; production editors; book designers; cover artists; and sales, marketing, and publicity folks at Berkley.

None of the writing would be possible without the friends—inside and outside the book world—and family who support me and never doubt that I can make my dreams come true. Thank you.

CHAPTER ONE

ON THE THIRD day of ninth grade, Jack Nolan asked Maggie Doonan to be his date to the Leo Catholic freshman dance. He blackmailed his older brother, Michael, into dressing up as a chauffeur and driving them in their father's baby-shit-colored Lincoln Town Car. Then he sweet-talked Mrs. Jankowski at the flower shop into finding lilacs in Chicago, in September, just because Maggie's sister had told him that they were Maggie's favorite flower.

After that, Maggie Doonan hadn't needed any more convincing that he was the perfect half-formed man for her. And the fact that he was an actual, honest-to-God choirboy had convinced Maggie's father not to even bother threatening him with the shotgun that still resided in the Doonans' front closet.

At the time, Jack had no idea what kind of power he had unlocked.

Two years later, he and Maggie had sullied the back seat of the baby-shit-colored Lincoln Town Car in unspeakable ways.

And, two years of near constant shagging after that, he'd watched her get in her parents' SUV to leave him for Harvard.

Watching Maggie's tearstained face drive into the distance had broken Jack's heart. But he'd been the only guy in his high school friend group to leave for college with valuable sexual experience not involving his right hand.

Still, he'd been sad.

Until he met Katie Leong during the third hour of freshman orientation at the University of Michigan. She'd winked at him while they'd learned the fight song at some stupid mixer for first-year students. That wink had hooked straight into Jack's dick and driven him to be the best college boyfriend ever—midnight burritos, romantic two a.m. walks to and from the library, and oral sex at least three times a week—six times during finals. Hell, he'd even started working for the school paper because Katie was going to be a journalist when she grew up.

The only thing about his relationship with Katie that had stuck past her semester in Paris, and her subsequent new relationship with some French douche named Julian, was his career in journalism and a broken heart.

But the broken heart had lasted only a few months—until he'd met Lauren James, his favorite ex-girlfriend. She was off-the-wall funny and could suck the chrome off a trailer hitch.

He and Lauren had lasted through their senior year at Michigan and a shitty apartment with six roommates in the Bronx while he'd studied for his master's at Columbia and she'd waited tables at a craptastic Midtown tourist trap and raced to and from off-off-Broadway auditions.

Lauren hadn't even dumped him when he'd moved home to Chicago for a shiny new job. She'd saved her tips and flown out twice a month until she'd met a British director who wanted to cast her in an all-female West End production of *Waiting for Godot*.

You're the best man I know, Jack. Such a great guy. I'll never have another boyfriend like you.

No, she wouldn't. Because she married the prick director after the very brief run of the show. That British guy hadn't been a Boy Scout, and he for sure didn't know all the best sex knots to tie.

As he stood at the bar of a speakeasy in Wicker Park, after waiting fifteen minutes for an artisanal old-fashioned made with, like, artisanal cherries and orange peels scraped off with the bartender's artisanal hipster fingernails or some shit, he'd been without a girlfriend for six months. It was the longest he'd ever gone, and that was why his buddies had thought it was a good idea for him to leave his couch—and the Michigan–Notre Dame game—to sit around and talk to them in public.

He *should* be working tonight. In addition to not having a girlfriend, he didn't have the illustrious journalism career he'd dreamed of. In a recent pivot to video, he'd become the online magazine's how-to guy. His boss told him he was "too handsome to break real news," but more important, he would be laid off if he didn't shift with the times.

Now his father grumbled about him "not having a real job" every time he saw him, and Jack kept his mouth shut because he was living in a condo his family owned. If he lost his not-real job, not only would he have to hold his tongue around dear old Dad, he would have to wear a sandwich board on the corner. Or worse, work with his dad. While his father could deal with his working a job outside of the family construction business, he wouldn't be underwriting Jack's lifestyle if he got fired.

He loved his father—looked up to him—but they would kill each other if they had to work together.

So, he was here with his buddies, trolling for ideas for his next bullshit column. Chris and Joey could be his guinea pigs for whatever he came up with. He'd grown up with them; they'd all graduated from Leo together. Unlike him, they were knuckleheads about women. The idea that they would need to stage some sort of intervention with him over the nonexistent state of his love life was freaking preposterous. As demonstrated by the fact that they were wearing suits for a Saturday night out in the hipster hell that was Wicker Park, so they could stand around a bar that served overpriced, fussy drinks while looking at their phones and not talking to any of the women actually in the room.

Neither of them understood that for the first time since Maggie Doonan had put her hand down his pants under the bleachers at the freshman dance, he was kind of happy being alone. He could finally do the kind of shit that he liked—watch the game with a beer or five, sleep until noon, bring bread into the house without ruining someone's gluten-free cleanse.

For the first time in his adult life, he was figuring out what he liked instead of contorting himself into the kind of guy Maggie, Katie, or Lauren needed. And he meant to go on that way.

Just the other day, he'd been thinking about getting a dog. Some slobbery beast—like a mastiff or a Saint Bernard. Lauren hated dogs. Which probably should have been his first clue that the relationship was doomed.

Still, he scanned the dark bar to see whatever other unfortunate souls found themselves ripped from the warm embrace of their college sports or Netflix queues. No one looked quite as miserable as him, though. Not a single one of the long-bearded hipsters littering the red leather couches and old-timey booths looked like he'd flash a nun for a beer on tap.

Looking around, he thought maybe his next video could be *How to Not Ruin a Saturday Night Paying for $15 Drinks at a Douche-Magnet Bar.* Name needed work.

His gaze stopped right next to Chris and Joey on the ass of a woman in a tiny black dress that didn't match her gray moccasins. He didn't give a shit about her sartorial choices because there was so much velvet-soft-looking light-brown skin between the shoes, which looked as though they'd seen better days, and the bottom of that dress, which made Jack's lungs feel like they were going to combust. He hadn't even seen her face yet, but he knew that she was like whiskey in woman form; he felt his judgment cloud and high-minded ideas about bachelorhood vacate the premises. In his head, she was already like the first puff of a cigar. Just her gorgeous legs made his throat itch and burn. Forty or so inches of skin had him choking on lust.

Thank freaking Christ the bartender showed up again with his drink. Jack knocked twice on the bar and, not taking his eyes off Legs, said, "Put it on Chris Dooley's tab." Jack was about to lose his wits to a woman, and it was all his friends' fault for making him leave the house. They were buying his drinks for the rest of the night.

He made his way back to Chris and Joey, still looking at their goddamned phones and not at the beauty next to them. No wonder they were constantly swiping and never actually meeting any of the bots populating most dating apps face-to-face. And no wonder Chris had been single since dumping Jack's sister, Bridget, a year and a half ago. They didn't pay attention.

Considering the sister dumping, maybe Jack should have drowned Chris in the kiddie pool when they were five.

But if they were aware of their surroundings, maybe Chris or Joey would be the guy getting to talk to Legs, and Jack would be left holding his dick. So, thank Christ his friends were idiots.

It wasn't until he was a few feet away that he noticed the other women with Legs. Both of the other women were knockouts, but they didn't rate for him. Jack had homed in on Legs, and he would not be deterred.

Maybe he could figure out how to keep things casual with Legs for the first three months or so. He doubted it. Once he'd tasted a little bit of a girl's magic, Jack didn't like to date around. He enjoyed flirting as much as the next guy, but he was—in essence—a commitment-phile. He liked having a girlfriend.

Maybe he and Legs could get a dog. He could compromise and live with a French bulldog. Small and cute, but still a real dog.

"Are you guys both swiping?"

"Yeah." Joey swiped left. "But I'm coming up empty."

"What the hell does that mean?" Because of his affinity for having one lady for years at a time, Jack had never been on a dating app. He didn't see the appeal. If he'd met Maggie on an app, he wouldn't have been able to figure out that the lotion she wore smelled like lilacs. He wouldn't have known that Katie's singing voice rivaled that of an angry tomcat, but that it was so charming he didn't care. He'd never have clocked Lauren's sassy walk across the stage in the production of *Hello, Dolly!* that he'd been reviewing for the *Michigan Daily* when he'd first seen her.

And he would have seen Legs's face first. To be honest, a picture of her face might be the only thing in the "pro" column for online dating. He needed to see if her face would captivate him as much as her rocking body did.

"It means he's not matching with any of the hot girls," Chris piped in as he swiped right multiple times. "I swipe right on everyone so that I get more matches."

"But he matches with mostly dogs," Joey said. "I'm not looking to get caught up with a girl so ugly I gotta put a bag over her head."

Yeah, he definitely should have drowned both Chris and Joey twenty years ago. Instead of clocking both of them, he pointed an angry finger in their faces. "Both of you are nothing to look at yourselves, so you get what you get."

He ran his finger under his collar, longing for his worn Michigan football T-shirt instead of a stupid button-down. It was damn sweaty in this goddamned hole of a bar that didn't have decent beer or a television.

"Yeah, you'll eat your words when you're forced to swim in the waters of Tinder, loser." Chris pointed back at him, finally looking up from his phone. "Then you'll realize that it's kill or be killed. The women on here are either bots or butt ugly."

That had to be the moment when Legs turned around. Jack could tell by the look on her—*beautiful, gorgeous, absolutely perfect*—face that she'd heard every word that his asshole, knuckle-dragging squad of buffoons had just said. Her eyes were so narrowly squinted that he couldn't tell what color they were. Her nose wrinkled up and her red-lacquered lips compressed with anger. Couldn't hide the fact that she was a knockout from all the angles. Not even with a raised middle finger partially obscuring her face.

She was like a sexy, rabid raccoon. And he was a goner.

Some dipshit with twinkling green eyes wasn't going to stop Hannah Mayfield from raining holy hell on the bros swiping left on the girls standing right next to them. *Two of whom happened to be her best friends.*

His tousled dirty-blond hair and the muscles straining his shirt's buttons didn't make her want to throw a drink in his face any less, and they weren't about to stop her from curb stomping his buddies. Didn't matter that the goofy fucking smile on his face said he couldn't read the room. She was about to de-ball all three of these assholes, and he was *smiling*. Maybe he was missing more brain cells than the average young professional man in Chicago—which is to say all of them.

"What the hell is your problem?"

Stupid-Sexy Green Eyes answered even though she'd turned her glare on his two bozo friends. "I didn't say anything."

No, his deep voice, which rolled over her with the subtlety of a Mack truck, wasn't one that had been calling all the women on Tinder, including her friends, dogs. But that didn't stop her from saying, "Well, then. Keep yourself busy sucking a bag of dicks while I disembowel your two friends here."

Although that was a harsh statement to lob at an innocent bystander, she couldn't risk showing any weakness in the face of the enemy. And all men were the enemy. Especially the pretty ones who looked at her like she was their favorite slice of cake. Those were the especially dangerous ones: the ones who could seep into her heart, which made it much harder when they left. And they always left—usually because they *just didn't want anything serious right now.*

"Why are you so angry?" He seemed genuinely perplexed, and honestly, she didn't know why she was so angry, either. It wasn't like she was on dating apps anymore. She'd given it the college try, but every petty humiliation suffered on those apps felt like a stab to the gut. And even when she'd met a few guys for drinks, she felt like she'd been at the worst audition for the worst reality show in the world. She didn't understand how people ever actually made it to sex with someone they'd never met before.

Probably drinks. Lots and lots of drinks.

"I'm pissed because they"—she pointed at Sasha and Kelly—"forced me to come to this hipster nightmare for drinks after I'd been working all damned day." She'd only been guilted into it because Kelly, a management consultant, was in town for the first time in months.

"The shoes." Green Eyes's gaze dipped to her feet.

"Not your business." She hated how warm his slow perusal of her made her feel, as though he'd already seen her naked. It was creepy, and she ought to have called him out. And the warmth melted some of her righteous indignation on behalf of her friends. *Not the plan here.*

"Working on a Saturday?"

"Event planner."

"Spent all day dealing with a bridezilla?" He took a sip of his drink, and she didn't roll her eyes at his stupid, sexist comment. The amber liquid rolling from the glass to his mouth was much more fascinating.

"That's a dumb, sexist thing to say when I'm already pissed." As if the only thing that event planners did was plan weddings. True, she wanted to plan weddings because that was where the money was, but she did so much more.

Then the stupid asshole smiled at her again. "Back to that."

She was surprised that at least half the panties in the room didn't incinerate under the force of his grin. *Good God.* He was so pretty that it hurt. Features cut from stone and stubble not quite artful enough to be on purpose. Drinking bourbon with his shirtsleeves rolled up. He was citified masculinity that wasn't quite civilized. A contradiction, and the kind of thing Hannah went crazy for. The dimples that bisected the stubble had a feral quality that made her want to touch him.

He'd moved a little closer since she'd turned around ready to tear his buddies apart. They'd retreated, but he'd advanced. It was kind of sexy that he wasn't afraid of her, that he didn't buy her painstakingly cultivated bitchy exterior. His lack of fear was working on her in a major way, and that terrified her. After Noah, she'd sworn to herself that she wouldn't be foolish enough to believe that someone could want her for something other than a few rolls between the sheets, and a *Hey, babe, that was fun, but I'm just not looking for a girlfriend right now.*

Because they were never looking for a girlfriend, especially not *her* as a girlfriend.

That didn't hurt anymore. *It didn't.* She'd accepted that she was just not the kind of girl men romanced. With her ethnically ambiguous looks, bawdy sense of humor, and filthy mind, men wanted to have sex with her. And then—once they realized that she wasn't entirely domesticated—they wanted her to disappear.

She had to remind herself of this, make it her mantra whenever this man was near. Never forget that men were the enemy, regardless of how friggin' sexy his smile was.

He stepped even closer, leaving only half a foot of space between them. Hannah clocked Kelly and Sasha in her peripheral vision. They'd moved over to one of the stand-up tables.

Great. Neither of them believed her when she said that she was done with dating and romance and men for good. Their seeing her charmed by the prime cut of Chicago man-meat in front of her would not do at all. And yet, she couldn't seem to turn around and run away.

Maybe she should slap him. He hadn't done anything slap-worthy, but he had her cornered. In the middle of a crowded bar, with multiple options for egress, she was pinned in place because he'd *smiled* at her.

"What's your name?" His voice softened, and she broke eye contact.

She looked around; his friends had made themselves scarce as well. "Hannah." She looked at his chest when she told him. Meeting his gaze was too intimate and it made her cheeks flush.

"I'm Jack."

That was a very good name. It made her think of hard liquor and sex.

"Of course you are." Damn, he smelled delicious. Like freshly showered man draped in freshly laundered shirt. With a little bit of citrus and bourbon on his breath. It was like a lethal dose of bro, but it appealed to her despite her struggle to maintain her antipathy along with her dignity.

His laugh surprised her. "Hannah, tell me something."

She didn't respond but made eye contact again. *Mistake.*

"Can I get you another drink?"

She looked down to the mostly melted ice and rye in her glass. It would be stupid to have a drink with him. If she spent any more time in his aura of good-natured all-American Chicago boy, she would think about him for months. She'd wonder if she'd been too harsh and why he didn't call. Because if she didn't leave right now, she was going to give him her number.

Green-eyed Jack was looking at her as though he was starved for her. He would ask for her number so he could try to sweet-talk her into no-strings-attached sex—if he didn't come right out and ask her if she wanted to bone that night. That was probably what he would do. If he did, he was so tempting to look at, and so not fooled into thinking that she was ready to hate him solely because he was a man, she would do it.

Then he still wouldn't call, and it would be even worse than if he was just some guy she'd talked to in a bar one night.

If she left now, she could be home in time and sober enough to pretend he was attached to her favorite vibrator. His tongue swept over his lower lip, and he must have taken her silence for assent. Large, blunt fingertips brushed her smaller ones as he took her glass.

He motioned to the bartender for another round without leaving her side. Probably sensing that she would leave if he gave her an iota of the space that she ought to crave.

"I don't date." It was only fair to warn him that she was done—so done.

He looked back at her. "Neither do I."

"I mean, seriously. I don't—um—" She just had to tell him that she didn't date, and she also didn't do the random hookup thing. Wouldn't be going home tonight and feeling his skin against hers. She hadn't clocked the light dusting of chest hair through the small opening at the collar of his shirt.

"We're just having a drink, Hannah." He smiled again when

he passed her a fresh tumbler of rye. "Think of it as an apology from my friends."

"Why are you apologizing for them?"

"I don't talk like that about women."

But she was sure that he thought that way about women. He was young, handsome, and well built. His watch and the quality of his clothes said he wasn't obscenely wealthy, but he probably lived relatively well. His straight white teeth said that his parents had been able to afford braces. So while he was smart enough not to seem like an asshole whose interest in her would be limited to a one-night stand or a string of booty calls, there was no way that he saw someone who would bust his balls every day at the end of his dating tunnel. Too bad she would really enjoy busting his balls.

"But I'm sure you think that way."

"No." His face hardened, and he took a drink. "I don't. My friends are assholes, but I think those apps make it easy to be."

"They turn people into commodities."

"Exactly." One cheek muscle flexed, and the dimple was back. She wondered what he'd do if she put her fingertip in it. "You shouldn't shop for a partner like you shop for groceries."

Advice wasted on her. "I don't do that. I told you, I don't date."

"I don't do the apps, either."

That surprised her. But then again, he'd never be standing here with her if he did. With the face and the muscles and the nice-guy veneer, he could have been getting a half-decent blow job instead of shooting his shot with her. "Why not? You'd do well."

Although she hoped she'd kept her voice neutral enough that

he wouldn't take her genuine desire to know why he wasn't on Tinder as a compliment, he totally did. "Are you saying I'm handsome, Hannah?"

She really liked the way her name sounded coming out of his mouth. Way too much for her own good. "You know what you look like, Jack."

The audacity of his wink had her fighting to keep from smiling at him. Even if he wasn't a total jerk, there wasn't room for both her and his easily stroked ego in this dank basement meat market. She drained her drink and put the glass on the bar. Reaching inside her purse, she pulled out a twenty and held it out to him.

"What's that?"

"For the drink."

"The drink was an apology."

"But that apology came with strings."

"No strings."

Then she did roll her eyes. "You're wasting your time."

"I don't see it as a waste."

She'd just bet he didn't. He liked that she was a challenge. "We're not going to"—she lowered her voice and leaned into him—"you know, do it."

He choked on his cocktail, and she barely fought the desire to bump his back until his windpipe cleared. Let him drown in his old-fashioned. If he died ignominiously, she wouldn't have to think about him tomorrow or next week and wonder if he wasn't a shithead of the same brand as every other man in this city.

Unfortunately for future Hannah, he caught his breath. "I never asked you for sex."

Her cheeks flushed. Maybe he really was just apologizing. "I'm sorry."

"For what?" His hand cupped her upper arm, good humor back on his face. "I'm flattered that you were thinking about getting naked with me."

"I wasn't." She shook her head and looked down at her shoes. The gray moccasins she'd thrown on after the last of the Lurie Children's Hospital people had left the event she'd thrown today for some local NFL players who had wanted to give a whole boatload of money to kids with cancer. They were terribly ugly, but her feet would have fallen off had she kept her heels on for ten more seconds. "I didn't think about that at all."

"I must be losing my touch, then." He wasn't. One smile and he'd melted part of her shell. A touch on her arm burned her skin through her dress. "I just wanted to apologize and share a drink with someone not staring at their phone."

"Oh." He couldn't seem to stop surprising her.

"But I was definitely thinking that I'd be lucky to get naked time with someone like you."

There it was. Jack was lethally sexy, dangerous to her equilibrium. The flutter in her lower belly just from being near him would lay waste to her inner peace, such as it was.

"I don't do that, either." Part of her hoped that he would argue with her. Try to convince her. She waited a beat for him to respond. When he didn't, she adjusted her over-the-shoulder bag and shifted away from him. "I've got to go."

He swigged back the rest of his drink and winced. It was kind of adorable on him—this totally gorgeous, seemingly self-contained man not used to the burn of bourbon in his throat.

The contrast between his manly appearance and that slight show of weakness attracted her even more. Her hesitation at this point was pure self-preservation.

"I'll walk you out."

"There's really no need."

He took her arm again, and she was sorely tempted to shake him off and maybe stomp on his foot. She was just about to, she swore, when he said, "There's a taco truck outside, and my stomach will hate me tomorrow if I don't eat something."

"That many drinks?" No wonder he was flirting with her. In her experience, guys like him did not flirt with women like her unless they were drunk or trying to slake their curiosity about dating a biracial girl.

Like Joe Osborne, the insanely good-looking but profoundly lazy stoner she'd dated sophomore year. He'd been into new experiences in general—mostly drugs, loose women, and never finishing a paper on time—but she'd mistaken his curiosity about her for genuine interest. Too bad that curiosity had never extended to whether she'd enjoyed their hookups. A few dozen orgasms might have made the shocked look on his mother's face when he'd introduced them over Parents' Weekend a little bit worth it.

Since her father had evaporated as soon as the pregnancy test came back positive, and her mother had been busy working to pay for her education, she'd been on her own with Joe's family. For two days, she was subjected to the *I'm Trying to Prove I'm Not Racist* variety show. At multiple points, she'd wanted to stop Mr. and Mrs. Osborne from talking about all their Black friends and tell them she believed them. But that would have made them even more uncomfortable. Considering their son's lack of sexual prowess and the fact that he was probably going to flunk out once Hannah stopped pressing send on his papers, she spared them and broke up with Joe as they were driving away.

Which brought her to Jack. He was probably just drunk enough to step outside of his comfort zone to hit on her. Once he sobered up and/or figured out that she was pretty much just like the white girls he dated, only she would make his parents feel weird, she'd never hear from him again.

"Nope." He bent down close enough that his breath touched her ear when he said, "I just want to spend more time with you. Buy you a taco and see if you'll give me your number."

USA Today bestselling author **Andie J. Christopher** writes sharp, witty, and sexy contemporary romance about complex people finding their happily ever after. Her work has been featured in NPR, *Cosmopolitan*, *The Washington Post*, *Entertainment Weekly*, and the *New York Post*. Prickly heroines are her hallmark, and she is the originator of the Stern Brunch Daddy. Andie lives in the nation's capital with a French bulldog, a stockpile of Campari, and way too many books.

VISIT ANDIE J. CHRISTOPHER ONLINE

AndieJChristopher.com
AuthorAndieJ
AuthorAndieJ
AuthorAndieJ